The Strange Death of Father Candy

Also by Les Roberts

MILAN JACOVICH MYSTERIES

King of the Holly Hop
The Irish Sports Pages
The Dutch
The Indian Sign
The Best-Kept Secret
A Shoot in Cleveland
The Cleveland Local
Collision Bend
The Duke of Cleveland
Deep Shaker
Full Cleveland
Pepper Pike

THE SAXON MYSTERIES

The Lemon Chicken Jones
Seeing the Elephant
Snake Oil
A Carrot for the Donkey
Not Enough Horses
An Infinite Number of Monkeys

The Strange Death
of Father Candy

LES ROBERTS

Minotaur Books

A Thomas Dunne Book
New York

This is a work of fiction. All of the characters, organizations, and events portrayed in this novel are either products of the author's imagination or are used fictitiously.

A THOMAS DUNNE BOOK FOR MINOTAUR BOOKS.
An imprint of St. Martin's Publishing Group.

THE STRANGE DEATH OF FATHER CANDY. Copyright © 2011 by Les Roberts. All rights reserved. Printed in the United States of America. For information, address St. Martin's Press, 175 Fifth Avenue, New York, N.Y. 10010.

www.thomasdunnebooks.com
www.minotaurbooks.com

Library of Congress Cataloging-in-Publication Data

Roberts, Les, 1937–
  The strange death of Father Candy : a suspense novel / Les Roberts. — 1st ed.
      p.   cm.
  "A Thomas Dunne book."
  ISBN 978-0-312-56633-3
  1. Family secrets—Fiction.   2. Italian Americans—Fiction.   3. Youngstown (Ohio)—Fiction.   I. Title.
  PS3568.O23894S77 2011
  813'.54—dc23
                                                                2011026225

First Edition: November 2011

10 9 8 7 6 5 4 3 2 1

To my darling grandchildren, Shea Thompson and Parker Roberts—always on my mind and forever in my heart

ACKNOWLEDGMENTS

My deepest thanks to those who taught me all about Youngstown: Chief James T. McBride, Sheriff Duke Wellington, and Bob O'Malley.

To the Doctors at the Cleveland Clinic: Michael Rocco, A. Marc Gillinov, and Robert Juhasz, who taught me how to get my wheels back on the track.

And always and forever to Holly Albin, who teaches me each day about love, friendship, loyalty, and courage.

The Strange Death of Father Candy

CHAPTER ONE

The high funeral Mass was held during the second week of October—the best-attended funeral service in Youngstown, Ohio, in 1985—and almost every mourner was crying. Even the ones who didn't shed obsequious tears struggled bravely not to. The church was mobbed with almost two thousand people, a larger attendance than most Cleveland Indians games enticed during the 1980s. The overflow—those who arrived too late to be seated in the main cathedral—were shuffled into the auxiliary auditorium of the parish social hall next door, where they could watch the service on closed-circuit television and do their crying in there. The lamenting in both rooms was loud and unabashed, the moaning rumble a counterpoint to sniffles and nose blowing.

At most funerals, the only ones who cry are the close relatives of the dear departed; everyone else simply looks sad, fights boredom, and tries not to sneeze away the fumes of burning incense. But this was no ordinary funeral Mass, because the deceased was not just an ordinary citizen who had lived honorably and religiously and who had died quietly of old age or an incurable disease. This one had perished long before his time, and the bishop himself was up there behind the ornate podium, droning away as he always did. The silent occupant of the closed casket had deliberately put a pistol in his mouth and blown out his brains.

He was Richard Candiotti—my elder brother.

His death was eating a hole in my liver, but I couldn't do a damn thing about it after the fact. One of the first things a kid learns as he's growing up is that no matter what else, gone is gone—for good. Still, I was one of the few sorrowing churchgoers who didn't cry. Not openly. I wept for Richard alone, inside, where no one could see it.

Richard had been the parish priest of Our Lady of Perpetual Sorrows in Youngstown for thirteen years, but older parishioners remembered him as a rangy, tousle-haired kid, growing up in the Italian neighborhood called Brier Hill, living with his two younger brothers and a sister in a tall, skinny mill house. Our parents rented the bilious blue home from the steel company, to which our father trudged to work six days a week, down the hill at Burlington Street with his metal lunch box under his arm, then crossing the road and moving over the walkway into the mill itself and onto the hellishly hot floor.

Brier Hill is a little world unto itself—with several bocce courts, a veterans' social club for Italian-Americans, an Italian Fair every spring, taverns where the bartenders were always named Vinnie or Mario, and an aggressive citizenry that took care of their own, decades before anyone ever heard of a "neighborhood watch." Nobody ever called the cops, because they didn't have to. Whenever a problem arose, we policed ourselves. Some steelworkers from the Hill got old and passed away, but many of them are listed as alive and on the payroll—even five and ten years after their deaths. Runners for the local mob still collect their paychecks.

It's that kind of a neighborhood. Tony Janiro—a big-deal middleweight fighter from the Brier Hill area—made his mark in the forties, although he never won a championship. They talked about him a little bit in the *Raging Bull* movie, but that was all about Jake LaMotta, who had nothing to do with Youngstown. But Janiro was Italian, and Youngstowners still sing his praises, even the people who weren't even born when he was fighting professionally.

Damn near everybody from Youngstown could fight professionally if they wanted to. That's how we survived—like my father. In his heart of hearts, he was a gentle man, but his environment, his neighbors, and the 120-degree summertime temperature of the floor of the steel mill at which he earned his living turned him into a guy with a quick temper and a quicker fist.

All us Candiotti kids were too smart to walk in our father's footsteps, and Richard was the sharpest of us. After a survey of careers available to him, he'd enrolled in a Catholic seminary in southern Ohio—bankrolled in large part by the head of an infamous and powerful Italian mob family—and dedicated his life to Jesus. At the time of his death, he'd become more than a priest. He was a neighbor, a friend, a teacher, a listener, and a spiritual guide—and according to all the younger kids who begged him to come outside and play with them on a brisk fall Saturday when the fallen leaves crackled under your feet and almost every house had a comically carved pumpkin on the front porch, he could toss a football a country mile.

That was before he went down into the basement to the game room of the church in the middle of the night and swallowed a bullet.

What makes a relatively young priest do the Dutch act in his own church, the church where he was baptized, confirmed, and accepted into the priesthood? I fretted over that, sitting miserably in the front pew with my remaining brother and sister, trying not to hear the uninspired voice of the bishop of Youngstown babbling about life and death and redemption, ignoring Father Richard Candiotti's method of death and saying he was enveloped in the loving arms of Jesus. Richard had grown up in the same house we had, though he was more pious and fastidious than the rest of us—even as a child, he always took too damn long in the bathroom every morning combing his hair. Every Sunday, rain or shine, he hassled his siblings about going to church and being devout.

Then he put on the turned-around collar and rode herd on everybody else to be good Catholics, too, until he threw in all his cards.

I would have cried about his death in any event, and I would have showed up for his funeral; he was the only living member of my family I had much to do with. But priests don't kill themselves—ever. It's against the rules of the Church.

I'm Dominick Candiotti—or Nick, as nearly everyone calls me—and I've *never* been a good Catholic. I've not been particularly sociable, either, which I guess makes me one of those loners. I dislike the label, but there's nothing I can do about it. I was a rebel from the beginning, and it was impossible for me to play the game like my three older siblings had.

My next-oldest brother, Alfonso, is a spit-and-polish homicide lieutenant for the Youngstown Police Department—a hypocrite who went through all the Catholic motions without believing them. Shorter in stature than the rest of his family, he learned quickly the art of politics and of power, and never looked back. My sister, Teresa, is a whining, scolding, boring pain in the ass who's raised bitching to a pure art form, marrying early the poor fool who'd stumbled onto her postadolescent virginity and didn't have the sense to back away. Teresa hasn't cracked a smile since she was ten years old.

And Richard—the late *Father* Richard? He was some kind of saint. It's too easy to say that about a Catholic priest, but with Richard it had always seemed well deserved, at least to me. I had feelings for all my family, because that's born into you, but I loved Richard Candiotti with all of what was left of my heart.

So how did he decide to put a cap in the back of his throat? I didn't know, either.

I'd tried every angle I knew to put the pieces together, and it frustrated me. I was angry as hell—at my brother, who should have talked it over with me before doing anything rash and stupid, and at the city in general. Richard had embraced Youngstown and everything that came with it, while I'd turned my back on it.

Why did I choose not to call Youngstown my home? It's a gritty, no-nonsense Rust Belt city that nourishes all its diverse backgrounds and ethnicities. Most of our citizens work blue-collar jobs, go bowling, drink beer, get into harmless punch-outs in tavern parking lots on a Saturday night, and veg out on the sofa to watch Sunday sports. It's a lot like Cleveland, only smaller.

Yet, sentimental magic came along with a Youngstown childhood, at least while I was growing up. It was a more innocent time, and we kids found our own fun on the streets and in the parks and in the after-school playgrounds. I learned quickly enough that everyone I knew was connected in one way or another to mob crime and civic corruption. It made me squirm, even while the industry that kept the town rocking and rolling, steel, was gasping its last.

It also made me squirm that everyone knew the town was controlled and actually run by two rival Italian mob gangs, and that no matter who you were, you had to go along to get along. If you didn't, you were hip-deep in trouble.

I couldn't handle any of that. It was like living in some kind of twisted fairy tale where the wicked witches and child-eating giants were the winners. So I ran, first to the military—a huge mistake—and then to a big city, Chicago. It was every bit as corrupt there as it was in Youngstown, but most Chicagoans were busy with their own affairs and didn't have the time to care. Besides, all Chicagoans knew that the civic leaders were openly corrupt, and they considered the graft they pocketed just another tax that had to be paid to keep the buses and trains running and the snowplows clearing off the streets all winter.

Richard loved his hometown, loved being atop the pinnacle on which every local Catholic had installed him, kissing his hand and his ring in the process—and probably, in their heads, kissing his ass, too. So he happily stayed where he'd been born.

He was the only human being to whom I could ever open up completely, because I was too young to connect with my parents or my other siblings. I didn't always follow Richard's advice, but I never failed to consider it seriously. Now I was furious enough over losing my brother and friend and mentor and adviser to make somebody suffer for it. I know how to do that. When I was in Vietnam in the early seventies, I made a living from that particular skill. And my brother's death, which everyone assumed was a suicide, was what brought me back to Youngstown. Not to sniffle and moan at his funeral, but to exact revenge from whatever guilty party had caused it.

But who was I going to hurt anyway? Hardly the bishop, who yammered away to the weeping survivors. He didn't deserve pain—only a strong suggestion to speak less, which I was sure he'd ignore. My octogenarian uncle Carmine, at the far end of the first row in a wheelchair, was gasping loudly through the plastic tubing he wore under his nose, connected to the oxygen tank he lugged all over town with him to counteract the sixty-five years of his life that he'd smoked. Some woman behind us in the church, a woman I'd never even met, was moaning and weeping as loudly as a wounded yak. I didn't know which way to turn, but my urge to injure was more frustrating than the incessant mourning.

The bishop, mindfully aware that the local media was videotaping his eulogy for inclusion on the six o'clock news and expanded coverage in the following morning's newspaper, was trying to convince us that only God understands the reasons a Catholic takes his own life and that no one should be judging Father Candiotti. This was a radical change from recent days, when a Catholic suicide was a mortal sin that denied the victim a formal funeral Mass and burial in sacred ground. Now, though, the Church hierarchy in Youngstown was thinking differently about it. In fact, Richard's grave had been dug a few hours after one of the church cleaning ladies found him dead on the floor of the basement, not too far from the Ping-Pong table.

I'm the only Candiotti besides Richard who attended college, studying art and creative design and ringing up a degree from Youngstown State. After graduation, the U.S. Army sent me to Vietnam in 1972, after rushing me through OCS and anointing me a second lieutenant in the Army Corps of Engineers. For whatever reason, I was coerced—or shanghaied—into Special Forces, given a green beret, and sent off into the fetid in-country jungle to perform covert tasks I never shared with anyone, missions that invariably involved the extinction of one or more human lives. The things I did in Southeast Asia, which still haunt me as the nightmares that wake me up screaming in the middle of the night, eventually earned me a major's gold oak leaf—but I never gave a damn for the rank.

When the Vietnam sort-of war ended in a wasteful draw, leaving more than 58,000 American soldiers dead, and more than twice as many forever maimed, and damn near every one of them who breathed Vietnamese air haunted by the way they'd lived, I turned my back on everything Youngstown and went to work for a construction company in Chicago, designing higher-end suburban homes. After three years, I bought half the business and moved into a smart condo two blocks from Lincoln Park and four from Lake Michigan.

I didn't weigh the knowledge that I'd rarely seen my family anymore. My parents had both died suddenly in a wintertime car crash, leaving us orphans. I never had anything significant to say to arrogant, self-important Al, and less to Teresa. I nurtured true fondness only for Richard. My wartime experience frightened away whatever faith I had left and drove the final nail into the coffin of the Catholicism I'd never really accepted. But I idolized Richard as a human being and not a man of God, and we talked at least twice a month by phone. I always listened to my answering machine when his call missed me, beginning with "Hi, it's Richard on the telephone." The "God bless you" always came at the end of the message, too. I didn't care about that "God bless" part, but it was a requirement for a priest.

What was left of the once-vital Candiotti clan, now impotent without our leader, sat like wax dummies in the front row of Our Lady, close to the coffin, which had not been opened for viewing. None of us understood a word the bishop said, but we weren't listening anyway. His well-packaged eulogy and quick addendum about the priest who had worked at his elbow was making him nervous and causing him to rush.

There was a stirring down at the end of the front pew, and I leaned over to watch Uncle Carmine stick himself with the tiny lancet of one of those glucose monitors he carried with him at all times to check his sugar level for diabetes. I found out later that he did it about ten times per day.

I wouldn't look behind me, but I knew the Severino family was paying tribute—the old man, Paolo Severino, his wife, Ruth, and his son, Paul junior, whom everyone called "Polly." Every Sunday morning, they sat where we were sitting now, in the front pew, which had become their right of rank and power—but on this special day, they graciously accepted the second row to make room for Richard's closest relatives. Nobody smoked inside Our Lady, but I could actually smell the fine cigar smoke that hung all over the Severino men.

The scent of crime, too.

Don Paolo Severino ran the rackets on the west side. Money laundering, loan-sharking, prostitution, gambling, and drugs were under his control. What everyone knew about, of course, was his casino.

This emporium never observed antigambling laws in Ohio, which, apart from Cleveland and Youngstown and Toledo, has always been a conservative, uptight state. This illegal club was owned and operated by Paolo Severino, and no one ever mentioned to him that he was breaking the law. No one dared. Like my father, Paolo was a man of temper and violence—but he never committed any himself. The people in his employ did it for him.

I wasn't angry at the Severino family. I just wanted to get away from them before they asked me for a favor that *would* make me mad enough to do something stupid.

Lucy Waldman was at the far end of the Severino pew, her eyes wet from crying over Richard's passing. About fifty but looking at least fifteen years younger, she'd managed Severino's casino for eight years. In her best days, she was Paolo's number-one extramarital squeeze, taken out to more places and parties to be shown off hanging on the old man's arm than were ever dreamed of by Mrs. Severino. Before that—long before, when Lucy was a kid just turning nineteen and was very beautiful indeed—she was a top-of-the-line Youngstown hooker.

Prostitutes don't often fare well as they age. Even the gorgeous ones wind up dead, broken, or used up. When the future disappears before their eyes, they marry one of their kindhearted johns—if they're lucky. The truly smart ones, like Lucy, not only find a rich and powerful client like old man Severino but maneuver their way into comfort and wealth of their own, too. Paolo rewarded her with 10 percent of the casino, and she plowed the rest of her money into blue-chip stocks. Now she's a rich, pleasant, good-humored woman—one of the uncrowned genuine duchesses of Youngstown, even in a working-class city where middle-aged whores are rarely treated like royalty.

Lucy Waldman sitting in the same row as the Severino family was apparently all right with Paolo's wife, Ruth, who knew of Lucy's history and position. But Ruth, nearly Paolo's age and running to obesity, didn't seem to care anymore.

I stole a glance over at the left side of the church. In the first pew, all wearing canonical black and looking determinedly grim, sat the bishop of Cleveland, the northeast Ohio auxiliary bishop, Richard's friend and mentor Monsignor Danny Carbo from Youngstown, and several other prominent Catholic clergy from all over the Ohio and western Pennsylvania area, invited to make the funereal turnout one local Catholics would recognize and respect.

Behind them, in the second row, was the wealthy Mangione family. They were entitled to the front left-side pew at Sunday Mass, in thanks for their generous donations to the parish and Mrs. Mangione's tireless volunteer work, but today they nobly moved one row back to make room for all the heavyweight Catholic clergy, just as the Severinos, on our side, had given up their front pew for us. As always, the Mangiones glared across the aisle at the Severinos, their sworn enemies. Both Italian clans were Youngstown natives, but the Severinos were connected through blood and business to the organized-crime bosses in Cleveland, ninety miles west, while the Mangiones were in open league with the Pittsburgh mob to the east.

Just as Youngstown citizenry's football loyalty is split—half the citizens plump for the Pittsburgh Steelers, while the other half roots for the Cleveland Browns—so was their fealty divided between the Mangiones and the Severinos.

The two families had feuded sixty years or more, although few remembered why it started in the first place—but there were many things far more important than who got to sit in the front pew at Sunday Mass. Crime and intimidation were primary colors on both their palettes, and in their single-minded competition, they splashed their hues all over Trumbull and Mahoning counties, touching every local cop and politician. I wondered whether either family had confessed their transgressions to my brother.

Richard hadn't grown up an innocent, but even in the confession booth he must have been occasionally shocked by the Severinos and the Mangiones. Those sins were lulus.

Both families kept coming to Our Lady because neither would

cede even that sacred ground to their rivals, although the Severinos come to the early Sunday Mass and the Mangiones to the later one.

At least twice a year, a violent killing chases other, milder news off the front page of the *Youngstown Vindicator*. The victim is invariably "made" or "connected" to one family or the other, and the tragedy invariably begets more tragedy as rival capos and their street soldiers gnash their teeth, simmer, and plot revenge.

As a kid, I learned not to take sides—I was afraid of both of them. That's one reason I left home as soon as I was old enough, and didn't come back.

Over six decades, there'd been many killings. Tough guys were stabbed or shot, a few were beaten to death, and more than half of them were discovered floating in a nearby lake or river. But the most popular form of gang revenge came when the designated target would innocently start his car in the morning and ignite a bomb placed under the driver's seat to blow him to bits. Before we were out of our teens, we all figured out how to construct a car bomb, even though only the rival families would actually put it into practice.

This form of execution has come to be known as "the Youngstown Tune-Up."

I remembered one particular Tune-Up. When Richard was in college and Alfonso was a rookie policeman looking around for important asses to kiss, a car explosion just down the street eliminated one of our good neighbors, Benjamin Zannoni. His son had hung out with us since we were old enough to remember. "Big Ben," as everyone called him, ran a dry-cleaning store close to downtown, but he filled in as an errand runner and sometimes informant for Paolo Severino. Benny junior, the eldest child in the family and one of my best playtime buddies, was eleven years old on that black morning and happened to be looking out the window at the time. His remaining family packed up quickly, sold the dry-cleaning store for pennies on the dollar, and moved to Warren some weeks after. I never heard from them again.

Some Italian guy who'd grown up on Brier Hill had moved to western Pennsylvania, where he opened a firm specializing in mine stripping—which meant he could get his hands on all the dynamite anyone might need, which explains the main ingredient of the Youngstown Tune-Up. I wasn't sure whether the mine-stripping guy was closer to the Severinos or the Mangiones, but as an independent, he sold dynamite to everyone.

I hadn't seen either mob family for many years, but as I sneaked looks at them, I carefully measured the men. The godfathers—Paolo Severino and Frank Mangione—were too old to worry about now, since one-on-one would never be a problem. But their sons looked tough and hard, and probably the underbosses, hit men and knee breakers who worked for them, wouldn't go down quietly. Still, in Vietnam I'd probably killed more men than all of them put together, and they didn't worry me much. What did worry me was the urge rising in my chest to mow all of them down where they sat.

What lived in my mind now was Richard's suicide.

Richard hadn't been a happy child—my parents were not Ozzie and Harriet—but he hadn't been *un*happy, either, especially during his skirt-chasing days, when more than one virginity—at least that's what the young women had sworn to—had been offered up to him. He'd tried to figure a way to college without having Papa pay for it. That's when he threw himself into Catholicism, winding up with a partial scholarship to the seminary—he worked in the kitchen on-site and at a discount shoe store evenings and weekends to pay for the rest of it—that eventually turned him out as a full-fledged priest.

He gave up a future job, marriage, children, et cetera, and swore a vow of poverty. But he received much in return—mostly the love that everyone showered on him. That love was now being expressed in loud and public grief.

They came to Our Lady from Brier Hill, which overlooks the belching smoke stacks of the mills, and from Smoky Hollow, just north of downtown, where Hollywood's famous moviemakers and studio heads, the Warner brothers, grew up. They came from Crab Creek, now a haunted wreck of a neighborhood but once surrounded on both sides by some of the busiest steel mills in America, and from the residential streets near what used to be festive Idora Park, in the old Fosterville neighborhood, where as kids we all enjoyed the Caterpillar Ride, the Fun House, and the Wildcat. A few years ago, the powers that be tried to sell Idora Park for peanuts, but nobody was interested. Then the whole park caught fire and burned to the ground, and they eventually had to close it. You think it might have been arson? No one knows for sure. But Idora Park is gone now, and that's a fearsome bite out of the ass of everybody's childhood.

The mourners came from Trumbull Road, too, which divides Trumbull County from Mahoning County and Youngstown. They came from Dearborn Street, and from side streets abutting Belmont Avenue, the neighborhood's north-south main drag, and from their childhoods at Jefferson School and Tod Woods School and St. Anthony's, too. They even came from Boardman, Poland, and Campbell, the Catholics who'd moved up in the world but had never changed their church affiliation. They all remembered Richard fondly.

Finally, the bishop's seemingly endless paean to the departed ran out of gas. The traditional rituals were performed by Monsignor Danny Carbo, and then everyone came gingerly to the front of the church and filed past the closed coffin. Most of them touched it with their fingertips. Several women and not a few men bent and kissed the gleaming cherry wood and said their good-byes and God blesses loudly and tearfully. As the casket made its slow-motion way up the aisle toward the front door, with four pallbearers on either side and the presiding bishop marching at the front like General Custer leading his men into suicide at the Little Bighorn, some of the emotional parishioners rushed to touch the vessel once more—to ensure their goodbye to Richard was noted. I know he'd always hated being patted and hugged and fawned over by people he hardly knew, so I was glad he was unaware of the hustling, touching, and nose dripping accompanying his final procession up the aisle.

Alfonso looked over his shoulder, checking who'd attended, nodding to a group of men sitting together about halfway back in the church and looking serious and chastened—fellow Youngstown police officers there to support him, with the police commissioner, the chief, and Al's immediate superior, Capt. Ed Shemo, in their midst. I watched Al's eyes as he took a silent roll call, remembering those who had come and making another get-even list of those who hadn't shown up. Like an elephant, Al never forgot anything. He'd arise every morning with a new and revised list of who he wanted to screw over.

Teresa sat quietly in her pew, embarrassed by her priest brother's having taken his own life and putting his family through the humiliating aftermath. Her good-natured, pussy-whipped husband, Charlie, paid attention only to her, holding her hand and whispering solace in her ear. It didn't matter. Teresa never sought help from anyone, tending to and polishing her martyrdom until it sparkled diamond-bright.

I just stared at the floor, waiting for the black limousine that would drive the family to the cemetery, which had existed long before Our Lady was built. The burial sites were well cared for, though the graveyard was perched on the side of a hill overlooking the now-polluted water of Crab Creek.

An elderly lady in her musty-smelling black dress stood in front of me, beads wrapped around her fingers and tears leaving tracks down her whiskered cheeks. I hadn't a notion who she was, but she squeezed my hand and said with an accent part Napolitano and part Brier Hill, "Father Candy always told us suicide wasn't the way out. He said that no matter what happened, bad or hard, we should always turn to God."

Father Candy. Anyone from the rough-and-tough Candiotti

family had to be damn well loved to accept a sentimental nickname like that one.

The old lady shook her head and shuffled away, still wondering why Richard had given up his own life.

Me, too.

The difference between us was that I would find out, one way or another—and do something about it.

CHAPTER TWO

"My baby is gonna be a priest."

Those special evenings happen to some families. In the early sixties, our small living room couldn't even hold Mama's pride. She was "crying happy" again—that's what she called it when her tears were for joy and not misery. Ever since Richard had announced his aim for the priesthood, Mama's eyes would fill up and overflow, her nose red. She cried every time she looked at him—and often when he wasn't even home, when her imagining him in his proud priestly vestments overcame her.

Though he was the eldest of four children and I was the youngest of the family, nothing ever rescued Richard from being referred to by his mother as "my baby." Every Catholic family yearned for an offspring to serve God with honor—and while the Candiottis always nurtured the hope that spiky, aggressive Teresa would mature, mellow out, and become a nun, she was only twelve years old at the time and hadn't made up her mind. Now they sent up thankful prayers that Richard would be God's personal messenger. There was a Catholic in the White House for the first time in America's history, and even though he wasn't Italian, the handsome, charismatic president was a matinee-idol icon to every Catholic kid in America.

Richard loved JFK, too, but otherwise he wasn't into politics. He disliked arguing, hondeling, fighting for his own ideas; he preferred quiet discussion to a snarled insult or a punch in the nose. He was always a gentle soul—not an easy task in our sweaty neighborhood. He'd begged his parents for a pet to care for and love—a dog, preferably, but a cat or rabbit would have been satisfactory, and he would even have settled for a gerbil, but Mama wouldn't hear of it. When he was eleven, he found a dog on the street and brought him home, but the mongrel was banished as soon as Papa returned from work. Papa wouldn't consider sharing our small house with another living creature who shed too much hair and peed and farted where it wasn't supposed to. But Richard eventually transferred his love toward animals to his genuine affection for every human he knew. In his heart, he never accepted the monsignor's unfeeling observation, as when Carbo attempted to slow down the crying of a young child whose dog had been run over by a truck by assuring him that animals did not have souls.

They did for Richard.

In school, Richard's patience and logic trumped knotted fists and bloody noses. He was even nice to Alfonso and me, never raised his hand in anger, hardly ever yelled, and wouldn't even consider inflicting a noogie or a wedgie on either of us—and he always stood up for and defended his sister, Teresa. He was an adolescent swinger who indulged in many one-night stands, but he was always gentle and thoughtful to women. Taking all things into consideration, it was no wonder that he wanted to be a priest.

Teresa was jealous of her big brother's news. If she eventually became a nun, she knew everyone would *still* pay more attention to Richard. Perhaps that's what turned her away from the veil and into a bad-tempered and unforgiving woman.

Al, on the other hand, didn't give a damn *what* Richard did with his life. He was too involved with being the tough guy in high school—not because he couldn't physically intimidate anyone, but because he'd grown hard and unyielding as a self-chosen leader. Everyone listened to him, especially his best friend, Paolo Severino, Jr.—Polly. Al was a guy to be paid attention to. His sarcasm was stiletto-sharp and devastating, and his personal decisions were handed down to followers and sycophants as the word of law. Al knew nothing about loving—only about using.

Richard and I had only one biblical argument. He was in his last year of priest training, and when he came back to Youngstown for the Christmas season, we got into one of those silly arguments about the New Testament.

"Look," I said to him as we were taking a walk in the chill but bracing December afternoon, "I'm willing to buy the Virgin birth, as far-fetched as it is. I'll even go for the Angel of the Lord and the star in the east."

"Good for you," Richard said. I amused him.

"Here's what bugs me, though. The three wise men."

"The three wise men bug you?"

"Yeah, they do. In the Bible, it says the wise men brought gold and frankincense and myrrh to the baby Jesus—whatever the hell myrrh is anyway."

"Myrrh is what makes perfume smell good."

"So who would bring perfume to a newborn baby?"

"Is that why the three wise men bug you, Nick?"

"No—and that's not the point. So they brought those gifts for the Christ Child, right? Well, I want to know what happened to it. Did Mary and Joseph schlep it back to Nazareth on the donkey? Now, frankincense is lightweight and compact, and myrrh you could probably stuff into the pocket of your robe. But gold—gold is *heavy*. It could break the donkey's back."

"Maybe it was small amounts of gold," Richard said patiently. "Not gold bricks."

"Okay, fine. But then when they got it home, what did they do with it?"

"The gold?"

"I don't remember reading about the Holy Family living large after that, or Joseph quitting carpentering and making investments. So if you're so smart, Richard, what's up with all that gold?"

"You're not supposed to question, Nick. You're just supposed to believe—happily. That's why we call it *faith*."

"Just like the Easter bunny and the tooth fairy, huh?"

Richard laughed. "I ought to give you twenty Hail Marys and twenty Our Fathers as penance for being such a smart-ass."

"You aren't a priest *yet*," I said. "You're just my big stupid brother, and you know what you can do with the penance."

Richard always took teasing well. I loved the hell out of him—and respected him.

Everyone else on Brier Hill held Richard in awed respect, too—even Don Paolo Severino. When Richard would return from seminar for a long weekend, the old man would invite him to his home for dinner and inquire as to how his education was coming and where he hoped to put down stakes when his priesthood became final and official.

"We need you *here*," Severino would frequently tell him, his chair pushed away from the table, his top pants button open after an Italian meal with more than one cannoli for dessert— all washed down with a bottle or two of the best homemade dago red. He cleared his throat, raspy since puberty, and took a healthy swallow of wine. "We want you looking out for our immortal souls."

Paolo's entreaty touched Richard deeply; he believed *someone* should care for the souls on Brier Hill. Youngstown was infamous for flouting the most elementary societal rules. A blue-collar steel town on the eastern edge of Ohio, a stone's throw from the Pennsylvania border and a long day's drive from New York, it still operated as the shoot-'em-up Wild West—and there was no Wyatt Earp to keep it clean. Youngstown was

America's most notorious "open city." Mobs ruled without interference. Honest citizens went along, and local law enforcement just closed their eyes or looked the other way.

Yet the city worked.

Don Paolo Severino knew many people who could grease the skids for Richard's dream to come true—every working-class family understood that. Those who were "connected" wore fancy knockoff wristwatches, snazzy shoes, and Italian suits they bought from a big hijacked van outside the back doors of certain bars, like the Tropics, on the corner of Market and Myrtle. It always started when the cops themselves, hearing about the waylaid vehicle before anybody else, would come by first for a preview look, buying items burglarized from the upscale homes in the Glen or bordering Mill Creek Park. Then they'd tell their friends about the great shopping, and before the week was out, most citizens visited the wheeled marketplace to spend their hard-earned money on bargains. It was a way of life, proudly displaying items scored off rich home owners or stocking their homes with things that fell off the back of a truck.

Richard never abandoned his plan to make Youngstown a finer place to live. When he finished his studies and was anointed a full priest, he was sent first to a small parish not too far away, in New Philadelphia, Ohio, where he was second in command to the elderly Father Navarre, celebrating the early-morning Masses every weekday and assisting on the more important ones on Sunday. As good as he was at listening to the troubled faithful, he proved inept at raising money for the church. Nearly retired Father Navarre was good at it, however, so Richard instead concentrated on his more humanist skills. Almost every Catholic in New Philadelphia invited him to dinner, often as an unspoken payback for confessions he'd patiently heard. He stayed in touch with the bishop, mostly through Don Severino. Six years later, when he transferred back to Youngstown, nobody bothered asking why—they didn't have to.

There was a chance Richard would be assigned to Saint

Anthony's, an old-time Italian church on Y-town's northwest side, but he prayed long and hard for what came to be—and proudly stepped into the job of primary priest at Our Lady. The rival Severino and Mangione families were members and regular worshipers, and Richard ensured there was no hanky-panky, name-calling, confrontations, violence, or even macho chest bumping between them at Our Lady. No matter whose side one was on, Sunday was a holy day.

Now it was hard for me to behave accordingly at his own funeral. I just stared straight ahead and thought other things—like, for instance, why my brother had inexplicably taken his own life.

After the Mass, Alfonso and his wife, Dolores, Teresa and her husband, Charlie, and I were led out of the church and loaded into the lead limousine along with the Youngstown bishop, who tried to speak kindly to the grieving family but wasn't able to work up much warmth.

"He was a fine man and a fine priest," he intoned, sitting on one of the limo's jump seats, facing backward, looking directly at Al. "He was devout, but as time went on, he seemed a little nervous—I don't know about what. In the past few months, he seemed—undecided about things."

Al nodded, but he was probably thinking instead of how many police officers, from Youngstown and from neighboring small towns and as far away as Akron, Cleveland, Columbus, and Pittsburgh, had showed up for the funeral, even including the assistant police chief from Indianapolis and another from Wheeling, West Virginia.

"It was as if," the bishop continued, "Richard wasn't himself lately."

"Is that why he shot himself?" I said. "Because he wasn't himself lately?"

The bishop looked miserably uncomfortable. "No one understands God's way—except God," he said. "We should not question; we should not wonder."

I wondered, though—and I'd do a lot of questioning about it, too.

The familiar landscape that was my childhood passed by the smoked glass—but I wondered anyway. Why was Richard *not* himself during the last months? He'd sounded normal on the phone. Why had he, who'd radiated acceptance, wisdom, and common sense, turned nervous and indecisive? And why hadn't I known about it?

Because I lived in Chicago—a bigger, tougher, more sophisticated city—a seven-hour drive from Youngstown on US I-80/I-90, and a million miles away from Richard and Our Lady in every other way. My twice-monthly calls with Richard took the place of face-to-face talks because the life into which I'd comfortably settled had inadvertently built a quiet wall between me and the family I'd left behind.

Now it was too late.

The hearse led the sad parade, two motorcycle officers cruising along on either side. Behind was our limousine, which the funeral directors referred to as "the family car." Uncle Carmine didn't come with us—he was in lousy shape generally, and certainly in no condition to sit out in the chill for an hour or more sucking on his oxygen tube. Our stretch limo was followed by two more, which carried important political mourners (Monsignor Carbo had begged off because of much work to do and disappeared before the caravan set out for the cemetery, and the Cleveland bishop had collected his priest driver and headed back to his own diocese), two big dark Lincoln Continental Town Cars belonging to the Severinos and the Mangiones, and finally more than 150 other cars flying magnetized purple flags and stopping traffic. Pedestrians, even Protestants and Jews, bowed their heads respectfully as the hearse passed; everyone had heard of Father Candy's suicide, casting a pall over their otherwise-uneventful day.

The long train of vehicles began its climb up the bumpy incline overlooking pathetic Crab Creek toward the cemetery. It took nearly an hour for all the mourners to park, find their way through the graveyard on foot, winding between the tombstones, markers, and several statues of saints or angels erected over the burial place of the more affluent, and assemble themselves around the freshly dug grave, shifting their weight from one foot to the other, anxious for the rituals to end so they could press the flesh of bereaved family members, chat up their friends, and get on with their lives.

I got a better look at the faces here at the graveside than in church, but not many sorrowers noticed whom I studied. I'd been away too long and was learning who was who all over again.

Don Paolo wore a dark gray suit, a gray tie that almost matched, and a stiffly starched white shirt and immaculately polished black shoes. He was a fireplug of a man, with hair dyed black and a tanning-salon glow to his features, and his sadness on this occasion looked genuine. His son, Polly, towered over him, surrounded by their higher-up captains and perhaps a few bodyguards unused to funerals. They'd pushed their way through the gathered mourners to the front of the crowd to make room for the don, and no one complained about it, nor about the small group in the front row on the other side of the grave—Don Frank Mangione and his two sons, Frank junior and Vincent. It was all for show, on both sides. No one would argue or push or begin shooting. This was neither the time nor the place.

Augmented by a solemn organ recording, Richard's casket trembled on the canvas straps that would lower it into the freshly dug grave. Teresa had stage-managed the entire funeral, an organizer who took charge of everything. She'd stepped forward to arrange the services and burials of our parents, too. As the crepe hangers gathered, Teresa counted attendees in her head and hissed at Charlie, whose mournful but resigned face stamped him as a perennial underdog.

Alfonso wasn't talking to my sister-in-law, Dolores. Looking back at their marriage, I couldn't remember them ever talking to each other very much. Al leaned backward and covered his mouth with his hand to pass words with his captain, Ed Shemo, who was taller than just about anyone else there and looked resplendent in his dress blues, generously garnished at breast, shoulders, and hat bill with medals, gold bars, and braid. He had to bend down to hear what Al was saying.

Dolores scanned the skies and the trees and the downtown skyline, looking anywhere but at the open grave itself. She always dressed to impress, even to go supermarket shopping, and on this particular afternoon her mink stole caressed her shoulders. She'd not eschewed generous use of her eye makeup, either, and her lipstick was close to the eggplant purple the cosmetic peddlers called "aubergine." She looked more like a floozie than a mourning relative. After she and Al had been married nearly two years—and, of course, Richard performed the ceremony—Richard took her to lunch and explained that she should settle down and be more of a wife and part of the Candiotti family, and not dress so revealingly that men looked at her hungrily when she slithered down Market Street or carelessly slid her silk-clad legs out of a car.

Dolores was resentful of Richard's interference, and she stopped talking to him altogether unless family was around. She did indeed take Communion almost every Sunday, but she hadn't been to confession since that lunch—at least she hadn't confessed to Richard after that.

I'm glad she didn't offer any confessions or revelations to me because I couldn't stand the sight of her.

Standing a few feet away from my surviving siblings, I realized someone *was* looking at me, someone I hadn't noticed at the church. Our eyes met, and that empty space inside my chest, too close to my throat, began to burn and throb.

Years have a way of distorting memories, but Diane Burnham had hardly changed in thirteen years. Her hair was shorter and a few shades blonder, and her fresh teen face had slimmed and matured. Her clothes, subdued for this solemn afternoon, were more stylish than those she'd grown up with on Brier Hill, when her born surname was Bottinelli and her father worked side by side with Papa in the hellish heat of the mill.

When we finally looked at each other at the same time, Diane allowed one corner of her mouth to turn up, and she nodded. I bobbed my head back at her, fighting the adolescent memories in which she starred. Her eyes were wet as she stood across the open grave from me—not quasi-religious tears when the laity publicly mourns a deceased cleric, but tears of friendship and loss.

Diane was the only blue-eyed Italian on Brier Hill, which might be why I'd fallen in love with her when we both attended Youngstown State. Maybe it was why she and I first tongue-kissed each other when we staggered, windblown and on a natural high, off the Wildcat roller coaster at Idora Park. At least 70 percent of the kids who grew up in Y-town scored their first real kiss or their first feel-up at Idora Park. That led us to learn together how to make good, exciting, imaginative, and always romantic love.

Maybe the blue eyes were just one of the reasons.

Idora Park's demise marked the end of Youngstown's old-fashioned amusement—the end of low-rent magical fun for kids and teens from every neighborhood for fifty miles around.

The end of Diane and me had started many years earlier.

CHAPTER THREE

The St. Aloysius Catholic Church in New Philadelphia, Ohio, was constructed in the 1920s of fat sandstone bricks, which give it a squat, earthbound look. It's the only Catholic church within the city limits, serving the Italians and the Irish, as well as a smattering of Hungarians and other Eastern European ethnicities who had wound up in the east-central Ohio town south of Canton.

Richard told me this story one night, years later, when he and I were having dinner at the Colonial House restaurant and we'd both had a lot of wine. No one ever looks askance at a priest drinking to excess. I remember it clearly, though, as if I'd been totally sober.

It was a rare free autumn afternoon for Richard Candiotti, his daily chores and his early Mass finished for the day and no appointments until later that evening, when some older women in the parish were hosting a weekly bingo game and he would drop by and say an opening prayer—as if bingo really *needed* divine intervention—when Diane Bottinelli came to see him. It was at the beginning of her senior year at Youngstown State University.

Richard hadn't seen Diane often after becoming a priest, and since it was a beautiful fall, leaves beginning to turn riotous colors that rivaled the leaf-peeping in New England, he suggested they take a walk together and enjoy the sunshine rather than shutting themselves up to talk in his small, stuffy office just off the main door of the rectory. They moved down the street together slowly, the domed roof of the historic courthouse looming over the horizon, Diane's arm hooked through his, enjoying the brisk, cool weather. They were easy in each other's company, their chatting almost gossip, and they reminisced over their naïve, guileless childhoods when they'd lived only three blocks from each other.

"I should apologize for our pasts," Richard said to her. "You were an impossible child, much too young for me to pay any attention to, and you were always underfoot. Looking back on it, you were adorable, with big blue eyes and a perpetual smile. You're still pretty adorable, but in a grown-up way."

"And you were skinny and gawky," Diane said. "From down there where I was, you were as tall as a tree." She hugged his arm. "You're still too tall—but now look at you! You've turned into a movie-star priest."

It made Richard laugh. "That makes me a bigger target."

Diane tossed her blond hair—it was long, more than halfway down to her waist, and she always wore it loose. "I paid attention to *you* back then, Richard. You were a really cute guy, and I had a major-league crush on you. Did you know that?"

"I never knew. I'm flattered."

She shrugged. "By the time I was old enough to say anything about it, you were wearing your priest duds and hearing some pretty hot confessions on Sunday mornings, so the discussion was moot."

He laughed aloud. "*Moot?* That's a big word."

"I learned it in college. Anyway, you flew away—so I started going out with your little brother instead."

"Nick isn't so little; he grew taller than any of us."

"He grew in lots of ways," Diane said, "especially inside his head."

"So," Father Richard said, "you drove all the way over here today to tell me that the inside of his head is growing?"

"I drove here to tell you," Diane said, her cheeks coloring and feeling warm despite the cool afternoon, "that I'm hopelessly in love with him."

That slowed Richard down a step. "Wow. Well, okay, then—congratulations are in order."

"Not really." Diane frowned. "He doesn't want to stay in Youngstown."

"Right where we grew up?"

"He hates it—the smallness of everyone he knows. And he hates the corruption."

"Everybody is corrupt in one way or another," Richard said. "But it's no more corrupt than almost any city in the country."

"Whatever Nick wants, it's not in Youngstown. I'm afraid I'll lose him. To the draft, probably—oh God, what if he goes to Vietnam?"

"I don't want him to—and I'll have to pray triple time for his safety. You should too, Diane."

"After that stupid war—assuming they're ever going to end it—who knows what Nick's going to do."

"There are lots of places where you can make more money," Richard said, shrugging. "Chicago, Boston, Washington—maybe even Atlanta. I understand where he's coming from."

Diane turned her face so Richard wouldn't see tears well up behind her eyes.

"You can always move with him."

She shook her head.

"Why not?"

"I've spent my whole life on Brier Hill." She sighed. "My parents are there, my friends. It—it scares me to think about going somewhere else."

"When you're married, whither he goest, there you goest, too."

"We're not married," she said. "Not yet. And if he goes into the service, he'll wind up in Vietnam." With the tip of her forefinger, she touched the outside corner of her right eye; she might have been crying. "What will he be like when he comes back, Richard? And will I be able to handle that?"

As a priest, it was his moment to intone something about God's will, but he approached it differently, as a dear friend of hers and a brother to me. "Nobody knows that until it happens, Diane. Don't get scared until you have to."

She was silent for a while, then cleared her throat and was glad Richard didn't look over and see her blushing. "Can I tell you something?"

"Of course."

"I don't know if I should be open and honest with you, as a friend, or scoot into the confession booth, where you can't see my face, and tell you about it there."

"Is this a personal secret, friend to friend, or is it a venial sin?"

She laughed without mirth, blushing deeper. "Oh, it's a sin all right."

"I don't want to hear about venial sins between you and my brother." And he covered his ears with his palms and softly sang "La-la-la-la-la" so he couldn't hear her.

She laughed. "I won't offend your holy thoughts, but Nick and I *are* grown-ups, and it's the seventies. So we spend a hell of a lot—oops, sorry, Father—a lot of our time in bed together."

"We've known each other all our lives, so knock off the 'Father' business," he said, suddenly struck by the absurdity. "I'm religious, but I'm not blind or stupid. So as a friend, I say enjoy yourself and revel in those tender, loving feelings."

"And as a priest?"

"I've got to limber up those Hail Marys and Our Fathers to give you for penance—if you ever make a confession with me."

Diane stopped, reached up and put her arms around the priest's neck, and pulled his head down for a kiss on the cheek. "I love you, Father Candy," she said.

"I love you, too," he said, guiding her elbow with his hand so they were now heading back the way they'd come, toward St. Aloysius. "I'm glad you came to see me. It perked up my day."

"Just spending time with you perked up mine, too."

Relief flooded through Diane's veins and she hugged Richard's arm close against her. Talking to him had made her feel good again, feel safe. Richard was one of those people always looking out for you—protecting you.

Praying for you.

Standing at the edge of Richard's grave, I still wasn't listening to the bishop, but staring hard at Diane. She was Diane Burnham now; her husband was a partner in a blue-chip law firm downtown. I'd met him once, briefly, after their marriage. I couldn't remember what he looked like.

But I recalled the public dinner with Richard when I was still in college. He'd aged a million years toiling for the church, and hardly resembled the older brother I'd grown up idolizing, now dressed in somber black and a stiff white collar. The waitresses at the Colonial House treated him as if he were the Pope himself. They didn't realize, or care, that he was the surviving leader of the Candiotti clan. But when he was a kid and our family was embarrassingly poor, Richard rarely broke bread at the Colonial House.

My resentment toward my hometown had started growing, niggling at my college brain, when Richard invited me to that dinner. I was ill at ease, a young adult sitting across from a priest, wearing my only suit and a garish medium-blue tie. Even though we talked often on the phone, I'd visited Richard's New Philadelphia church only twice. Unlike the rest of the family, I hadn't been going to Mass at Our Lady in Youngstown, either. I never followed any Catholic rules or habits.

He was just my brother, not my confessor. He advised me to go for a master's degree to keep me out of Vietnam, which I chose to ignore. He told me to marry Diane, which would also lower my number in the draft. He said if I left for good, the family would be disappointed—and that some, like Teresa, would never forgive me.

But I was too busy thinking of Diane—the way her skin felt beneath my hands, how her hair smelled. I thought about the first time I'd seen her naked—the first time I'd seen and touched the nude body of someone of the opposite sex. Remembering it in front of my priest brother, I flushed with embarrassment. And lust.

Diane and I lost our childhoods together. I haven't the foggiest idea of where she learned some of the things to which she eventually introduced me in bed. She said she read about them in romantic novels, and I thought them strange, abstruse, and kinky. But the first night that she took my penis in her mouth and made it hard with her tongue, and then swung her body around so her knees were on either side of my head and told me to eat her out, it was an entire sex education within minutes.

I didn't want to leave Diane back then, but she wanted to stay where she'd been born and raised, to pursue the small, rusty dreams so many locals accepted as their right and due, and I yearned to move away and discover the rest of the world. Richard was all over my case about it at that dinner—and it irritated me.

"Get your head out from under your cassock and look around," I said. "Everybody in Youngstown is either a gangster or *wants* to be a gangster."

"That's not true."

"No, everybody else is the *friend* of gangsters—one gang or the other, because they're too scared not to be friends, and too terrified that one morning they'll go out and turn on their car and—" I made the childish sound a kid makes playing war and exploding his enemies. "Surprise! The good old Youngstown Tune-Up. Then a week later, someone in the other family gets wiped out, too. It's always war on the next block, and it never ends. How can anybody live in this goddamn town?"

"Don't curse," Richard said.

"You have a limited vocabulary—and a limited outlook. The real world doesn't stop at the borders of Mahoning County."

And then he forgot about cursing and told me I was acting like an asshole. Normally, you don't hear that from priests.

It was hard hanging on to that resentment now that I was mourning Richard, who'd eschewed anger for kindness, sanctity, and charity. Yet he'd turned the tables on me, bringing back my inner rage and a raving hunger to avenge him when he'd placed a gun between his teeth and pulled the trigger.

Why the hell *was* that?

CHAPTER FOUR

Finally, mercifully, it was over—the prayers and chants and rituals, the burning incense, the crying and sniffling. The Candiotti family came forward to drop roses onto Richard's casket as it was lowered into the grave. Richard wasn't being interred beside our parents but instead would rest for eternity on slightly higher ground. The headstones that surrounded his plot were almost all inscribed with the names of priests and nuns, or the very rich. There were a few towering angel statues on the graves, too, of marble and granite. On the clergy graves, they were pretty small angels.

The crowd thinned out fast, but the road downhill was narrow and the cars moved slowly, stopping, chugging a few feet ahead, then stopping again.

Don Frank Mangione paused for a moment to talk to me, our first conversation for at least twenty years. He didn't offer a handshake but moved close to my ear and spoke softly.

"Your brother was good for people in this city," he said. "Good for all of us. This death, it breaks my heart." He tapped his chest where his heart might have been. "Why would he do such a thing, Dominick? It breaks my heart."

I didn't know why Richard had done such a thing—nor *if*

he'd done it. But I'd returned to Youngstown to discover the reasons, and to mete out punishment where it was richly deserved. I couldn't say that to the old man, though—at least not yet. "I thank you for your kind words, Don Mangione."

"You and me don't know each other so good, but Richard was my confessor and my friend. So I offer whatever assistance you want." He patted me on the arm and stepped away. His son Frank junior took more than a moment to meet my eyes before he moved away. It wasn't a friendly look—just curious. His resemblance to his father was obvious; they were both short men with wide faces and bodies like fireplugs.

The Youngstown police came next in line, crowding around Alfonso, shaking his hand or patting his back. Capt. Ed Shemo was at least six inches taller than Al, and when he put both arms around him, Al almost disappeared within his hug. Shemo looked at me over Al's shoulder, nodding. There was little I had to say to cops anyway.

The other mourners passed in front of my family—neighbors, parishioners, high-placed clerics and high-rolling laity contributors, mayors of Youngstown, Warren, and Niles, city and county politicians, and two Jewish community heavyweights and their wives who owned huge parcels of real estate in Trumbull and Mahoning counties. I shook more than three hundred hands and kissed more than two hundred cheeks at the hillside cemetery. I had no idea who most of the mourners were, but the scents the men had splashed on their cheeks were stronger than the perfume worn by the women.

Diane Burnham had disappeared after the service ended. Those who remained to brave the chill had watched the first shovel of dirt thud against the lid of the coffin, then headed for home.

Alfonso and Dolores walked back toward the limo with me. Ahead of us, Charlie was holding Teresa's elbow to steady her as she maneuvered between the monuments and tombstones. She appeared to be scolding him as they walked—or maybe she'd grown into her married thirties always looking that angry. Al, on the other hand, marched in military fashion, his shoulders back, his uniform cap worn squarely on his forehead, a few steps in front of his wife, whose moving was difficult in her high heels and short, tight skirt—as if she'd wandered into the funeral by mistake on her way to lunch with a lover and really wasn't part of the Candiotti clan at all.

When we were all in the limousine except the bishop, who was riding back to his office in his own limo, Charlie and I were on the jump seats, facing the rear. Alfonso took off his gold-billed cap and leaned forward to put his hand on my knee.

"Nick, we're having people to the house," he said. "Not a big crowd—just friends close to us. Even the caterers and bartenders who'll be there—they thought the sun rose and set on Richard. You're coming, aren't you? It'd be funny if you didn't show up. Everybody wants to see you."

"Everybody," Teresa added, "who hasn't seen you since you were a kid." Her voice grew sharp. "People who loved Richard and respected our family—even though they forgot about you."

"Let them remember how they loved Richard while I go back to my hotel," I said. "They won't give me a second thought."

"*I'll* give you a second thought." Teresa's jaw had turned to concrete, angled out and upward like a stone bench in the cemetery, her lips nearly invisible. "This is your family, too—even if you turned chickenshit and ran somewhere else a lot of years ago. So you're coming to Alfonso's whether you want to or not, and you'll be polite to everybody. You'll nod, cluck your tongue, and be kind. I know you don't give a rat's ass for us, but you *will* show Richard the respect he deserves—or you'll answer to me."

It was easy remembering how much I'd always disliked my older sister. I'd had plenty of fistfights in my childhood—I won most of them, and, like any kid, I lost a few, too—but the worst beatings I ever suffered were administered by Teresa, whom I would never hit back, even though she always doubled up her fist. There are two generations of Catholic kids somewhere who lucked out that she never became a teaching nun.

I slouched against the back of my jump seat and looked out the window. Gray morning had turned to dark afternoon, and a rainstorm was imminent.

Why were the mourners visiting Alfonso's? They'd prayed, wept, and shuffled past the family, murmuring sympathy. Why prolong this day and extend their connection? Were they desperate to stretch their relationship to Father Richard for another hour or two? Were they troubled by a priest's suicide that had no answer and hoped that by pressing themselves close in Dolores Candiotti's elegant, soulless living room, they'd learn a solution at last?

Or did they just want the free feed?

The drizzle began when the limo pulled into Alfonso's driveway behind a caterer's truck. Cars were parked along the street for several blocks in every direction, and windows inside the house glowed with false cheer against the pewter sky. The driver from the funeral home jumped out and opened an enormous black umbrella, under which both women crouched so they wouldn't get wet on the way to the front door. Alfonso sat quietly, unsure as to whether the umbrella would return for him. When I turned up the collar of my coat and got out of the car, Charlie followed meekly, and Al figured he'd look sissified if he waited for someone to hold the umbrella over his head, so he got out, too, keeping his cap down by his side so it wouldn't be ruined.

Inside, one of two young men with military haircuts—rookie police officers volunteered by Captain Shemo for in-house services—disappeared with my coat. About forty people were crowded into the great room, all drinking wine. Several others had started on the dining room buffet spread. Three young women wearing outfits from the caterer's stood behind the table, spooning food onto the extended plates of the mourners. The caterer himself, Glenn Keeney, who avoided looking like a server and wore a well-cut gray suit instead, circulated among the guests, shaking hands. Glenn once owned an upscale restaurant in Boardman, and he knew personally every high-level cop, politician, business maven, and city reporter for the *Youngstown Vindicator*.

The great room was stuffy, despite its size—looking bleak, as if no one really lived there, like a stage setting on which to play out the end of the long afternoon of obsequies. It was a large, expensive house, far more pricey than most local police lieutenants could afford on Alfonso's salary.

It didn't take me long to find Diane. She was at one end of the living room, standing by the floor-to-ceiling glass window and looking quietly out at a well-sculpted flower garden in the backyard, where costly hosta, planted strategically in rows, bowed beneath the onslaught of the rain.

"I was hoping you'd be here," I said when I finally reached her. I wanted to hug her, as an old friend there to support my bereavement—and I wanted to kiss her the way I used to. I did neither. "I wanted to talk to you at the cemetery, but I guess it wasn't the time or place."

Diane sighed a little. "There are no times and places. You look well, Nicky." She studied me up and down. I was a shade taller than Richard had been, although I packed a few more pounds around my shoulders. My hair was slightly longer than anyone else's in the room.

"You're the one who looks good, Diane. Fantastic, even." Diane's eyes mesmerized me. They always had. "Is your husband here with you?"

She hesitated before saying "No."

I recognized the beat of hesitation, and decided to ignore it. "Did you see a lot of Richard before . . ."

She smiled ruefully. "I'm not the world's best Catholic, but I tried to get to Sunday Mass at least once or twice a month. I always loved Richard's sermons. He was so—what? Wise, I guess. He was a wise man."

"You're a CEO now, I hear."

"I'm a *co*-CEO, yes, along with a woman I met—after college. It's a small marketing business, mostly local, but we're pushing hard." She looked out again at the rain, falling heavier now. "How long are you staying in town?"

"I haven't decided. There are things I have to find out."

"Yes," she said, but she didn't really mean yes.

"I'd love to talk more with you. It's been too many years. Can you find time for lunch? Maybe tomorrow, or the next day? We should catch up." I felt foolish as soon as I'd said it. What was there to catch up on? We'd been each other's first lovers. But when I graduated, my number came up too soon. I was drafted and sent to Vietnam's Special Forces, where I killed people.

Personally. Up close.

There was killing in Youngstown, too—in my neighborhood, among my friends and schoolmates. It was during my last year at Youngstown State when someone close to me was efficiently and heartlessly disposed of—and it hit me hard in a very personal way.

His name was Jim Gaglione—another Italian, naturally, but he wasn't from Youngstown, or even from Ohio. Born and raised in Queens, New York, he'd earned his bachelor's and master's degrees from New York University, taught in New Jersey for a few years, and then relocated to Youngstown, where he became assistant professor of sociology. I took his course in my junior year, and since he was only about eleven years older than I was, we became buddies, drinking companions, eventually good friends. I learned a hell of a lot more from Gaglione over a pitcher of beer than I ever did in his classroom—but that's not unusual for college teachers.

What can I tell you about Jim? He cheered for neither the Browns nor the Steelers, but he frequently wore a red-white-and-blue New York Giants jacket. Like most other Italians, he listened almost religiously to Sinatra and Tony Bennett records, but he loved all kinds of food, especially Mexican, and would complain there weren't many good Mexican restaurants within driving distance.

As far as the Vietnam War was concerned, Jim Gaglione gobbled up the news every day. He wanted America to go in there, level the place, and bring home the blue ribbon. We argued about it sometimes over a beer, because I just wanted us to quit fighting a hopeless war and bring our guys home.

Jim was around during the sixties and admitted he'd smoked some pot, but he was dead against drugs, too—especially heroin. That's what got him into trouble.

A young woman, a freshman at Y-town State, had been kicked out of school for prostitution. I didn't know her, so it only touched me peripherally. But Jim knew her from one of his classes, and he reached out to help her straighten herself out. When he learned she'd started turning tricks because she was hooked on horse, he found out the name of the man who was supplying her with the drug and who was pimping her, as well. He went to the police with the story, and when he got no satisfaction, he went higher, to the DEA headquartered in Philadelphia. The drug pusher/pimp was arrested and an investigation started, ending up with the indictment of two distant members of the Severino family. The young woman was moved somewhere out west—I think it was Denver—and went through withdrawal treatment and psychological counseling. Jim figured it turned out all right in the end, and he was pretty proud of himself because of it.

About two months after the indictment, he was found unconscious in Mill Creek Park. Both his arms and most of his ribs were broken, and his face was completely smashed in. Nobody seemed to know who'd done it or why, but even the *Vindicator* reported there had been more than one attacker.

I knew who'd done it, or at least who'd ordered it done, but I had no proof and was handcuffed from doing anything about it. Jim Gaglione lingered in the hospital in a coma for almost a week and then died quietly—almost a year to the day that both my parents had been killed in an automobile accident.

So much violence, so much death, and the local police wouldn't even stir their asses unless they had to. That made me not want to live in Youngstown anymore. I waited until graduation and then quickly joined the army, was put through Officer Candidate School and Ranger training, and was sent to Vietnam as a professional killer for Uncle Sam.

After the war, I came back. Richard was still celebrating Mass at his church in New Philadelphia, Teresa was now mothering her second child and was well on her way to becoming a solid-gold bitch, and Alfonso was too busy kissing important asses and learning how to be a political cop. There was nothing left for me in Youngstown except Diane, and it was very hard for me to readjust to civilian life after the long nightmare of war I'd lived through. I asked her to move away with me—I was ready for her. I was not, however, anywhere near ready for marriage, and when I failed to pop that particular question, Diane chose to remain in Youngstown with her family and friends. She begged me to stay there with her, but that just wasn't in the cards.

So I packed up and moved to Chicago, and Diane married someone else. Shortly after that—in September of 1977—Black Monday hit northeast Ohio, and most steel mills shut down. In the next few years, fifty thousand workers queued up in the unemployment line, and the Youngstown area never recovered.

Now, in 1985, there was no catching up left to do.

"You can tell me about Richard," I said. "About his last years."

"Are you going to trade stories with me?" Diane Burnham asked. "And tell me about these last years for you?"

"That'll be a short story."

"Sometimes short stories are the best."

Alfonso was calling my name, waving me over to the other side of the room to talk to a visitor—an elderly lady who was crying all over again because Father Richard was gone forever. Diane and I made a quick appointment—a lunch date for 12:30 the next day at Courtney's—and then I moved away and tried not to think about her any more that evening. Tried and failed.

While I was talking to the red-eyed old woman, Paolo Severino came up and tapped me on the shoulder.

"I want we should talk, Dominick," he said. "How many years since you and me had a real conversation? About a million, I think."

I thought he might be right, as he *looked* a million years old. He was in his late eighties.

"I don't live here anymore. I hardly ever come back."

The old man nodded. "This business with Father Richard—it makes me sad. I loved him. I cried when he died, and I cried at church today." He made a gentle fist and tapped his chest where the ribs came together. "Your brother Al, he been like a son to me, too. Ever since your father died, they were like my boys."

"Kind of you to say."

"Your brothers always been close to me. But you, Dominick—" and he held out his hand, palm downward, and tipped it back and forth—"you, not so much." His tone was kind. "Why? I wonder. I done anything which offended you?"

"Times just change, sir. After Vietnam, everything was different. I wanted to live somewhere else, and do my own thing." I wasn't lying well, and I knew it.

"But you're back now."

"For a few days is all."

Severino reached into his pocket and pulled out a business card and a pen—not a ballpoint, but an old, elegant fountain pen from thirty years earlier. He opened the cap and held it between his lips, signing his name on the back of the card. "Here," he said. "Come to my club. Eat, drink, gamble—whatever you want. You don't spend a nickel in my place, and there'll be lots of nice girls for you to talk with."

"I'm in mourning."

"Me, too, but I ain't dead. Neither are you. Understand what I'm saying to you?" He threw his arms around me and hugged. Then he broke away, heading into the crowd near the door. The people stepped back like the parting waves of the Red Sea, murmuring to him as he brushed past them. They all used his honorary title, Don.

On the back of his business card, Severino's signature was boldly unreadable. On the front was the name of the casino he owned and operated.

In 1985, legal gambling existed in the United States only in parts of Nevada, Atlantic City, and some casinos on Indian land, run by the local tribes and answering to no one. But Severino's gambling club operated in northeast Ohio as openly as if it were on the Las Vegas Strip, and everyone accepted it—the police, the Church, the business community, the university, the state legislature, and anyone else over the age of nine. Wealthy gamblers treated the club like an unending Hollywood premiere, gawking at visiting celebrities, but the casino was criminal and everyone knew it, including off-duty cops who acted as parking lot valets and security.

I slipped the business card into my wallet as my sister-in-law, Dolores, approached me. Her lipstick was slightly smeared, and her walk—always provocative—had somehow turned into a burlesque of gracious hostess. She was smiling crookedly, and the sharp aroma of whiskey surrounded her like a force field.

"Hello, brother dear," she said. "You're receiving your subjects like a king—and not paying any attention to your family. Shame on you, Dominick." She put a hand on my arm, leaning heavily on me, one of her breasts pushing aggressively against me. I wondered how many bourbons she'd consumed already. "You want something to drink?"

"I'm fine, Dolores."

She nodded. "You're always fine, aren't you? That's what's so neat about being you, isn't it? Always fine." She half-turned from me, checking out the crowd. "What do you think of our elegant house anyway?"

"It's a very nice house," I said.

"That's nice," she said. "It's so nice that you think it's nice. *Nice* is right up there with *fine* in your vocabulary, right?"

"It's a lovely house, but *lovely* isn't the kind of word guys use. I've been here before, you know."

"I know, baby," she said. "Your infrequent visits are front-page news. How many times have you been here since Al and I moved in? Twice?"

"Today is number three."

"Whoopee," Dolores said, dry as dust. "We ought to have funerals every day; then we'd see more of you."

"Hold your breath until the next one, then."

She took it like the backhand slap I'd intended it to be. I moved away from her, hating being anywhere near her or my family, and hating the shared history I'd been party to. The only relative I'd cared for was Richard—last of the Mohicans—and he was gone.

Glenn Keeney, the caterer, assailed me. "I'm sorry to meet you under these circumstances," he said, solidifying my guess that he'd had no idea who I was until someone pointed me out to him. "I knew Richard very well—as a priest and a friend. I play poker a few times a week with some pals—people like your brother Alfonso—and Richard enjoyed playing with us."

"A few times a week?" I said.

"No, no—only when he could get away from his duties." He shook his head sadly. "What will we do without him?" He produced a card and pressed it on me like a magician traveling from table to table in a restaurant, picking customer's pockets for fun. "If there's anything I can do for you," he said, "don't hesitate to call." He leaned in closer to me. "If you're thinking of a party or anything, I'll make you a good deal." He clapped me on the shoulder and walked away. I glanced at the card; it was a business card promoting Keeney Catering. I wondered how many guests there to mourn my brother were carrying newly acquired business cards from Glenn Keeney. I stuck it in my pocket so I could throw it away when I got back to the hotel.

I left without bidding good-bye to anyone except, in an off-hand way, Al. I hadn't approached Teresa, who was too busy tormenting her husband, and as for Dolores, I doubted she'd ever speak to me again. I recalled that her family was connected distantly to the Severinos, but I wasn't sure how and didn't care.

My stomach was empty, and I'd had nothing to drink, either, but I didn't want to hang out in a bar or restaurant, nor hole myself up in my impersonal room. I just wanted to drive around the city and look at it for a while.

In autumn, the darkness comes early to Youngstown, so only a smear of orange remained in the western sky as I pulled out from the long line of mourners' cars and headed toward the part of Youngstown I knew best.

I hadn't seen Market Street for many years. It was now only a dim memory of how it used to be when I went to Y-town State and shared a small studio apartment with two of my college classmates, who never moved farther away than Boardman. Market Street, south of downtown and over the bridge spanning the Mahoning River, had been popping back then, with restaurants, clubs, and seedy bars. College kids hung out there every night, and the aggressive strolling hookers who lined the sidewalk would trot out into the street to rap genially on the window of a car stopped for a red light. Youngstown was a good place in which to be young—when everyone looked for fun, adventure, some decent beer or booze, and to learn all about life and verve and sex.

It was different now, in 1985—except for the hookers. Some were still there, well into middle age, and others were newcomers, but they all looked alike to me.

I hadn't been back in this neighboorhood since before Black Monday. On almost every block was a burned-out house or two, charred and mute among occupied homes. Someone with money and power owned fire insurance on those houses, and set fire to them as often as they dared to get rich on the payments.

There were houses that had not been torched, but these were abandoned, too. All their windows were broken, the front doors were sealed shut with raw boards, and the lawns hadn't been mowed for a year and grass had grown up around the front steps, swaying and blowing in the wind like a tragic savanna. It was almost as if some army like General Sherman's had marched through here, laid waste to the houses, and salted the land so no one could even raise a crop.

These houses were ghosts that wouldn't let me forget that before the economic tragedy that slammed its door on Youngstown in 1977, this city had been alive, vital, and bustling. Most of it was run by the unlawful and corrupt back then, as it always has been. But it was still a good town.

The farther south on Market Street I drove, the sleazier it became. Finally, at Indianola Avenue, I turned right and then right again on Hillman Street to work my way back downtown to my hotel.

Hillman Street jolted me even worse. Bad enough when it was daylight, at night it virtually screamed danger. On nearly every corner, tough-looking men hung out, almost all of them African-Americans. They kept their hands in their pockets, but their eyes were constantly alert and aware, staring both ways down the street. I watched a few cars stop, their passenger-side windows rolled down, and some sort of conversation took place between loafer and driver. Several of the cars were high-end luxury vehicles, driven by well-dressed white men who obviously had some sort of business to transact with the street-corner sentinels.

I'd been away from Youngstown for a long time, but not *that* long, so I knew that whatever anyone wanted to purchase—heroin, cocaine, crack, crystal meth, prostitutes of either sex and any age, or weapons—was easily available on Hillman Street. Hillman Street was a crowded Farmers' Market for the Depraved.

Half the men whom I'd served with in Vietnam and who'd survived to return to postwar America—even though Washington never admitted it *was* a war—carried a drug monkey on their backs. The government wouldn't admit that, either. If they came back to Youngstown, many of them cruised Hillman with their passenger windows down.

I shivered, squeezing my eyes shut, but when I opened them again, nothing had changed. I looked for a side street and got the hell off Hillman Street as fast as I could.

After a few minutes more of driving, when I was downtown again, close to the Holiday Inn where I was staying, I found a bar.

CHAPTER FIVE

The next morning, I woke with a hangover, the haunting essence of a headache behind my eyes. Maybe the funeral made me realize I'd never see my brother again or hear his voice on the telephone. One expects parents to die eventually, but I never thought Richard would go before I did.

He hadn't been to war like me, going out into the fetid Vietnamese jungle alone at night, breaking necks and efficiently cutting throats the way I had. But Richard, kind and generous by nature, had been trained by the Church to save souls, not to send them untimely into hell. As for me, I still wasn't sure whether the Vietcong I'd killed—were they all Vietcong, or were they unfortunate ordinary citizens who got caught in the squeeze of a senseless American war?—had immediately been dispatched to Hades to roast slowly, or had risen upward to Paradise.

Like a wife, Heaven and Hell weren't issued by the military.

I called room service for coffee and then I showered, standing too long under the stinging-hot needles until the water cooled.

I arrived at Courtney's about ten minutes early. I wished we could have lunch at the elegant old landmark restaurant, the Mansion, on Market Street, but it had burned to the ground the year before. When some Youngstown building goes up in flames, nobody ever asks why. Most often we know anyway—hearing the insurance company grinding its teeth in frustration as it issues the check.

I asked for black coffee, and sipped it quietly until Diane Burnham showed up. She one-upped me—she was fifteen minutes late.

I stood up, took her elbow, kissed her cheek. Her skin smelled the same as it always had, fresh and natural, with only a hint of perfume. It wasn't the same scent she used to wear, though; it was more mature and aggressive.

"Thanks for coming," I said, hoping no one in Courtney's would notice how I looked at her. Diane was dressed for a day at the office—a dark blue business suit with an at-the-knee skirt and an emerald silk blouse. She looked the way she was supposed to—a marketing executive—but I thought her as beautiful and sexy as ever, and a long-forgotten memory pulled hard like a stretched rubber band inside my chest.

How long had it been since I'd felt that tug from my youth? Had it never faded away? I'd nodded at Diane at church with her husband about six years earlier when I'd visited Richard's Sunday-before-Christmas Mass, but we'd said little more than hello.

"I can't remember my last meal in Courtney's," I said as she sat down. "Probably before Vietnam—when I was with you."

"I've lost count how many times I've been here since."

With her husband? I tried not to feel envy or resentment. It was the wrong time. I hadn't been to bed with Diane for thirteen years, had hardly spoken to her. We'd both moved on, but jealousy felt far too familiar.

She looked at my coffee cup. "Aren't you drinking these days?"

"Sure—just waiting for you."

Diane checked her watch. "Sorry I was late getting here. Bad habit of mine."

"It never used to be. You were always right on time."

Her smile was wry and bitter. "That was many moons ago, White Cloud."

I looked around for the waitress and we both ordered drinks. "It was good seeing you yesterday," I said. "Your being at the cemetery made me feel more comfortable. Did you see Richard often?"

"In the past few years, I only saw him at church. Now I probably won't go back again." She shrugged. "He and I used to squeeze in an occasional midweek lunch, but we just ... drifted apart. He was busy."

"Being a priest?"

She didn't answer, just lowered her head and looked up at me with her amazing eyes. "Are you still a lapsed Catholic, Nicky?"

"I couldn't even tell you the name of the Catholic church nearest my house in Chicago." I toyed with my coffee cup. "What was Richard like toward the end, Diane? Was he different?"

Diane had to think about it. "I guess—different *sometimes*."

"Was he losing his faith?"

"I think he was more serious about religion than ever before. He was more serious about everything."

"Oh?"

"He didn't laugh much in the past few years. As a young priest, he was very jolly. He relished a good joke as much as anyone—and they loved him for that."

"You loved him, didn't you?"

Her smile was tired. "Of course I did."

"I'm glad you transferred your crush from him to his younger brother."

Diane looked away, glancing around the room for a moment. "A crush," she murmured. "He told you that story?"

"After you told him you'd been crazy about him." I leaned forward and put my hand on the tablecloth, not touching her. Holding her hand when she was wearing someone else's wedding ring was too intimate—almost obscene. "You're beautiful as ever, Diane."

"Nobody looks as good at thirty-five as they did at twenty. I've gained about ten pounds since college. It went right to my hips."

"Liar."

"I wish."

"Well, *I* think you're drop-dead gorgeous—like always."

"Just memories talking," Diane said. "You think of those days with sugary emotion and get all sickly sentimental. When you go back to Chicago, you'll hardly think about Youngstown anymore."

"You're wrong."

"Am I? I bet you don't even remember what my home address was."

I recited it without even thinking about it.

That raised her eyebrows a little. "Very good," she said.

"You want to hear your old home phone number, too? Your favorite food was gnocchi because your mom made it so well," I went on, pronouncing it the old-world way, *nyOH-kee*. "Your favorite color was green. Your favorite music was Simon and Garfunkel, and your favorite book was *To Kill a Mockingbird*. You loved the movie."

"My mother doesn't cook much anymore," she said, "and we don't often go to her house for dinner, so I miss the gnocchi. I miss hearing 'Scarborough Fair' on the radio, too. But I still like green—if you didn't figure that out from the blouse. And *Mockingbird* is still my favorite book of all time."

"Let's see," I said. "What else? During your school years, you preferred those big fuzzy socks. When you wore a dress, it was a size four. You wore size seven and a half shoes, narrow. And your bra was a thirty-four B."

Embarrassment splashed Diane's face pink. "My God, Nick. You remember *that* thirteen years later? That's creepy."

"I remember everything about you—everything about *us*."

The waitress returned with a single-malt scotch for me and a vodka martini, straight up, for Diane. She caressed the stem of the martini glass, then stirred the lemon twist with her little finger. "The good old Pete Penguin days at Y-town State . . ."

"Pete Penguin," I said, thinking of our school mascot. "Cute little guy."

"He seemed cute at the time." She shook her head to clear away cobwebs she didn't know were there. "But it was mean keeping a penguin as a mascot. Ohio wasn't a good climate for him, and he died a few years later. So sad." She looked over my shoulder, not meeting my eyes. "Childish, wasn't it? And weren't *we*? All that old shit clutters up your mind, makes it hard to remember what's new—what's important. You ought to empty out your memories every once in a while."

"You can't toss out the important stuff."

"If it was so goddamn important at the time, why didn't you come home after you became a civilian again? Why did you leave to hide in Chicago?"

I shook my head to tell her I wasn't going to answer. Instead, I clinked my glass against hers. "Cheers," I said.

A man approached our table. He was close to my age, wearing an elegantly tailored black suit with pinstripes, and a pair of absurdly tiny John Lennon–type glasses tinted with a touch of gray. I'd seen him rarely, and not for many years, but I recognized him immediately. Of course I didn't like him, but men are like that sometimes—*more* than just sometimes.

He leaned down and kissed Diane's cheek the way one might kiss one's old Sunday school teacher—not the way one kisses one's wife. But he was looking at me instead. "Taking a lunch break, Diane?" Bob Burnham said. "Good for you—you work too hard."

Diane cleared her throat. "Bob, I think you remember Dominick—"

Her husband pumped my hand heartily. "Yes, sure," he said, interrupting her before she pronounced my last name. "I think we met several years ago, didn't we? I've heard a lot about you. From Diane."

"That was kind of her," I said.

"More than kind. Oh, she praises you to the skies, Nicky."

Shocking that he used my nickname. Only my family calls me Nicky—and Diane, naturally. But when Burnham pronounced it, "Nicky" came out of his mouth like a dirty word.

"I was sorry to hear about your brother," he went on, adjusting his glasses on the bridge of his nose. "I tried to get to the funeral, but I had an important meeting."

"Father Richard made the funeral just fine," I said. "I guess he didn't have any important meetings."

Bob straightened, blinking. Diane drummed the tabletop, red-polished nails clicking. I remembered that gesture of annoyance from thirteen years earlier.

I could tell the way he worked on setting his face that he was going to ignore the shot I'd taken at him—or at least pretend to. "So—you two are remembering the good old times, huh? They were all good times." His eyes launched daggers at me. "They were good times until Father Richard, uh, passed away. Everybody loved him, you know. I'm not the first one to tell you that."

"No, you're not the first one."

He threw his shoulders back, standing up as tall as he could so he could look down his nose at me. "Even the Severinos and the Mangiones loved him—and of course I did."

"You did? I had no idea. Were you his personal attorney?"

Diane jumped in, slightly out of breath. "Priests don't need attorneys. At least Richard didn't."

"That's right," Bob said, smiling so his teeth showed the way Doberman pinschers look when Hollywood makes them snarl and appear vicious in movies. "He gave a hell of a lot more help and advice to me than I ever did to him."

"What a wonderful guy he was," I said. My mouth was nearly dry, and I yearned for a sip of my drink, but I was damned if I'd do it while Bob Burnham stood at the table.

Diane tried not to let her question sound anxious. "Are you here for lunch, Bob?"

Bob shook his head. "I had an early lunch, so I'm just leaving. Oh, well—important meetings again, like every other day. But that's my life, isn't it, Diane? Nicky, it's good to see you again, but I wish it were under different circumstances." He started toward the exit, waving good-bye to Diane without looking at her.

"He's prosperous-looking," I said to his retreating back, possibly too softly for him to hear me, "and maybe a little chubby."

"He *is* prosperous."

He looked over his shoulder once when he got to the entrance. He didn't look like a Doberman any longer—now more like a vulture.

"He doesn't seem upset that we're having lunch together," I said, watching as he turned the corner toward the front door and disappeared from my sight lines.

"It's a public place," she said. "Besides, we're old friends."

"Does he know that? I mean about how good friends we were?"

She nodded slowly. "Bob knows just about everything. He makes it his business to know. That's *why* he's so successful." She reached for her drink. "I asked you a question before."

"I forgot."

"Liar. I asked why you didn't come back here after your war. Why you chose to hide out in Chicago."

"Didn't I answer that?"

"No, you just clinked my glass and said 'Cheers.' Don't give me that 'Cheers' bullshit."

I tasted the scotch I'd been longing for since Burnham had joined us. "I had things I was running from."

"What things?"

"Vietnam things, mostly. You don't want to hear about them."

"Yes, I do."

I didn't smile. "Then click your heels three times, turn around under a bright star, and make a wish, because I don't tell war stories. Tell me your stories instead."

Another sip of her martini twisted her mouth. Maybe the martini had a big kick to it. "I don't have any stories. Just an old novel I keep adding to."

"What about your business? Marketing, is it? You majored in accounting."

"I did. I worked for my cousin Jerry for a while—he had a restaurant in Boardman, remember? Well, I did his accounting every month, and offered unsolicited business suggestions—but it wasn't full-time. I quit a few months before I got married. I didn't have a job again until three years ago, when a friend started this company with me. Her name is Betty Mazzi—she's married to Pete Rizzo, who used to play baseball for the Penguins in college. Did you know him?"

"No," I said.

"Well, anyway, that's what I do. My business. See, I told you it was boring."

"So you're skipping over the novel—not even giving me a plot line?"

"The novel is that when I figured out you weren't ever coming back, I counted my problems on all my fingers—and then married Bob Burnham."

I clenched my teeth, wondering if the muscles around my jawbone were visibly jumping. "Was he a big-shot lawyer even back then?"

"He was in law school. *Then* he became a big-shot lawyer. He represents movers and shakers in Mahoning and Trumbull counties, but he also represents some foreign companies. I don't even know which ones they are, but Bob's great at making profitable connections." She chewed the inside of her cheek.

"Whoa, now I'm impressed. Is he a good Catholic, too?"

"Not really."

"Ah, then he doesn't go to church to pray, but to be seen by the right people. He mumbles prayers he doesn't even know, kneels and makes the sign of the cross, and writes a nice check to Our Lady every six months, so his important law clients think his conscience is clear and his sins confessed to and cleaned up neatly. Then, when they need a virtuous lawyer to screw the little guys, the ones they've fucked over—or to keep them from stepping on their own dicks—they call Bob Burnham."

"Stop being an asshole," she said. "Why do you hate him so much? You don't even know him."

"Do I hate him?"

"You're making fun of him."

"I used to make fun of Jerry Lewis, too. Remember? I used to imitate him, the way he walks, the way he yells 'Hey, lady!' That doesn't mean I hate Jerry Lewis."

"Is it because Bob married me? Because he sleeps with me?"

I should have been more cautious, or even taken a beat before I answered her. But I didn't. "Yes," I said, "because he sleeps with you."

Diane pushed a lock of hair from her forehead. "You dumped my ass thirteen years ago. Have you been celibate ever since? I doubt it. So why is it different?"

I absently patted my left jacket pocket, only then remembering I'd given up smoking nearly ten years ago. I suddenly wanted one desperately. "Because I'm an asshole. Okay?"

This time, Diane's laughter was genuine. "Okay," she said.

We ordered lunch. I chose a steak sandwich with french fries—one of my favorites. Diane picked a Caesar salad. "So I won't gain any more weight," she said.

"You look fantastic; you always look fantastic."

Her smile was a secret one—from everyone but me. "College—and you—that was a long time ago. A long, skinny time."

I leaned back in my chair, keeping one hand on my glass, playing with it, almost stroking it. "So," I said.

"So."

"You didn't have kids?"

She didn't look at me. "Bob didn't want children."

"*Bob* didn't."

"No."

"A good solid Catholic like Bob doesn't want a houseful of rug rats? The church would faint if it knew he uses prevention. Did you confess that to Father Richard? He would have laid a penance on your husband that would have made his eyes roll."

"Give it a rest, Nicky."

"A rest," I said. "Sure. I'll close its little eyes."

The restaurant was getting crowded. Many of the customers—lawyers and judges and executives—were in suits of various shades of black and gray, with quiet, dull ties. Some of them waved at Diane before they sat down, and two of them actually came over and said hello before repairing to their own tables to order the first in a series of martinis or manhattans. Despite their looks at me, Diane didn't introduce us.

I wondered if I had stayed in Youngstown and married Diane whether *we* would have had kids. I didn't feel like a father. I couldn't imagine raising children and instilling in them the values I'd learned and practiced in Nam.

When we were halfway through with lunch, Diane said, "I suppose I should tell you Bob and I are on the verge of a separation."

"Oh."

"He's been sleeping in the guest room for more than a year now."

"I'm—sorry."

"Are you?"

"I'm sorry you're having a bad time."

"It's not entirely his fault. Things just happen, I guess."

"You don't have to tell me about it."

"I think I do. I don't confide in my best girlfriends because I don't have any."

"You and I share lots of things, Diane, but the toughest one is loneliness."

She shook her head as if she hadn't wanted to hear me. She gulped down the rest of her martini, caught the eye of the waitress, and waved the empty glass for another one. Then she said, "Bob's been having an affair for a long time—with one of the other attorneys in his office. She's a damn good lawyer. Seems like a nice person."

My hands curled into fists without my being aware of it. "Don't make it sound so fucking sweet. Your husband is a bastard."

"Not really. He figured out I didn't love him."

"Because of his affair?"

"Before his affair. That's why he's having one."

"Then why did you stop loving him?"

"Why did I ever start?"

When her second martini arrived, she attacked it. Then she tossed the romaine around in her salad bowl before pushing it away. "I'm a shit, aren't I, Nicky?"

"Why?"

"Because I'm tired of this Caesar salad—and all I want is to fuck your brains out."

CHAPTER SIX

My skills had been college-age supple, and I'd undressed Diane hundreds of times. Her underwear had always been white—or, for a fancy dance or party or special occasion, a peach color. The bra she wore this time when I unbuttoned her emerald blouse was dark green, too—or possibly bluish green. Like most men, I can't identify hues more sophisticated than the primary colors.

When the underwear wound up casually tossed onto the floor of my hotel room, though, I remembered vividly how she looked the first time I'd seen her completely naked—and the second time and the hundredth time. A decade and a half later, she excited me just as much.

More.

She'd mentioned at lunch that she'd gained ten pounds since college, but I hardly noticed—except for her breasts. They were fuller and slightly heavier. I took her left nipple between my teeth and tormented it with my tongue, and she moaned and writhed as my hand caressed and explored between her legs. She'd been wet before she was completely undressed.

The first time we made love, two nights before our high

school prom, we were virginally nervous, awkward, and clumsily ineffective. By college graduation, we'd enjoyed sex together so many times, we were confident, and very good at what we did.

The last time we shared a bed together was during a two-week leave from my violent duties halfway around the world, and the reunion sex was cautious and strange. Almost every night, I woke up screaming from the kind of nightmare I'd already lived. In both our minds, the bad dreams signified a drawing away, a drying up of what we'd believed for too many years would last a lifetime.

This time, in my room at the Holiday Inn downtown to which we'd rushed, lust-driven, from an unfinished lunch at Courtney's, lovemaking provided a new wrinkle. We'd apparently forgotten the gentle, adventuresome sex of our days of young love. Our return to it this time was mean and selfish—almost like antagonism. Her nails scratched my back as never before, leaving bloody claw marks. Her teeth nipped my dick sharply. When she climbed on top of me and lowered herself with roughness and abandon, she kept murmuring "Oh fuck me! Fuck me!" into my ear as she strained, riding me. After the second mutual orgasm, we were breathing heavily. Diane looked at me, her mouth no longer smiling and flirting, but with a cynical sneer.

"Well? Isn't this the time to ask me where I learned what I know?"

"I don't want to find out."

"I had thirteen years to study, Nick."

"Write a term paper on it," I said, "but don't ask me to read it."

She rolled over, half on me, and bit my lower lip again, too hard for my liking. It started to bleed. "You never were a reader anyway," she said, and her tongue entered my mouth and went halfway down my throat as she straddled me, pinning my wrists against the pillows. When she took her mouth away from mine, my blood was smeared over her lips. In what vampire movie had I seen her before?

Finally, after the third go-round, when I faced not being eighteen any longer and was practically worn-out, Diane leaned over the edge of the bed and groped for her purse on the floor. She took the ashtray from the nightstand and placed it on her naked stomach, then fired up a cigarette.

"Well—*that's* different," I said.

"What?"

"I never saw you with a cigarette. How long have you smoked?"

"I can't tell you, exactly. I didn't make a note of that particular date." She looked at her watch.

"Do you have to get home?"

"When I feel like it."

"Will Bob be mad if you're not there for dinner?"

"I think not."

"Is he suspicious?"

"Not anymore. He's rarely home for dinner, and I'm rarely there to cook it for him. Okay?"

"Okay."

I shifted around on the bed until I was relatively comfortable, tasting her on my mouth, tasting my own blood. She took deep puffs, not seeming to enjoy her cigarette, and blew smoke up toward the ceiling. No lamps were turned on in the room, but the fading day came in through the window. I watched her smoke twist and dance lazily.

"My husband's interests are elsewhere," she said. "And I'm not living like a nun." She ground her cigarette out in the ashtray.

"Why don't you divorce him?"

"When I'm ready," Diane said. "I'll do pretty well. He's a good lawyer and he knows lots of other good lawyers, but so do I. Does that make sense to you?"

"Yes, it does."

"Good."

"So who are *you* cheating with?"

"At the moment? You."

"What about other moments?" I said.

"Why? Are you writing a book?"

"Is it anybody I know?"

"That," Diane said, her voice like the edge of broken glass, "is none of your goddamn business." She slid out of bed and over to the chair near the window, picking up her lingerie from the floor as easily as an all-star shortstop scooping up a ground ball. I had to catch my breath as I watched her glide across the room, her muscles working in concert. As in the beginning, she walked almost like a cat when naked. She kept her back to me, as if after all the sexual gyrations with which we'd whiled away an afternoon, she was almost embarrassed to be seen full front. She leaned against the back of a chair and slipped into her panties. They were bikini-style and also dark green. "What's the difference anyway?" she said.

"Because I care about you."

"Not enough. You didn't care enough. That's why you went away. That's why I slept with several different men after you'd gone—until finally Bob Burnham asked me to marry him, and I thought, Why not?" She looped the bra straps over her shoulders, reaching behind her to fasten the clasp. Then she faced me again, looking sexier and more erotic in her underwear than when she was completely nude.

"Well, it's been a fun afternoon, Nicky—almost like old times. Thanks for the laughs," she said. "Going back to Chicago tomorrow?"

"I don't think so."

She buttoned her blouse, one eyebrow raised. "You're sticking around for a while? Surprise, surprise."

"I want to find out about Richard. He took his own life. I want to know why."

She frowned. "You'll upset people for no reason."

"What people?"

"Everyone—starting with me."

"You don't get it that Catholic priests preach against suicide? That it's a sin? That they never do it themselves, no matter what?"

"Rules are made to be broken," she said.

"Not that rule. Not for a priest."

"Richard was human, like everyone else. What's your point?"

I swung my legs over the side of the bed and felt around on the floor for my briefs. They're dark blue, I thought at this inappropriate moment. Back in the early seventies, I used to wear what they now call "tighty whities." Diane and I both had changed the color and style of our underwear as we grew older. "My point," I said, "is there was no reason for Richard to kill himself—and maybe he didn't."

Diane was putting on her left shoe, steadying herself on the edge of the dresser. She stopped before it was all the way on and stood there, the shoe dangling off the end of her foot. "Don't be a damn fool. You know who the tough guys are around here."

I pulled the briefs up around my waist. "Tough guys don't scare me."

She was completely dressed now. "They *should* scare you. That's why they're called 'tough guys.' I've known you too long to see you get hurt."

"That's kind of you," I said, putting on my shirt.

"So am I supposed to be your Youngstown girlfriend for as long as you stay in town? Am I supposed to come over here tomorrow so you can fuck me again?"

I stopped buttoning the shirt. "I never fucked you, Diane. We made love hundreds of times, but I never once fucked you. Not this time, either."

It made me glad I'd finally gotten to her. She didn't say anything, though, so I picked up my pants and walked into the bathroom, shutting the door. The drum of the shower was loud, the needle spray almost too hot. She was gone by the time I came out.

Sunsets in October take the light down with them by seven in the evening, and I looked for a quiet little place for a bite to eat. There had been a lot more mom-and-pop eating places in Youngstown when we kids ran the streets, Italian places where the owner was the chef, the hostess was his wife, and the waitstaff their sons and daughters. But corporate thinking had sunk in all over America. The neighbors who owned small local joints had been forced to close, and now chain restaurants were everywhere, serving boring, unimaginative food. I had a thing about restaurant chains and made a point never to eat in any of them.

I wasn't kidding when I told Diane that our young times were a lot more romantic—more real—and more important than just knocking off a quick lay. She'd changed since then, grown hard, aggressive, and sexually adventurous, even touching and kissing me in places no one ever had before.

I'd changed, too. Tough guys never scared me. *Nobody* scared me anymore.

That was my goddamn trouble—I never forgot anything. I'd awakened to my own sexuality and adulthood by desperately loving Diane Bottinelli. But then I went away—to Vietnam and Chicago—and she became the married Diane Burnham.

I found an Italian restaurant. It was small and unobtrusive within a gaudy strip mall—the only business in the mall that wasn't part of some franchise. I sat at a table covered with a red-and-white checkerboard cloth, ordered a half bottle of Chianti and linguine with white clam sauce. Later, I passed up the tiramisu the waiter tried to force on me. He brought the check and I handed him my Visa card, then waited.

I was surprised when the Visa card came back to me via

the owner/chef, a white-coated elderly man named Umberto Pellegrino.

"Mr. Candiotti?" he said, holding the Visa card with my name on it. His English sounded good—only a trace of *Siciliano* remained in the rhythm, rather than in the actual pronunciation. "Are you any relation to Lorenzo Candiotti?"

"He was my father," I said.

Pellegrino squeezed his eyes shut. "Lorenzo, he was my good friend. I worked in the mill with him a lotta years. When he got killed on the highway that night—him an' your mama, God bless their souls—I never got over it. I got outta the steel business altogether an' got into this restaurant with my brother-in-law. But I never forgot Lorenzo." He cocked his head at me. "I bet I seen you an' met you when you was a kid, prob'ly at one of the Italian festivals—your parents always took you kids around with them. I seen you at their funeral, too. Broke my heart."

It broke my heart, too. My father and mother were returning one blustery winter night from a pre-Christmas party at the home of one of the third-level people from the Severino family, several miles out of town, near Austinburg. The tires skidded on highway ice and the car hit the railing of a bridge they were crossing, smashing it and going on through. They found my father dead, wedged in the front seat with the steering wheel column embedded in his chest, the mangled car half-submerged in the water. My mother was discovered about a quarter mile downstream in Meander Lake, and the autopsy revealed that the impact of her forehead against the dashboard had killed her, not floating out through the jammed-open door and drowning.

It turned me into an orphan, but no one was around to take care of me. That's when I grew closer with Richard, even though his calling took him to New Philadelphia. Teresa was dealing with her marriage and first baby, and Al was too involved with a rapid rise in the police department. It turned out well for him, but I was now without a family who cherished me. Only Diane was left.

Mr. Pellegrino was thinking about us Candiottis, too. He pulled out a chair and sat down across the table from me. "Your brother, the priest," he said, shaking his head. "I read about it in the newspapers. Sumbitch, that's such a terrible thing. I woulda gone to the funeral, but I run this place all by myself now an' I hadda get here and start things up—you know, making the sauces an' stuff." He squeezed my hand. "You had the white clam sauce, right? You enjoy? I make the sauces, but white clam sauce I do the best." He looked for the waiter. "I'll get you another bottle of wine over here, okay?"

I put up a hand. "No, I've had enough wine, Mr. Pellegrino. But I thank you."

"I loved your papa like my own," he said. I know your cop brother, whatsisname, Alfonso, pretty well—and I'm embarrassed how many times I made confession with Father Candy. Hey, you gonna come back an' live in Youngstown now? Well, don't matter you live in China. Anything you want—ever—you give me a call." He handed me a business card with the restaurant's name, his own, and a phone number printed on it. "Whatever it is, I'm your guy, okay?" Then he grinned, returning my Visa card. "Your money's no good in here," he said. "You can come in here an' eat for nothing for the rest of your life, okay?"

I didn't argue with him. I knew you never won a dispute like that one with a loving and generous Sicilian. But I left the waiter a ten-dollar tip.

CHAPTER SEVEN

Once you've seen Paolo Severino's casino in Youngstown, Ohio, you'll never forget it.

It's a former mansion, which had about a dozen bedrooms, twice as many bathrooms, and a living room, dining room, and ballroom that could each hold sixty people at a time before it grew too expensive for the original residents to heat it—before the Severinos bought it. The building is four stories high, painted a too-bright yellow, and there once must have been secret staircases and passages galore inside, created by overly imaginative turn-of-the-century architects reading too many Fu Manchu mysteries. From the road, its arcane architecture and strange towering turrets make it look like a medieval castle. Severino's button men—some veterans from the same Southeast Asian war as mine—take turns standing guard in those turrets with automatic rifles in case any unwanted visitors arrive or put up too big an argument in the parking lot.

There's rarely trouble at the casino, though, because the valets who park your car, also doubling as security specialists, are usually off-duty Youngstown cops. Tough and authoritative when they stop you on the street for speeding or running a red light or making an illegal U-turn, they are polite and helpful to the casino customers in their off-hours, working on Paolo's payroll. They make nice money for an evening's work, and pocket tips, as well—a more remunerative job than wearing a blue uniform all day.

The valet who opened my car door was tall and rangy, about twenty-eight years old, and looked familiar to me, although at first I couldn't place him.

"Good evening, sir," he said, and stepped back as I got out of the car. Then he took a closer look at my Illinois license plates. "Mr. Candiotti, isn't it?"

"Dominick Candiotti, yes."

"I thought it was you," he said. "From the Illinois plates. I'm Mike LeBlanc. I was at Father Candy's funeral. My sympathies," he said. "I've gone to church almost every Sunday since I was a teenager, and he was an inspiration to me." He shook my hand with both of his, and it felt genuine.

"I appreciate that, Mike. Do you work here full-time?"

"Just two nights a week. During the day, I wear a badge, the way I did at the funeral. I work for your brother—your *other* brother, Lieutenant Candiotti. He comes here a few nights a week, too—to shoot craps. Most nights, he gets lucky."

Lucky my ass, I thought. Alfonso is a high-placed, influential cop, and I was certain the people running this gambling joint made sure he won almost all the time.

"You're a police officer, then."

"Sergeant. But the extra money I make working here helps—with the family. I have three kids."

"Good for you."

"Have fun tonight," he said. "I'll take good care of your car."

The man at a podium just inside the main door had a reservation book open in front of him. He was big enough to play on any offensive line in the NFL. His white-on-black name tag told the world he was Joey Sposito and that he was the assistant manager. I recognized the name. He'd gone to the same high school as I had—he was a senior when I was a sophomore. Tough kid, as I remembered—and it wasn't a difficult assumption that he'd grown into a tough man.

Now, I invariably take the measure of every strange man I meet. Could I whip them hand-to-hand? Could I outthink them, or outdraw them? So I casually but carefully studied Sposito and thought I could defeat him one-on-one if push came to shove. I could think faster than he could, too. But there was no way I could draw a weapon more quickly than he could, because I wasn't carrying one, and from the bulge on the left side of his jacket, it was apparent even to lamebrains that he packed heat.

I identified myself, told him I remembered him from high school, and gave him the card signed by Don Severino.

He gave me a curt nod and not much else. "Welcome to the club." He scribbled something on a slip of paper and handed it to me. "When you're ready to gamble, give this to the cashier inside. She'll take care of you."

I didn't look at what he'd written—I didn't want to be rude. But after I'd moved away from him, I saw he'd scrawled "$500" and his initials.

What would I do with five hundred bucks? I couldn't drink that much in a month—and it seemed weird to me to gamble with other people's money. I pocketed the paper and walked through the main door into the casino.

Las Vegas and Reno casinos are bigger, but all look as tacky and overdone as this one. High rollers who show up in the Nevada desert to win money or spend an evening with an expensive hooker don't have a smattering of good taste—just the cash they hope will convince everyone that they are cultured and sophisticated.

Everything the Vegas casinos have, Severino's has, too, except perhaps superstars in the main showrooms. I vaguely remembered Italian crooners, headliners like Don Cornell, Jerry Vale, and Dean Martin singing for old man Severino twenty-five years earlier, when I was too young to get inside. In the main casino room, what used to be the ballroom, there were crap tables, roulette wheels, blackjack tables, noisy slot machines, and pretty girls dispensing free drinks and flirting. They were waitresses, but I wondered what else a hundred-dollar tip might buy from them.

In addition to the craps table, the casino offered a game of chance known as "batuk." It's also a dice game, but this one originated in Turkey. The Italian mobs swiped that and made it their own, like they've swiped everything else.

Humorless employees in dark suits watched everything. In the ceiling, surveillance cameras were spaced evenly every fifteen feet, so that any player who as much as scratched his nose was being observed by *someone*.

Tobacco smoke hung in the air like fog, moving only slightly with the whirring fans and air conditioners that kept the crowded room breathable. No one wore tuxedos, though the women customers, what few there were, had arrived in dressy dresses—and all of them had come on the arm of a man. The only unaccompanied women in the place were either Severino employees or "independent vendors" who'd signed in at the door. Maybe those were the "nice ladies" the don had mentioned.

Most of the male customers looked relatively prosperous, but they probably didn't have as much money in the bank as Las Vegas high rollers carry in their pockets. Unlike Caesar's Palace or the MGM Grand, old man Severino's gambling club didn't smell like big money.

It reeked, however, of big power.

I didn't recognize all the mingling locals, but some were easy to spot. Two Mahoning County supervisors, a federal congressman from Trumbull, several judges, a state senator and a state legislator, one of the deans at Youngstown State, and the

Mahoning County sheriff himself were customers that night, drinking, gambling, and socializing, some smoking cigars illegally imported from Havana. At least half of them were with dates—young girls wearing too much makeup and hair spray and showing too much bare skin—who were not their wives.

A very pretty young girl whose name tag announced that she was Taya—a name I'd never encountered before—appeared at my side and asked me what I wanted to drink. I ordered a single-malt scotch but didn't specify my favorite brand, Laphroaig, because I doubted the Severinos had ever heard of it. When she delivered my drink, I tipped her ten dollars and wondered if she was allowed to keep her tokes.

I saw a man I thought I remembered from college—back then, he was majoring in prelaw. He stood at the blackjack table with a healthy pile of chips in front of him. He looked at me for a long time, too, until finally his memory kicked in and he came up to me, hand extended.

"Dominick, right? Dominick Candiotti?"

"That's me. And you're—let's see, now—David Ratner."

I thought we were both pretty good at remembering. We weren't friends; we'd studied different subjects at Youngstown State and run in different social circles, too.

I don't think he was aware of my brother's suicide, or if he was, he ignored it. Maybe it was only churchgoing Italians who were upset by Richard's passing, but either way, Ratner did not offer his sympathy.

Catching up with the present took us about a minute each. I told him I designed and built homes for a living, and he rather proudly announced he was now one of the top prosecutors in the Mahoning County district attorney's office.

Apparently, we *still* ran in different circles.

So an assistant DA, all dressed up and looking sharp, was gambling illegally in a casino owned by the mob. If I could believe the size of Ratner's pile of chips, he was doing quite well at it—or playing a fixed wheel for quiet profit. I tried not to laugh.

Anxious to get back to the table, he gave me one of his business cards and pleaded with me to have lunch with him before I went back to Chicago. Later that evening, I thought it might not be a bad idea.

I watched him return to the twenty-one game, slipping his arm around the slim waist of his pretty, brassy-looking blond companion, who, behind her overdone makeup and bold eyelids, looked no older than eighteen. Ratner didn't bother to introduce us.

All Youngstown big shots have wives. The ladies don't make many public appearances, and hardly ever at the casino—just often enough to assure people their husbands get along with everyone who doesn't cross them egregiously. Wives give their important spouses a patina of respectability, and make sure nobody really knows their wifely secrets—that they are drinking themselves unconscious while their husbands are out every night, or banging off the belly of the guy who comes to cut their lawns. The men have families to take care of, and the wives take care of the husbands, who have responsibilities. They are regular American husbands, and they show up at Severino's to socialize, press flesh, risk a few bucks at a table, and let everyone see they are, at heart, good fellows—with sexy, too-young mistresses, even if they are only mistresses for a night.

I found the cashier's window and presented the girl behind the glass my chit from the man at the door. This one was probably the daughter of a Scandinavian couple, and she had a lovely smile and blue-green eyes that went perfectly with her long blond hair. I wondered why she was working in a joint like this.

"Welcome to the casino, and good luck," she said automatically. Apparently, all the employees had been instructed to greet visiting suckers with a welcome. She gave me five hundred bucks in ten-dollar chips—fifty of them.

The chips were bulky and heavy, stretching the fabric of my suit when I pocketed them. When I moved, they banged against my right thigh, like the heavy-duty sidearm I'd always carried in Vietnam. I understood why the casinos prefer their risk-taking patrons to carry chips. Inveterate gamblers feel better when they lose them, which is not half as painful as watching actual cash leave their hands and disappear into slots that eventually find their way into Severino pockets.

I wandered around the casino, more interested in people than in games of chance. Some gamblers were having a good time, but most had that hungry look—that *losing* look. I watched three blackjack players, their nervous eyes, their twitchy hand movements, and the perspiration breaking out on their foreheads. Then a hammy, heavy hand fell on my shoulder.

"I'm surprised to see you, Dominick," Polly Severino said. He was shorter than I am, with too-white teeth and silver-and-black curly Italian hair. "So close after Richard's funeral. But it's good you're here." He waved an airy hand, at home within his kingdom. "This is a place to have fun, not to feel bad or mourn."

I didn't like Polly. He was good-looking in a sensual, who-gives-a-damn way, but arrogance emanated from him like a poison cloud. He was secure—because he was the old man's number-one son. He wouldn't have been so cocksure if he didn't have important relatives and had to work the graveyard shift at the 7-Eleven.

"I'm just in town for a few days, Polly. Your dad invited me, so . . ."

"He don't get here most nights. That's where I come in. I show up early afternoon and stay here till the last dog is hung. Then I have a nice quiet drink and lock up the joint." He seemed amazed by what he'd just said. "I work too fucking hard."

I nodded. "Sorry I won't get to chat a little more with your dad."

"He got nothing to chat about except he don't sleep so good and his feet hurt and he mainlines stool softener every night. He don't work so hard no more; he takes it easy. But hey, he invited you here, so enjoy yourself."

I shrugged. "I'm not a big gambler. Once in a while a few bucks on the Super Bowl, but . . ."

"We could cover that bet here, anytime you want."

"Polly, you have a minute to talk?"

He frowned. "I guess so." He looked down at my bulging pants pocket. "Is that hardware you're packing? In *my* joint?"

I patted the chips so they rattled around. "Your chips," I said. "I'm not carrying."

"Me, neither. I don't have to."

He led me out to the hallway near the front door and up a sweeping flight of stairs to the second floor. There were two intimidating hitters standing at the bottom, looking very serious and completely connected. I could tell at once they were not just employees or off-duty Youngstown law-enforcement officers. With them guarding that stairway, I figured no one ever got up to the second floor unless they belonged.

"It's cool, Vinny," Polly said. "He's okay, Chet. Stay loose."

They nodded, and Chet moved his neck around inside his collar to look even more tough. They were Polly's personal bodyguards.

Polly Severino's upstairs "office" looked like a cubicle in an insurance firm—inexpensive metal desk, a worn leatherette swivel chair behind it, and two mismatched metal chairs in front of the dented metal filing cabinets. There was also a sagging leather sofa against one wall. The only decoration was a cheaply framed color photograph of the Pope. My Chicago construction business office was utilitarian, but it looked like the Taj Mahal next to Polly's.

I sat down and put my drink on the desk. There were no coasters, and I didn't worry about them—there were more wet-glass rings on the desktop than I could count.

"Whaddya need?" Polly said. "You see some twist downstairs that makes your dick stand up and salute? Let me know, and I'll arrange it for you."

"Not interested," I said.

"No? What are you, a fag?"

"Why don't you ask me again, Polly," I said, "when we're not in your territory."

He swept his hand from left to right as if we weren't crowded into a small, ugly room. "The whole world's my territory, Dominick. But I didn't mean nothing, okay?"

I nodded.

"So what brings you here, then? I mean up here in my office."

"Do the waitresses downstairs get to keep their tokes?"

"Huh?"

"When they're tipped by the customers—your customers—do they get to pocket those tips, or do they have to kick back to the, uh, management?"

"What kind of shitass bastards you think we are?" Polly growled, his eyes turning to slits. "We make enough from our gamblers. We don't rob the waitresses and dealers. They keep whatever you give them, okay?"

"Okay," I said.

"Is that all you wanted to know?"

"No, but it's got nothing to do with your father's casino here. Mainly, I'm trying to figure out what happened to my brother."

"I think we all know what happened." He made a pistol out of his thumb and forefinger, putting it in his mouth and squeezing the imaginary trigger. "It sucks."

"Yeah, but why did he do it?"

Polly shrugged. "Who knows? Offing yourself is a personal thing. He didn't mention nothing to me."

"You saw him a lot?"

"Some."

"Besides at Mass." It wasn't a question.

"Some."

"He spent time with your father, too?"

"*Some.*" The third time in a row he used that word, he practically spit it out. "My old man and yours—Richard's old man—they were friends from a million years ago."

"Did my brother come in here? To the casino?"

He smirked. "Everybody in town with two nickels to rub together comes in here."

"To gamble?"

"Richard played the wheel sometimes."

"Roulette?" I couldn't imagine Richard with enough money to throw away on the green-felt gambling table. "How did he do?"

"I guess he was lucky," Polly said. "Couple a bucks here, couple there . . ."

So they fixed the wheel for him, too, I thought—not so he hit any big money, but enough so that he'd go back to the vicarage smiling.

Now why would they queer the wheel for a priest?

"Did he do anything for you in return?" I asked.

Polly always looks hard at everyone—it's always been part of his persona. But there was annoyance this time—and an unspoken threat. "He heard my father's confession on Sunday."

"Yours, too?"

"Not so often—'cause I never do anything wrong, okay?" He didn't even try not to smile at himself.

"Did he ever do anything else for you or your father?"

The smile turned to anger, and his face grew red. "Ya think he come over to my house to do my laundry? What the hell you talkin' about?" He took a few deep breaths for control. Polly was known for his temper tantrums. So was I. I didn't lose my temper very often, but when I did, it was a pip.

He gulped a few more lung fulls of air until he finally located the calm place and forced himself back into it, but it made him seem even more intimidating. "Listen," he muttered, "Richard took his secrets to the grave, whatever they were. You can't push into other people's lives and ask a bunch a questions."

"I didn't mean to bug you."

"Then don't, cuz I don't like it a damn's worth." He rose from his chair. "I was always more your brother Alfonso's friend—because I'm closer to his age than yours. I never got to know you that good. Now I know you even less, and to be honest with you, that's the way I like it, 'cause you're not like either one a your brothers, or your father, neither. Take your time while you're back in town. Spend some money at the tables and you might even get lucky. Pick out some fluff chick down there to haul your ashes—all on the house. Then spend some family time, cry a little over Richard, and move on." He leaned toward me, both palms flat against the desktop. "*Move on*, Dominick. You hear what I'm sayin' to you? That's what we do—we keep movin' on."

I went back downstairs, feeling exactly as if I'd been summarily dismissed. Vinny and Chet, standing sentry at the foot of the stairs, looked at me without emotion—the way they might look at an ant crossing the floor, just before they stepped on it.

It took me a moment to find Taya, the pretty cocktail waitress, and ask her for another drink. When she brought it, I fished a fistful of chips out of my pocket and pressed them into her hand without counting them. She looked nervous for a moment, afraid the tip was to reward her for something more expected of her than bringing me a single-malt scotch, but when she thanked me profusely, I told her to take her boyfriend out for a terrific dinner on that money.

Her grateful smile broke my heart. It doesn't break easily.

I moped around some more, watching the players, still not tempted to gamble. If I didn't play one of the games of chance pretty soon, I'd have to hunt Taya down again and give her the rest of my chips.

Then I saw a familiar face.

Lucy Waldman always wears clothes that get people's attention, and tonight was no different. Her dress of vivid crimson wasn't really a ball gown, but it looked like one anyway. And when she threw her arms around me for a hug, I sniffed the same perfume that Diane had worn that morning. They'd both developed expensive tastes.

I returned the hug, feeling a thin roll of fat around her waist that I didn't remember—but it was the first time I'd hugged her in nearly twenty years, and we'd both grown older, so it didn't surprise me.

"I'm glad you came by, Nick," she said. "I wanted to hug you in person, but at the church . . ."

"It's good to see you, Lucy. You look great."

"It's all done with smoke and mirrors," she said. "Paolo invited you to stop by?"

I nodded.

"We're all mourning Richard—in our own way. He made such an impact on so many different people. . . ."

"You, too?"

She blushed beneath her artfully applied makeup. "And I'm not even Catholic."

"Can we talk somewhere private?"

Lucy shrugged. "It's not really private, but we can sit in a corner in the bar. Hardly anyone goes in there to drink—they're too busy out here losing money."

She took my elbow and led me into an intimate lounge in what I assumed had once been the mansion's dining room. The bartender was skinny and tall, somewhere in his sixties, and I recalled having seen him around back in the days when I first began drinking legally. Not here, though—it was in one of the old hopping places on Market Street. I waved at him. I was sure he didn't remember me, but he waved back anyway.

"Want your usual, Lucy?" he called out.

"Sure, honey. And bring a cigarette, too, would you?"

"And you, sir?"

I lifted my nearly full drink to show him. "I'm good for the moment."

We sat at a table in a shadowy corner. The bartender brought her drink, along with a pack of Marlboros and a Bic lighter.

"I recognize you from someplace else," I said to him. "I used to hang out on Market Street a lot—fifteen, twenty years ago, when I was a kid."

"I never paid no attention to kids," he said, "unless they got in trouble." He was trying to remember me. "Did you get in trouble as a kid?"

"No," I said. "I waited until I grew up to get in trouble. Dominick Candiotti." I stuck my hand out for a shake.

He looked concerned and sad as he squeezed my hand with his own. "You're the padre's brother? Jeez, I was so sorry to hear about his untimely passing. I'm Ray. I didn't go to church all that much, but if I did, I always confessed to Father Candy."

He went back behind the bar and lit his own cigarette. I turned my attention to Lucy. "Is that a Bloody Mary?"

She shook her head. "I quit drinking a while back, so this is a Virgin Mary—and no smart cracks, please." She clinked our glasses. "Your health."

"And yours, Lucy. But you're always healthy. When's the last time you had so much as a cold?"

"November 1963," she said, smiling as she remembered. "The day of JFK's funeral. I'd been crying since he died, and it raised hell with my resistance. I had hangovers, though—lots of them. But about four years ago, I quit drinking. Cold."

"Good for you."

"I sure want a shot right now, though." She played with the drink, not taking a sip. "I'm gonna miss Richard something awful."

"What happened to him, Lucy?"

"Everybody knows that, honey."

"But why?"

"How should I know? I'm not God—just a weary, retired hooker old enough to start getting hot flashes."

"Did Richard come in here often? To the casino?"

She shook her head. "Not much for the past year or so. I asked him once why he didn't come around more often. He said he didn't want to set a bad example—a priest patronizing an illegal gambling joint."

"But you saw him frequently?"

"Maybe once every few months. We'd run into each other—or sometimes we'd just meet for breakfast or lunch. We were *old* friends—I knew him from when he was about fifteen. That was about thirty years ago—when I first . . . hooked up with Paolo." She sighed. "He hung around a little with Paolo, too. Him and Alfonso."

"I remember that."

"You never thought it was strange your two brothers got buddy-buddy with the head of, um, of this family?"

"That was the way things were around here. *Are.*"

"Were, are, always will be," Lucy said. "But tall, gangly, funny Richard . . ." She shivered, gulping back real tears. "He left us too soon. He was one of my special pets."

"'Pets'?"

It made her laugh. "Don't let go of the past, Nick, 'cause it makes the present, whatever that's worth. I was the one who introduced your brother to . . . one of the joyful mysteries of life. And I don't mean the priesthood."

"You took Richard's cherry?" I said, unbelieving. "When he was fifteen?"

"Fifteen or sixteen—around there somewhere."

"Jesus." I desperately gulped my drink. When I finished, there wasn't much left of it. I waved at the bartender. "Single malt, please," I called.

"Don't be such a prig," Lucy said, laughing. "Don't be a tightass."

"But—you were Mr. Severino's girlfriend."

"I was and am," she said. "But I started out an ambitious whore, looking for a step up in life, and then another one. Even when I was Paolo's number-one squeeze, he never forgot what I was, and every so often he asked me to take care of certain people for him—as a favor, or a business deal. He took a particular liking to Richard and asked me to educate him. So I did."

I shook my head, getting used to the idea. "If you'd done it on a regular basis, he might never have taken the celibacy vow in the first place."

"Oh, he got around. Before he entered the seminary, lots of girls made him smile, but he took it to a way higher level—after what I taught him." Her lips tightened. "Everybody has happy memories. It's the present that makes them eat their gun." She grimaced. "Damn, I'm sorry I said that, honey. I didn't mean it that way."

"What *did* you mean?"

"I don't know zilch. I'm guessing." Lucy stopped talking as the bartender arrived with my new scotch, puffing on her cigarette until he moved back behind the bar and out of earshot. "I got a good life," she said, lowering her voice slightly. "My only job is to come in here every night, look terrific in brand-new clothes I go to New York to buy every three months or so, and make sure everybody's having a good time—and that they pay for it at the gambling tables. I own a small piece of this casino, a share the old man gave me, and it buys me my clothes and the house I live in, because I damn well earned it. As far as Paolo is concerned—he's about three years older than God, and all he wants me to do now, whenever he comes in—maybe two or three nights a week—is to go upstairs to his private office. I pour him some homemade dago red—we stock it here because that's all he ever drinks—and I take off his shoes and socks. I rub his feet and legs, because now he's got varicose veins, and he actually groans at that massage. That's the extent of it these days. And if and when he dies, I'll be taken care of—I got a legal piece of paper says so.

She sipped her Virgin Mary. "So don't ask me to guess. I won't fuck up my life and lose everything—and I'm too old to start over, selling my ass—so don't ask me."

She stood up, leaned over, and kissed my forehead. "I'm glad you came by to say hey. I love you, and I loved Richard. Hold on to that back in Chicago." She smiled sadly down at me, and her grip on my forearm tightened. "Go back soon, okay? Soon."

I watched her walk away. However old she was, she still knew how to walk so every man in the place would stop whatever they were doing and look at her.

I stayed at the table and finished my drink. Some people think single malt tastes like medicine, and this one left a bad taste in my mouth.

Not too many clients came in to the bar—just waitresses filling orders. Taya noticed me sitting alone in the corner and came over while Vinny mixed her drinks. "Hi again, sir," she said. After I'd tipped her earlier, her smile was genuine. I waved good-bye to the bartender, but he didn't wave back—just gave me a glum nod.

I passed Joey Sposito on my way out the front door. He didn't smile, either. Maybe everyone who works here runs out of smiles at nine o'clock in the evening, I thought.

"Enjoy your evening, sir."

"Hey, you can knock off that 'sir' stuff. Remember me, Joey? We went to the same high school, except you were a few years ahead."

He hardly looked at my face. "No."

"No? Just no?"

His look was noncommital, but his voice tone was cuttingly sarcastic. "Just no," he said.

I laughed, even though nothing was funny. "Jesus, Joey—we

went to the same high school. Have you been taking manners lessons from a wolverine?"

"I take lessons from a higher authority than that." This time, there were more teeth in it. "Was everything okay with your visit—*sir?*"

"I'm swell," I said.

CHAPTER EIGHT

I wasn't swell, though—too haunted by my own demons to drink any more casino booze, and even more annoyed by the brush-off from Joey Sposito. Maybe that was the rule at Severino's casino club—the pretty young girls were pleasant, beautiful, and accommodating, and the rest of the employees were sour apples like Sposito. Well, screw him anyway. Screw them all.

I made my way home through quiet streets, remembering how lively they'd been when I was younger—fun bars and clubs, fun booze hangouts for the college kids and other crazy people, as opposed to now, when Market Street had turned lonely and depressing. I hoped that, like other midwestern cities that had stumbled on their own antiquated and outdated politicians and businessmen, Youngstown would someday turn around and be a great little city again. But if it did, it'd be too late for me.

I spent most of the night staring at the hotel room's ceiling. My trip home wouldn't end as soon as I'd hoped. Questions nibbled me, and to make them go away, I'd have to jump in the deep end of the pool to learn about the end of my brother's life; otherwise, I might never sleep again.

And if some of the local hotshots, the mob guys, the self-important people who ran Youngstown chose to get offended—well, I could handle that all right, too.

I managed to catch some sleep but only a few minutes' worth at a time. In the morning, the hovering clouds were only mildly menacing. I put on a sports jacket, slacks, and a tie, threw on my raincoat in case the skies opened up, and took my first step toward collecting pieces of the truth.

David Ratner's office was in the county building, offering a view of the old Beaux-Arts Home Savings and Loan Building, with the well-known clock tower that dominates downtown. The Beaux-Arts looks old-fashioned—it always has—but in Youngstown, it's become a symbol for the city itself. I could see it through Ratner's only window—he hadn't yet advanced to a corner office in the district attorney's department. He looked composed as he listened to me, toying with a pencil. He hadn't expected me to arrive at nine in the morning, but he was too polite to turn me away. We exchanged our up-to-date histories again. He was married to a high school teacher, whose photograph was displayed on his desk, along with one of their three kids, and he played racquetball twice a week. He didn't offer me any background on the young woman in his company at Severino's the previous night.

I'm afraid he grew uncomfortable as I told him why I suspected all was not as it seemed with the death of my priest brother.

"I feel like a stupid schmuck," he said. "I never put the names together—that's why I didn't extend my sympathies when I saw you last night. Naturally, I knew about Father Candiotti's passing; everyone does."

"'Passing'?" I said. "'Passing' is a kind way of putting it."

"Well, it *was* suicide," Ratner explained, as if I hadn't heard it fifty times before. "Why not accept it?"

"Because Richard wouldn't do that."

"You don't live here anymore. Maybe you stopped knowing him that well."

"You're not Catholic," I said. "You probably didn't know him, either."

"I saw him around, talked to him. Sometimes he seemed . . . troubled."

"Troubled about what?"

He shrugged. "His job was to *hear* confessions. He didn't *make* them—at least not to an ADA like me."

"Priests don't commit suicide."

Ratner nodded sagely. "And yet, here we are. Forgive me, but if you were going to kill yourself, would you share the reasons with everyone—or with *anyone*?"

I sat quietly for a few moments—long enough for him to begin checking his watch. Finally, he said, "I'm sorry, but I'm not sure what you're here for. I mean here, in my office."

"You know the Severino family pretty well, don't you?"

"Everybody knows them," he said, trying to seem like a good guy with his smile.

"Even people on your side of the law. They don't bother you, do they?"

"They mind their business," he said, "and I mind mine."

"Letting you win at the casino is their business?"

"I'm just lucky. I always have been. As far as I know, the casino is honest," he said. "That's why we let them operate here." He clamped his lips together as if to stifle an impolite burp. "I mean, we don't *let* the Severinos run this place, because we know it's not legal. We just ignore them."

"My brother was close to them, though. Both my brothers."

Ratner cleared his throat. "Your brother Richard was their pastor."

"And my brother Al, the homicide cop?"

"I hardly know Al."

"Ever run into him at the casino?"

"I don't hang out at the casino every night," Ratner said. "I go there every few weeks to relax, talk to people."

"I saw the lady you were with last night. You looked very relaxed."

He coughed again, unnerved. "I'm sorry, but I have work to do. I wish you'd made an appointment—we could have talked longer."

"Should I make an appointment now, David?"

"Well," he said, looking everywhere in the room except at my face, "my schedule is kind of crazy for the next month or so." He stood up, leaned across the desk, and offered a handshake.

I rose, too. "Well, I hope you can find some extra time to . . . relax," I said. "So you won't be so crazy."

Outside, the rain had started—just a sprinkle so far, but making *pitter-pat* sounds on my raincoat, the cold drilling right through to my bones. I shoved my hands into my pockets, walking without a particular destination. But when I found myself in front of police headquarters, I knew why I'd come.

I told the sergeant at the doorway I was Alfonso's brother, and showed him my driver's license, along with a small photo of Father Richard I keep in my wallet. He earnestly ushered me in, extending his sympathies over Richard's death. "I tried to get to Mass at least twice a month," he said. "He was a terrific priest."

Al's desk was on the third floor, and to reach it I stepped into the small, creaky elevator that had been infamous for decades. Within the tiny confines of that elevator, arresting cops sometimes imposed "attitude adjustments" on bad guys they'd just brought in off the streets—and many outlaws with multiple arrest records could attest to it. Some of the more belligerent criminals often emerged from that elevator not looking the same as when they'd entered it. I didn't examine the floor or the walls too closely, because ancient bloodstains were still faintly visible—a rusty brown color, not like in the movies. I don't think anyone had cleaned that elevator in twenty years.

It smelled rank—of sins and screwups, of bravado and authority and cruelty—and mostly gave off the stink of fear.

Alfonso's desk was one of four in a sprawling dun-colored room with two widely spaced windows on one wall. Between them were three dark green filing cabinets. Another wall was caged off, not for criminals-in-waiting, but for storage.

Al in shirtsleeves, was the only occupant in the room at the moment. A half-drunk cup of coffee stood on the edge of his desk. The jacket of his brown suit was on a hanger behind the door, and his tie was pulled down two inches from his throat. He didn't seem to be doing anything more strenuous than reading the morning paper.

"Hey, kiddo," Al said. He put down the paper, stood, and hugged my neck. "What the hell you doin' here? Came to see me at work?"

"Something like that."

He grinned amiably. "You want coffee?"

I'm a coffee drinker, but police stations always brew it too strong, and I could tell just from the smell that it would strip the enamel off my teeth. "Not for me," I said.

"I drink it all day long, maybe a pot and a half. It keeps me alert." He looked around the empty office. "So I can catch the bad guys."

We stared at each other for a moment; then he said, "Sit down, why dontcha?"

I did sit down, but I didn't remove my raincoat. We continued the eye contact for too long.

"So, Nicky," he said.

"Al, tell me," I said, "what went wrong for Richard?"

"Is that what you came up here for? Aw, Jesus! I'll miss him every day for the rest of my life. That's bad enough without digging at his memory and turning up dirt."

"Cops turn up dirt for a living," I said. "So how come you're going to let him sink into the sunset without even asking why?"

"Will it bring him back? Look, everybody has secrets. So

they keep quiet about it, and eventually they either take it by the horns or not."

"And 'not' means they swallow their gun?"

That made him wince. "Look out the window. All those people walking around out there—they all have problems, but none of them chewed on their hardware; they stepped up to the plate. Whatever bothered Richard, maybe he couldn't handle it."

"He handled his gambling jones, though, didn't he? He gambled at the casino."

"Sometimes."

"And he played poker, too."

Now he smiled, and I tried to remember the last time I'd ever seen Alfonso smile, even when he was a kid. Ever since adolescence, his expressions had ranged from mildly troubled to mad as hell. He'd been a surly child and a nasty teenager. Nothing had changed. "He wasn't a serious gambler; it was relaxing. Even priests need to relax."

"He played with you every week?"

"Not every week. *Nobody* plays every week—we got other things to do."

"But pretty often, wasn't it? Glenn Keeney told me that."

Alfonso scoffed. "Keeney. Where'd you hear that from him?"

"At your house."

"Oh, yeah," he said. "I meant to talk to you about the other night. You really pissed Dolores off."

"Dolores doesn't like me—and she had too much to drink to keep it to herself. Besides, we're talking about Glenn Keeney."

"What does Keeney know?"

"He plays poker with you, too."

"He brings the sandwiches!" Alfonso protested. "He caters, just like at my house that day. So we let him play once in a while, for grins. But he's not one of the guys."

"We? Who are 'the guys,' Al? Besides you?"

He looked away, pretending he was checking the weather

outside the window again. When he answered, his voice dropped to a near mumble. "Different guys every week. Cops—like Ed Shemo, for one."

"Your boss?"

"My friend. You think police captains like Ed are so goddamn holy that they never kick back and have fun?"

"Okay. Who else?"

"Political people sometimes," Alfonso said. "And businessmen."

"Gangsters?"

He shrugged.

"The Severinos?"

"The old man doesn't play poker."

"How about Polly?"

Al rubbed at the back of his neck. "The game is always at his house. Polly's."

"A priest shows up for weekly poker at the home of a Mafia chieftan?"

"'Mafia chieftan'?" There was no humor in his staccato laugh. "Where'd you learn that expression? Some fag college?"

"*You* barely finished high school. To you, *every* college is a fag college. Right?"

"College isn't everything," Al said, smug. "Look where I am without college."

"With a brother whose suicide doesn't even stir your curiosity."

"Sometimes it kills the cat."

I said, "That sounds like a threat, Alfonso."

He held my eyes longer than necessary. "Don't be a lurp, Nicky. You're my kid brother. I love you. I don't wanna see you get hurt."

My next question rode its way across his desk in a dead voice; I couldn't make it sound any other way. "Who's going to hurt me?"

Alfonso licked his lips. "Nobody's gonna hurt you. You

don't live here no more, but you're my brother—and nobody fucks with you, or they'll answer to me."

"Why would they fuck with me?"

"Because you're messing in their business!" he shouted, slamming his palm on the desk, making the newspaper jump. "You ask too many questions! That's my job. Let me do the asking."

"Who will you ask about Richard's suicide?"

Alfonso's anger became a frustrated whine. "Nobody killed him; nobody stuck a gun in his mouth. He killed himself, and if I knew why, I would of stopped him. There's no questions to ask anybody, and that's why they're pissed off at you."

I put both hands on the edge of his desk. "Who's pissed off with me, Alfonso?"

Al expelled most of his breath and slumped down in his chair, already looking exhausted and beaten. It was silent in that office for more than a minute except for the traffic noise outside the window. Finally, he said, "I got work to do. I can't sit here and chat with you."

"Is that what we're doing? Chatting?"

He hauled himself to his feet. "We never got close, Nicky, but I love you. There's no questions to ask, 'cause there's no answers. Pack your bag, drive by the old house on Brier Hill again and take a look—just for a sentimental jolt—and then go back to Chicago and live your life."

He walked around the side of the desk and hugged me, but there was no passion in it. I think I'd worn him out.

As I was leaving through the front door downstairs, I almost bumped into Mike LeBlanc coming in. He grinned as he shook my hand. "We run into each other in different places, I guess," he said.

"I just stopped by to see your boss."

The grin dimmed a few watts. "Yeah."

"I've got some questions about my other brother—about his death."

He looked around, taking in the sergeant at the desk, and

subtly moved away from him to the other side of the lobby. "I understand why you might feel that way."

"Sergeant LeBlanc, do *you* have any idea why Father Candy killed himself?"

Now the grin completely disappeared and he looked deadly serious, having to discuss matters like death and suicide. "No one really knows," he said. "He only did good things, you know? Like the kid's recreational center next to Our Lady High School? Four years ago, it wasn't even there—and somebody else owned that land. But Father Candy, he was determined to give the kids someplace safe to hang out, and he fought for that center and twisted a few arms and talked real pretty to some others, and that land got donated and somebody else kicked in almost a million bucks to build it. Everybody knew Father Candy was behind it. We worshiped the ground he walked on."

"Who coughed up the million bucks?"

LeBlanc shrugged. "It was listed as anonymous. I didn't ask, and nobody else did, either. That's one of the reasons Youngstown is broken up and mourning over Father Candy's . . . demise."

"His killing himself, you mean."

He didn't answer.

"Did the police check the suicide weapon for prints?"

He looked blank. "Uh, ballistics isn't really my department."

"Does anyone know if it was actually his gun, or somebody else's?"

"Jeez," LeBlanc said, frowning heavily. Then he turned both palms upward, a signal of helplessness.

"You're a good Catholic, right?"

He ducked his head. "Probably not as good a Catholic as I should be."

"Have you ever heard of a priest carrying a weapon? Or even owning one?"

"No," LeBlanc said. "But Father Candy might have—because of his brother."

"Alfonso?"

"He's a homicide policeman. Sometimes people get mad at him and want revenge. They might have thought about taking it out on Father Candiotti."

"Or on his other brother," I said.

"Well, you'd be harder to get to. You live in Chicago."

"Yep, and my name and number are in the phone book."

LeBlanc seemed genuinely surprised. "I don't know anybody who has their name and address in the phone book around here. You'd better be careful, then."

"Meaning?"

"Meaning—well, just take care of yourself, Mr. Candiotti."

"If Richard had been taking care of himself, this might not have happened."

LeBlanc looked away for a second. "I guess you're right. Listen, I gotta get to work." He shook my hand again—like he meant it.

I found my car in a lot a block away and set off, not quite sure of where I was going. I had to think about Richard's death, and to examine what Alfonso and Mike LeBlanc had said, to see if there were hidden messages I hadn't gotten the first time.

I started driving, and eventually I found myself on Brier Hill, where I'd grown up.

It took me another ninety seconds to find the house where I'd lived until I was an adult. I almost didn't recognize it. In my day, it had been painted a dingy blue. My sister and brother kept it for a while after my parents died—Richard and I also owned a piece of it—but Teresa decided it was too much trouble and they sold it. I don't know how many different families had lived in it since, and I had no clue as to who'd repainted the house light pink with perky yellow trim. I thought it looked ridiculous.

Neighborhoods change. During the 1920s, there were more Slavic surnames on the Hill, and on the employees list at the steel mill, than Italian. But one ethnic group moves out and upward and another ethnicity moves in. On Brier Hill, nothing had changed for about forty years now, and my guess was that it never would again. It was the hardscrabble, hard-hat guinea neighborhood where everyone puddles steel. The military veterans hung out at Italian Post 12, and every June entire families got dressed up and attended the Brier Hill Italian Fair, where they ate sausage sandwiches with red sauce that stained their mouths, followed by spumoni ice cream or cannolis from the hastily erected portable stands. They high-fived all the neighbors they saw every day and usually didn't talk to, and they bowed and scraped in the presence of men like Paolo Severino and Frank Mangione, who walked among "their" people, chucked babies under the chin, "accidentally" fondled the breasts and asses of teenage girls and, on occasion, those teen girls' mothers, and never reached into their pockets to pay for anything. They were the godfathers, and everyone dug into *their* pockets to make them happy.

I was still longing for a taste of coffee, so it was a fortunate happenstance that I drove by Di G's Pizzeria, about eight blocks from my old house. The owner and chef, Marty Di Gregorio, was once a Y-town cop himself, until he tried to arrest a hoodlum who'd severely beaten up his common-law wife. The abuser resisted arrest by shooting a hole in Marty's kneecap and another one in the side of his face, and Di G's police career was over. His police pension, plus a generous low-rate loan by the Severinos, allowed him to open up a pizza joint. He specialized in thin-crust pizza—none of that thick-crusted Sicilian shit that became popular for a while in the late seventies.

I parked and went in, ducking between the raindrops. Marty looked up, saw me, and the corner of his mouth—the corner that hadn't taken a bullet—moved upward about an eighth of an inch in the beginning and end of a smile. "Hiya, Dominick," he said. It'd been fifteen years since I'd seen him, and all he could come up with was "Hiya, Dominick." Marty Di G was a quiet man.

He looked at his watch. "Kinda early, ain't it? You wanna small pizza for lunch?"

"Just coffee, Marty. Black."

"Lemme whip you up a pie. Sausage and black olives, like that."

I looked at my watch. "It's ten in the morning—too early for pizza. Just coffee."

"It's your funeral," he said, and the realization of what he'd said made him jerk.

Downcast, he waved me to a chair by a small table. When he brought the coffee, he said, "I didn't mean nothin' by that last remark—I forgot about Richard. I couldn't get away from here the other day for the Mass, but I sent flowers."

"Did Richard come in here for pizza?"

He looked sad. "Not so much no more, just once in a while. He was a busy guy—lots of people needed him."

"To confess."

Di G shrugged. "Everybody got somethin' to confess about. So thank God there's priests out there who listen and keep their mouths shut. Hey listen, Dominick—you want a lottery ticket? I sell lottery tickets now. I make almost as much money on them as on the pizza."

"When did you start selling lottery tickets?"

"From the beginnin'. Back when all there was was The Bug."

I nodded. "The Bug" was Youngstown slang for the old-time numbers racket, controlled by the two local mob families. In New York City, it was called "policy," and in Chicago it was simply referred to as "the numbers." I never wound up going south of Chicago's Roosevelt Road in the years I'd lived there, but the numbers racket was part of the city, too—as in every major city in the United States.

"The way things go," Di G went on, "the only ones that play now are the coons, and they don't come around here in this neighborhood no more. So I sell The Bug to friends and neighbors who eat my pizza."

"The state lottery *is* pretty big," I said.

He winked broadly. "Don' kid yourself, Dominick."

I took a dollar from my wallet and gave it to him. "At least that's what I hear in Chicago. Here—I'm in."

He nodded, tucking the dollar into his pocket. Then he went behind the counter and fished a numbers slip from one of the drawers beneath the cash register. "I'm givin' you one of our own lottery tickets, not the official ones." He winked. "We got different rules here. You know what I'm sayin'?"

"Different rules?"

"About lotsa things." He came back and handed me the slip, then leaned over and poked me in the arm. "C'mere, I want you to see this."

I followed him behind the counter and into a storeroom in the back. There was a big refrigerator to store the pizza cheese and the meat toppings, and next to it there were several stacks of ten-gallon cans marked TOMATO SAUCE, from a company in Indiana. Over in the corner, there were four more cans, marked similarly, but they were from a different company—imported from Sicily, or at least that's what the labels said.

"You store pizza stuff back here?"

He closed the door so no one would hear him—never mind that we were the only two people in the restaurant. "Every couple a weeks, I get a shipment of tomato sauce—from Sicily." He said "Sicily" as if it were the punch line to a bad joke.

"So?"

"So you ever hear anybody in Sicily growin' tomatoes and shippin' them all the way to Youngstown?"

I cleared my throat to keep my voice from breaking like a preteen's. "So?"

"I don't never open the cans, but I know what's inside 'em. Money. Lots of it—laundered money from the five families in New York. They ship me the cans, and I store 'em back here for a while." He pointed to the four ten-gallon cans. "Then, when I get told—like once a month, maybe—somebody comes and picks them up and takes them away. After that, somebody else comes in here and orders a couple pizzas to go—maybe some cold pop. Garlic sticks, too, dependin'—and they leave me a really great tip."

"A tip?"

He grinned good-naturedly. "Ever heard of anybody gettin' a grand for a tip?"

"Marty," I said, "you're connected."

His shoulders rose. "I don' even understand what that means. Listen, I never done nothin' wrong. I never hurt nobody. I never stole nothin'. I never cheated. I help out friends when I get asked to—like they helped out me openin' this place. What's the problem with helpin' friends?"

"Everybody does what they ask—if you know what's good for you," I said.

"Everybody does, sure. They go along, or they get chewed up and spit out like yesterday's bubble gum." Di G shook his head emphatically. "Not gettin' beat up, not no Youngstown Tune-Up or nothin'. I'm just sayin' those who help, who're what you call 'connected'—when it's time for cookies for dessert, they get a bigger helpin' than their neighbor who plays by the old-fashioned rules and never gets his head out of his ass."

"Cookies," I murmured.

"Here's the thing," Marty Di Gregorio said earnestly. "Two, maybe three years ago, the city Health Department inspector comes around, tells me I gotta replace a lot of the wirin' and plumbin' in this place, all the stuff that keeps the refrigerator cold. It's not like it ain't sanitary the way it is—I keep this place so clean, you could eat off the floor. But the city makes its rules. I figured it'd cost me about twelve to fifteen grand to make all those repairs and changes, and I couldn't afford that—or afford schmearin' the city inspector, neither. So I make a call, sit down with Polly Severino and make arrangements, and two days later, the whole thing goes away."

"Just like that?"

"Just like that."

"And after that, you started getting shipments of tomato sauce from Sicily."

He nodded. "All my life, I was good to the Severino family. I bought insurance from the company they said to, I bought stuff they invested in, and I was respectful, even fixed the old man a big deluxe pizza whenever he come in here, and I didn't charge him nothin', neither—and he was respectful right back. So when it come time to exchange favors, I was the lucky one. And I make a couple bucks on the side, so's I can't lose. You know what I'm sayin'?"

"I know what you're saying," I said. "It's okay."

Marty's crooked smile widened, showing his gold tooth about three teeth off center—inserted after the bullet had blown out the real one. "Hey, lemme whip up a deluxe pizza for you, too. For your lunch—on the house."

I sighed. "Just a small one."

"I make a big one; you take home what you don't eat."

"I'm staying in a hotel. I've got nowhere to keep half a pizza."

"God dang," he said. "Well, while you're in town, your money's no good in here. You can eat pizza till it's comin' out of your ears." He tugged on his apron, rearranging it. "The works, now, huh? Everything but anchovies. Neither o' your brothers ever liked anchovies, so I'm figurin' you don't, either. Am I right or wrong?"

"You're right, Marty," I said, sighing. "I don't much like anchovies."

I ate the small pizza he made for me—pepperoni, sausage, mushrooms, black olives, and green peppers. I'd begged him to leave off the onions, too. He sat with me while I ate, slugging on a can of Dr Pepper, talking about old friends, half of whom I couldn't remember. But I wasn't concentrating. I was thinking over what he'd said earlier—that everybody in town did what they were asked to by the mobs. It got me wondering. I knew my elder brother had been close to the Severinos before his death, and even played poker with Polly.

What had Father Richard been asked to do by the Severino family? What price had *he* had to pay—to get along?

CHAPTER NINE

Was I going a little crazy? Were my suspicions punching their way to the surface out of my own incipient paranoia? Maybe. My supersecret Vietnam missions had made me nuts for several days, but I'd felt like I was the only one losing it—except I'd lost it quietly, deep inside my own head and not where my comrades in arms could see it. But ever since I'd picked up the phone in Chicago and heard my sister, Teresa, tell me in her dry, annoyed voice that Richard had committed suicide, I'd fretted over it. I worried he'd been diagnosed with incurable cancer and decided to end his life before the suffering kicked in. But he had too much guts for that. He wasn't that kind of man, or that kind of priest.

After talking with elderly Marty Di G over a pizza, it seemed Richard's involvement with the Severino family was similar to that of everyone else in town who was, in one way or another, connected. He did things he was asked to do—*told* to do—whether he liked it or not. Maybe that was the payback for the help given to him and to the church for all those years.

Nothing ever comes without a payback. If you get to be about fifteen years old and haven't learned that simple truth yet, you're probably a dumbass.

Teresa lived in the upper south side neighborhood, in a pleasant weathered gray ranch house at the crest of a modestly inclined hill, surrounded by a ragged green lawn about two weeks past its last mowing—the kind of uninspired but efficient house you look at and then forget fifteen minutes later. It was supported by what money my brother-in-law, Charlie, brought in, because Teresa had gone from her trundle bed to her marriage bed with no beds in between. She'd never had a paying job in her life.

She wasn't glad to see me sitting in her living room, and it never crossed her mind to offer me anything to eat or drink. No harm, no foul—I didn't want anything anyway. But the thought would have been nice.

She checked her watch uneasily, as if she had important appointments of her own encroaching on the time I was stealing from her. But I guessed her only pressing appointment that day was doing her laundry. There could be no pleasant conversation between us, so I got right to my questions. But when I asked her about Richard's last years, she became furious, her nose wrinkling and her eyes narrowing. I kept waiting for flying monkeys to zoom around the room before someone spilled water on her and she'd melt away.

"You got some nerve!" she snapped. "For years, you turn your back on this family. Now your brother dies and here you are in our faces, pushing people around and asking stupid questions. Who in *hell* do you think you are?"

"I'm part of the family, Teresa," I replied. "I'm just trying to figure out why Richard did what he did—so I can understand it."

"Is that what you're here for?"

"I can't get Youngstown answers in Chicago. Was he involved with the Severinos? Besides being their priest?"

The hardness fled from her face, escaping like a horse that had been penned up in a tiny corral. "He never discussed it with me," she said stiffly. "He was friends with Don Paolo—from years ago."

"The old man subsidized his seminary studies."

"Yes, 'cause he was friends with our father—in case you forgot that."

"So Richard hung out with the Severinos when he wasn't hanging out at church?"

"Don't be silly," she said. "He ate dinner over at the don's house sometimes."

"And Polly? Paolo junior?"

She shrugged defensively. "I guess he played cards with him. Not often—he was a priest, not a gambler."

I rolled it over in my mind. "What about you, Teresa? Do you hang out with the old man, too?"

"Full-time mothers don't hang out with anybody."

"How about Charlie?"

Teresa didn't mean to speak of her husband with a kind of weary contempt, but it slipped out anyway. "He fixes furnaces for the Severinos and their people, and the air conditioners, too, in the summertime. Of course, he'll work for anybody who calls him on the phone."

"Convenient," I said.

"Don't be such a snotnose all the time. *Everybody's* got a furnace."

"So everybody in this family's hooked up with the Severinos one way or another."

"Not *me*."

"Of course not you," I said. "You're Miss Goody Two-shoes."

She contemplated me as if she'd been rummaging through an old drawer and had come across a long-dead mouse. "You're out of the nineteenth century," she sneered. "You make me want to barf! You judge everything. You look at it *your* way and judge it—whether it's wonderful and perfect or it's really, really bad. Your head is too far up your own butt ever to take a look at what's in the middle."

"*You* tell me what's in the middle, if you're so goddamn smart."

"Everything! Your family, your friends, this city, the world! Our parents died, so you had to get away from Youngstown. You got shipped to Vietnam to do some mysterious shit. You came back home and saw everybody else palling around with mob guys, and Alfonso an up-and-coming cop, and you had to get away again, to hide. So there you are in Chicago, and except for talking to Richard on the phone, and sending the rest of us Christmas cards like we were distant acquaintances, you changed your spots, Nicky. You don't belong here anymore."

Teresa stopped and took a deep breath, as if she faced her next step as the most challenging leg of her journey. "And now Richard's dead," she said more quietly, "and you—perfect, moral *you*—ask stupid questions of everybody and cluck your tongue and wring your hands because a priest took it in his head to kill himself."

Then her voice got louder again, climbing an octave in anger. "Give it up, for the sake of Jesus! I have no idea what went on inside Richard's head. Nobody has an idea—least of all you. Kick off your shoes and relax. I'll even make you a sangwich. We'll reminisce until my kids get home to say good-bye to their uncle—who, I bet, doesn't even remember their first names. *Then* you can leave town."

"I don't want a sandwich, Teresa. And your kids are Charlie junior, birthday June seventeenth; Loretta, birthday September seventh; and Joanne, birthday March fifth." My smile was way too smug, even coming from me. "Just so you know that I know," I said.

After I left my sister's home, I sat in the car for a while, fumbling in my wallet for Glenn Keeney's business card. Keeney

Catering, like his now-defunct restaurant, was located in Boardman. It didn't seem like a bad marketing idea—there were more well-off customers in Boardman than there were in Youngstown.

The office, located on Market Street in a mini–shopping center shared with a Laundromat next door, was hidden behind a dirty plate-glass window. Inside, it occupied only two rooms, as far as I could see, and there were no facilities for preparing food. I wondered where they did that.

A middle-aged woman with exceptionally blue eyes sat in the front room, and Glenn Keeney leaned over her desk. Together, they were reading a catalog showing colored photographs of food. With raised eyebrows, he greeted me by name and, without introducing me to the woman, ushered me into his office, past a coffeemaker with half a potful that had probably been sitting there since early morning.

"I'm pleasantly surprised," Keeney said. "We didn't have time to talk the other night. Sit down, sit down." He lowered himself into the chair behind his desk. "Are you planning a party? I'd love to take care of it, throw you an elegant affair, large or small. I'll make you a nice price." He whipped a menu and price list from his top drawer and handed it across the desk with a conspiratorial wink. "Your whole family—the Candiotti family—is friends to us here."

"Us?"

He pointed carelessly toward the woman at the desk in the front room. "To my wife and I." So that's his wife out there, I thought. What a rude little son of a bitch he was, not bothering to introduce us. And what a careless grammarian to boot.

"I'm not planning an elegant affair," I said, which made him frown. "I'd just like some information."

"For information," Keeney said, pointing at the Princess telephone on his desk, "call four one one." He wasn't even attempting humor. "All I do is cater parties."

"For the Severino family?"

He shrugged elaborately, as if I'd discovered a deep, dark secret. "For anyone with enough money to give a party."

"You cater Polly's poker games every week."

"I don't *cater* them; they're not fancy. I bring sandwiches, snacks—things the boys like to eat. Polly supplies beer and soft drinks."

"You make good money doing that?"

"I don't make money just doing a favor."

"And does Polly do you favors, too?"

"Naturally. Like, whenever anybody else does a party or benefit, or even a big-deal meeting of some kind, Polly or the old man recommends me—and that's where I make my best money." Keeney pointed a manicured finger at me; the colorless nail polish glistened. "You're in business, too, right, Nicky? In Chicago? So you understand half the business in the world gets done through favors and friendships."

I said, "Nobody calls me Nicky except my family and close friends."

"Ah. People call you Nick, then?"

"They do when I ask them to." I shifted my butt in the seat. "You knew my brother pretty well, didn't you?"

He just nodded, as if expending more unnecessary words would cost him money.

"But he didn't throw parties."

"He was *invited* to parties. Priests don't *give* parties."

"And he got invited to the poker games?"

Another nod.

"Priests can't afford to lose money gambling."

"Well," Keeney said, "when Richard won, great! If he lost—I can't guarantee how it was handled, but I don't think he ever left a game with an empty wallet."

"So Richard lived on favors," I said without warmth. "That means he *did* favors."

"*Everybody* does favors. You should know that."

"What kind of favors are we talking about?"

"I'm not discussing favors at all," Keeney said. "Unless you're totally stupid, I'm sure you know what I'm talking about."

"*I'm* talking about my brother."

"Your brother must have been deeply depressed. I have no idea about what, but it caused him to take his own life."

"You have no idea, but you saw him every week at church, and at the poker game, too."

"At church, he saved souls," Keeney said. "At the games, he liked to play Texas hold 'em. That's all I know. You're asking complicated questions when there's a simple answer. You're wasting your time."

"Wasting yours, too?"

He indicated the menu in my hand. "I'm at your service—if you want a party."

My fantasy of having a party choking the shit out of him enlivened my imagination, but I chose not to think about it. I put the menu down on his desk, too polite to suggest what he should do with it. As I passed through the front office, I said, "It was lovely meeting you, Mrs. Keeney."

She looked stunned and confused. Too bad for her.

I sat behind the wheel of my car for a while, adjusting the rearview mirror so I could see into the catering office. There was a glare on the plate glass, so my sight was limited, but I could tell he didn't go out into the front room for a while. His wife looked over her shoulder at him; then she got up from her desk and walked to the door of his inner office, where she stood with her arms folded, listening. At one point, she glanced out the window, saw I was still parked there, and looked upset. She quickly moved into his office and out of my sight, talking and gesturing to him as she entered.

I couldn't tell, but my guess was that Glenn Keeney was on the phone, telling somebody about me and my questions.

Who's on the other end? I wondered.

CHAPTER TEN

About a decade and a half ago, I found myself a member of the U.S. Army. My service to them was spending two-plus years in Vietnam, doing a lot of violent things I try every day to forget. But I never got hurt myself. My worst physical injuries in-country were deeply splitting a fingernail (which hurt like hell), fighting a hellacious bout of dysentery from eating in a suspect restaurant in Saigon, and spending a few weeks trying to cure athlete's foot.

The emotional injuries were something else again.

My body is not without scars, but I collected all of them in my youth, before I ever left Youngstown. On my right hand, between the third and fourth knuckles, is a glistening white badge of honor I earned when I was ten, fighting with a slightly better-off kid in fifth grade who made some scornful remark about my father's dirty-hands work in the steel mill and observed that I was part of a "poor" family. Among other things, I knocked out his front tooth—it was imbedded in my punching hand until the school nurse extracted it. The incisor caused a mild infection, which left a scar.

I have another white slash on my forehead, just over the left eyebrow. I added it to my collection outside one of the college hangout bars on a Saturday night when some muscle-bound asshole, who, I found out later, didn't even attend Youngstown State, observed that Diane looked like a really hot fuck, and he was going to take a shot at it if he could. His ring was big and thick, with a healthy turquoise stone that he probably wore only as a punching ring, and it cut open my forehead with his first punch, drawing more blood than either of us expected. It was also his last punch because I did a hell of a lot more damage to him than he did to me. I broke his nose, which was attended to in the emergency room that evening, along with several stitches to keep his cheekbone from falling out.

Does it sound like I grew up rough? Damn right. On Brier Hill, there was no such thing as "fighting dirty" or "fighting clean." One fought to win with every advantage one could wangle or steal. Otherwise, one lost and suffered the consequences, whether loss of face, loss of honor, or, more frequently, physical harm. The object of the game, always, was *not* to lose. I fought to win, and I matured tough. When you're the youngest kid among four siblings, living on a small block inhabited by at least two dozen kids close to your age, you'd *better* get tough.

I'm out of practice now. I've never gone hunting in my whole life—unless it was in-country, where they had a fair chance of hunting back at you—and now I even try not to step on bugs. But here, close to home and mourning my brother's death, those splenetic toxins were boiling up inside me again. Richard, I was convinced, had not committed suicide.

What the hell was this about a priest "doing favors" for the gangsters who ran the entire fiefdom of northeast Ohio? His "job" was to pray for them, but I *wouldn't* believe he'd been carrying water for Severino or any other mob bosses while flaunting a turned-around collar—even for thugs who laughed and smiled and invited him to dinner.

So I had to find out what favors he'd done, and for whom—and if it was true, why hadn't they helped him with *his* problems so he'd have been able to deal with them comfortably?

I didn't know who else to ask—and I felt impotent because of it.

Uncle Carmine—my mother's eldest brother—still lived in Brier Hill in the old mill house, now painted a too-bright blue, where he'd spent more than two-thirds of his life. In his older years, when he suffered from emphysema, he always wore his oxygen tank on his hip. The tank was connected to a ribbon of tubing under his nose. And whenever he left the house, he—or someone else—took his wheelchair along because it was too difficult for him to get around on foot for too long, due to his diabetes and a bad heart. He'd been widowed for a quarter of a century.

I had no idea how he ever got up the steps until I saw that his downstairs sofa, which looked less than ten years old, was the kind one could pull out and easily convert to a bed. That answered only part of my question, as the house, built in the 1920s, like so many others in the neighborhood, had only one bathroom, which was on the second floor. I didn't want to think of how Uncle Carmine got up there when he needed to.

I felt strange visiting him after all this time. At Richard's funeral, he'd joined the Candiotti family in the front pew of mourners, but to me, he was little more than a stranger. Even seated in his wheelchair, this craggy, angry guy was a giant, wide as a panel truck. He was the toughest man I'd ever met. He'd made a living doing the dirtiest and most dangerous jobs in the steel mill. As a small kid, I'd seen him on more than one occasion bearing fresh scars from serious fights, although no one ever told me with whom he'd traded blows. I know he was stabbed at least twice, and there was talk that he'd actually been shot, but during that time I hadn't see him in person for almost a year, and apparently the wound had healed by then.

He'd always been in endless trouble with the police, and one of his beatings, I'd heard, was at the wrong end of three police batons, although he was never arrested or charged. He'd butted heads with the hard guys, too, at odds with the Mangiones from across town as often as he was with the Severinos. One of his many tales was that four hitters had beaten him half to death on orders from the Mangione family, then left him bleeding and teetering on the edge of unconsciousness in an alley just south of downtown. As they dusted themselves off and walked away, Uncle Carmine grabbed the ankle of one of them, brought him down with a vicious twist to his foot, and bit off most of his ear before anyone could stop him.

Now he was disabled and in disintegrating physical shape, but I didn't know if the rest of his ruination was from disease or from the multiple drubbings he'd received—and given—through the years. His hands and knuckles were twisted and misshapen, probably from bouncing off too many hard skulls.

He hobbled to the door to greet me, leaning on a tripod-base metal cane. He was wearing too-loose Lee blue jeans, which his ass would never again fill. His old brown sweater bore a busy plaid design and a shawl collar, probably from the early fifties, but he still looked shivering cold. It took him almost a minute to get back to the living room and into his wheelchair, having refused my help, and after thudding into the uncomfortable seat, he raised his hand for me to wait until he caught his breath.

The chair was packed and ready to go at a moment's notice. Faux-leather pockets hung all over it, and in the various compartments he could transport sandwiches, a thermos, Kleenex, eyeglasses, a lap blanket, and God knows what else. There was also a silver 9mm in a holster strapped to the right side of the chair.

You don't often see armed men in wheelchairs.

He sat facing a small TV set on a high table, watching a soap opera featuring beautiful babbling actors at least fifty years younger than he was. When a commercial appeared—one that looked like the soap opera itself—he was finally ready to talk.

He pointed a remote at the screen and clicked the TV into mute, sighing with soft relief at the quiet.

I handed him a bottle of Jack Daniel's in a paper bag. "A little present," I said. "For giving up some of your time for me."

He laughed sardonically, but he took the bottle, slipping it out of the bag. "That's all I got," he said. "Time. I got all the time in the world to drink this, too. Thanks, kid." He looked at it lovingly, almost caressing it, before he put it on an end table next to him.

I pointed to the holster. "You carry heat around with you in that chair?" I asked.

"Except when I sleep at night. Then I slip it under my pillow."

"Why?"

"*Why?* Look at me, fa God sake. I got more medical things wrong with me than some broad on a soap opera, and I'm not strong enough to take another beatin'—I took too many of 'em already over the years. So if I have a problem with somebody now, we sit down and discuss things. If we don't have a meetin' of the minds—if they try to punch me around again—I'll shoot their fuckin' eyes out."

I sat down in the only other chair in the room, a stiff-looking armchair upholstered in a faded flower print. "I couldn't blame you for that, *tio*."

"Nah," he said. "Everybody blames me—for everythin'. I lived my whole life gettin' blamed—even for stuff I didn't do." He adjusted the tube that was stretched across his upper lip, blowing oxygen into his nostrils, and inhaled deeply. "I'm glad you come around to see me before you go back. Chicago's good, right? I ain't been there in maybe thirty years. But it was good back then."

"It's a good town."

"Good town, lousy baseball club. Last time the Cubs won the World Serious was way before I was born." He sighed.

"Sorry you had to come back here because of Richard. You was close when you two was kids."

"He was the best in the family," I said.

Carmine nodded. "I only saw him like at Thanksgivin' and stuff. I never went to his church. I gave up bein' Catholic a long time ago. After my wife—your aunt Mary—died, I didn't see no point in it." He raised his head and scratched idly at random bristles on his neck. The skin beneath his chin hadn't been shaved carefully, and his wattles had turned to crepe. "Your brother Richard got pissed off sometimes—lately."

His words clanged around inside my head like Chinese temple gongs. I tried not to look eager. "What about?"

"Bein' a priest, hearin' confessions, bein' famous in your own town. Everybody was in his face all a time, askin' him for stuff."

"Who was everybody?"

"He never told me."

"What about the Severino family? Did they ask him for stuff, too?"

The bones in Uncle Carmine's face and skull rearranged and compressed under his skin, as if all of him were growing smaller. His faded brown eyes flashed anger. "Those cocksucker bastards!" he snarled.

"What," I demanded, "did they do to Richard?"

"Look, your old man, my brother-in-law, he was tight with Don Severino. They looked out for him, for his family. Especially Richard, but they looked out for you, too, even when you din't know nothin' about it. It was a family thing."

"And they didn't look out for you?"

His staccato laugh was more of a cough. "I'm not a Candiotti—and I'm not in the Severino or Mangione family, neither. That got them cheesed at me, and they was in my face all a time. They both had me beat up more than once. And when they weren't doin' it, the cops were doin' it themselves, like when they'd haul me in for questionin'. You know how many times I got punched in the stomach in that fuckin' police elevator? The last few years when I still worked at the mill, I'd have three different guys, buddies a mine, come by in the mornin' and drive me to work because I was scared shitless of startin' my own car, knowin' the last thing I'd ever feel was the Youngstown Tune-Up." He made that same explosion sound in the back of his throat, flittering his fingers as he raised his hands and then lowered them slowly, illustrating pieces of car and driver flying into the air and then drifting down to earth like tiny snowflakes.

"Who was trying to kill you?"

"Screw it. Old news."

"What about Richard?" I said. "That's *new* news."

He lifted both hands again, then dropped them into his lap. "Whatever his business was with mob guys, it was *his* business. Favors, you could say. It ain't like it used to be in this town, like protection and out-and-out theft. The Severinos, they got different interests now." He shrugged his massive shoulders. "Legit business—along with hookers, money launderin', and politics."

"Are you saying, *tio*, that Richard was actually a bagman for the mob?"

"I ain't sayin' nothin' like that," he mumbled, "an' don't tell nobody I did." Then he raised his chin to point it at me, challenging me. "Richard never got beat up all a time like me, he never got shot at, and he never turned on a car that blew up under his ass. Nobody killed him off, kid. He ate his own weapon."

He stopped talking, sucking in as much oxygen as he could. Then he dug into his pants pocket and brought out his little glucose monitor. "I gotta check my blood sugar," he said. "It's four o'clock almost."

I watched while he extracted a few drops of blood from his finger. He waited for about ten seconds, then looked at the number displayed in the little window.

"Are you okay?" I asked.

He nodded. "Close enough." He replaced the monitor in his pocket.

"Richard was a priest, *tio*. He didn't own a weapon."

Uncle Carmine frowned, thinking about it. "So what?"

"So," I said, "where did he get it?"

I wasn't hungry, even though it edged close to dinnertime, so instead of finding a restaurant, I bought myself a few drinks at a bar not too far from Uncle Carmine's house. Then I went to a movie downtown. Ten minutes after I left the theater, I couldn't even remember who was in it or what it was about. All I recall is that several of the actors and even one of the actresses carried guns, and by the end of the film, they were spraying lead all over the place.

Then I stopped and had a few more drinks, feeling my anger again. When I was a kid and then later in Vietnam, I *knew* who the bad guys were, and I was assured of what I needed to do to them. In Youngstown, I was furious with shadows, with rumors, with maybes and might have beens—and with all the weeping, crying, smiting of chests, and dabbing at leaking eyes by people who didn't really gave a damn whether Richard had been murdered, committed suicide, had a heart attack, or just simply fell down the stairs. He's gone; that's too fucking bad. Now let's move on.

Not me, brother.

The air was damp and chilly, but it wasn't raining, and I cranked my windows all the way down to get plenty of fresh air to straighten me out a little bit as I headed to my room at the Holiday Inn, hoping I could get some sleep. Father Candy's suicide bothered me more than I'd ever imagined; the tragedy and the weight of it sucking the air out of my chest. Sleep would be a temporary escape.

The parking areas were on the side of the hotel, and when I

arrived, I figured there must be a lot of out-of-towners visiting. Most of the vacant spaces were toward the back. Few rooms overlooked the parking lot, since most overnighters would prefer gazing at something more pleasant than a small sea of cars.

I knew the side doors to the hallways were always locked at 9:00 P.M., so I slipped out of the car, locked it, and started toward the front entrance. I hadn't taken too many steps before two figures emerged from between parked cars and stood where it would be nearly impossible for me to pass by them. I couldn't see the faces, but the tall, wide, hulking man who stood slightly ahead of the other was built exactly like Joey Sposito.

I sighed. It was starting.

"Candiotti," Joey growled. It was loud enough for me to hear, but soft enough that nobody in the hotel could understand what he was saying.

"Joey," I replied.

"You're a real bother, you know that? Buggin' everybody, askin' lotsa questions, makin' yourself a pain in the ass."

The shorter guy rotated his head around on his almost nonexistent neck and adjusted his shoulders. Then he began moving, almost in a circle, trying to get behind me. He didn't have his hands in his pockets, though, nor did Joey Sposito. I figured they weren't planning to kill me, at least not here in the parking lot of the Holiday Inn.

"To make an omelette, you gotta break some eggs," I said with a shrug.

"The word is you should stop breakin' eggs."

"Why's that? Somebody think those eggs are rotten and'll make a stink?"

"Funny," Joey said. "You're a funny guy." He looked at his companion. "Am I right?"

"He's a funny guy," the sawed-off one said, still moving.

"Sure I am."

"Everybody wants you to go away," Joey said. "Back to

Chicago—or wherever the fuck you wanna. Just get out a Youngstown."

My hands hung down at my sides, and I tried not to flex them. The short one was almost behind me. "When I'm ready."

Joey Sposito shook his head sadly. "You jus' don't lissen, do ya? You're ready now, you dumb fuck."

The short guy grabbed both my arms just above the elbows and squeezed them almost together behind me, breathing garlic and booze over my shoulder. He was strong. In front of me, Joey Sposito was advancing, slipping a leather glove onto his right hand. There was enough light from a high carbon lamp halfway down the lot that I could tell it was one of those weighted gloves—made for the single purpose of hurting someone else badly.

I didn't have time to think it all the way through, but then, in Vietnam, when I was out on one of my "missions," I often had to make lightning-quick choices. I made the first one by grinding my heel all the way down the right leg of the man behind me, probably removing most of the skin on his shin, and ended with stomping my heel, hard, against his instep. I heard the bones cracking even though his shoes.

The pain made him howl and let go of me. My left elbow smashed back on him, hitting him in the neck, just below his chin. He was silent for a few seconds, and then he started making strangled, gasping noises.

But I didn't wait for his choking heaves, because with my right hand I reached out for Joey's, which at the moment was up near his face as he pulled on the glove. I think he expected me to pull his arm toward me, but I fooled him and pushed it backward into his face. His own reinforced knuckles smacked him right in the mouth, not hard enough to hurt him badly, but it slowed him down enough that I could drive my left fist deep into his abdomen.

It bent him over from the waist and buckled his knees, giving me enough time to turn and chop the side of my stiffened hand into the short guy's neck again, this time just below his ear. He fell heavily, his forehead bouncing on the cement, and I knew he'd stay there for a while, so I turned my full attention back to Joey Sposito.

He started to straighten up from the body punch, and I put both hands behind his head and drove his face down toward my knee, which was coming up fast. He went down on all fours and I practically jumped on top of him, my fist mercilessly belaboring his kidney. I knew him from high school and now he worked for the Severino family, which made me madder than ever. He groaned loudly at each punch, struggling beneath me, but I had the leverage. I kept slamming into his kidney until he pissed in his pants, the puddle spreading beneath him.

I stood up. He pushed himself up on his hands, and I leaned down and hit him on the side of the head. Joey went out quickly—like a cat hustling out into the night when you leave the door open too long. A concussion, I thought, at the very least.

I went back over to the shorter man, who was now beginning to stir. I pulled him up by his lapels and slapped his face twice with my palm and twice with the back of my hand. He whimpered and started to come around.

"Wake up. The party's over," I said.

His eyes opened. Then they scrunched closed again as he grimaced in pain. "You broke my fuckin' foot," he managed to say.

"That was the beginning." I slapped his cheeks again, almost gently. "Who are you?" I asked. "What's your name?"

"Dellarosa," he told me, pissed off that he had to. "Gabe Dellarosa."

I nodded. "Listen up, Gabriel Dellarosa, because I'm only sayin' it once. You, or Joey, or anybody else from the Severinos comes around and tries roughing me up—or worse—you're all dead men. *Capisce?* I just cleaned your clocks and I didn't even break a sweat, so imagine what happens when I get really mad." I shook him a little, and his eyes opened wider. The last time I saw anyone's eyes bug our in fear like that, it was a nine-year-old kid watching a *Nightmare on Elm Street* movie. "Don't come around, Gabe. I don't play by the rules, and if you try playing with me, you're not gonna like it one bit. So go back and tell Polly Severino that. And take Joey with you. Understand?" He didn't answer me quickly enough, so I slapped him again, this time across the lips—not gently, but not brutally, either. Just enough to get his attention.

"Yeah," Gabe croaked. "Yeah, awright."

I started away, then turned back to him. I told him my room number at the Holiday Inn. "If anyone knocks, Gabe, I'm going to shoot him through the door without opening it. Tell Polly that, too."

I headed for the main entrance to the hotel, not looking back. I guessed Gabe Dellarosa was heeled, but I didn't worry about it. I'd scared him into doing whatever I wanted him to. I figured he—and maybe Joey, when he woke up—would actually think I was Superman. Maybe so, because if you can make other people believe you're unbeatable and invincible, then naturally you *are*.

It wasn't until I got up in my room that I started to shake. If anyone knocked, I sure as hell couldn't shoot them, because the two guns I owned were locked in a little safe in a closet of my house in Chicago. I'd made it through relatively unscathed.

Physically, that is—because now more than ever I knew something had happened regarding Richard that had caused his death. And I was goddamned if I'd leave Youngstown until I found out what it was.

CHAPTER ELEVEN

I'd spent little time with my brother Alfonso in the past ten years, and on this trip I suddenly realized he looked different. Every grown-up takes on a different look from when they were kids. The world changes us all the time, whether we like it or not.

In our childhood, we dressed like kids, clean but rumpled dago ragamuffins—except on Sundays, when we wore suits to church. Because I was the youngest, I was doomed to hand-me-down clothes until my last year of high school. But after Al became a cop, my only recollections of him were in his snappy tailored blue uniform or wearing a suit. The uniform never looked right on him—it made him appear as a little boy wearing a costume of influence and authority that didn't fit his personality. He looked perfect in suits, though, especially after he was promoted to lieutenant and was able to afford really good dress-up clothes. They made him look important, too—as someone who had power and was listened to when he talked.

But when I dropped by his house unannounced after dinner, Alfonso wore faded jeans and a light blue sweatshirt with gold letters promoting UCLA. I don't know why he had the shirt, as he'd never been anywhere near Los Angeles. The farthest west he'd ever traveled was to a law-enforcement symposium in Kansas City.

I was still in my sport jacket and dress pants, but I'd loosened my tie and opened the neck button on my shirt. Initially, he was surprised to see me, but he thawed a bit and welcomed me in. Now we were drinking Iron City Beer out of tall, icy mugs he kept in the freezer.

Dolores disappeared into another part of the house, probably to put as much distance between us as possible, and he and I holed up in a little downstairs room off the kitchen that he called his office. Nothing in there looked like anything other than a retreat for a married man who wanted to spend time alone in his house. No desk, typewriter, or books—just a seventeen-inch TV set atop a small bar. Two leather chairs were in front of the TV, and a sofa along one wall looked ideal for a quick nap. A pleasant aura of good cigars hung in the air—a male smell. I wondered whether Dolores had ever been inside that room for any length of time.

"I don't know where Richard got the gun," Alfonso was saying. "He sure as hell didn't own one."

"Then whose was it?"

Upturned palms. "Who knows."

"You didn't run ballistics? You didn't check to see who the gun belonged to?"

"I wasn't the investigating officer, Nicky. Captain Shemo wouldn't let me anywhere near the case because it was my own brother. He thought it'd be too painful for me, that I couldn't of handled it." He raised the mug in a silent toast to his boss. "I appreciate Shemo for that."

"So who was the lead cop?"

He looked annoyed "There was no 'lead cop' because there was nothing to investigate. Richard committed suicide—period."

"Who took charge of the gun?"

He shrugged. "I don't know."

"Alfonso, do you even know what goes on in your department?"

"My department," he said, "is homicide."

"*Homicide* rhymes with *suicide*."

He spoke through his teeth. "And *luck* rhymes with *fuck*—but it's not the same."

"So?"

"So I don't know anything about it."

"Who does?"

He set the mug down too hard. "*Nobody* does. Get it through your thick head; it wasn't a police matter. If your dog takes a dump on your neighbor's lawn, no cops come around with weapons drawn, waving warrants. We got better things to do."

"Like what? Running errands for the mob?"

He flushed pink. "I don't run no errands!"

"Sure not," I said. "You draw the line at washing Polly's car for him every week."

His mouth was one thin line slashed across the lower part of his face. "I don't have to take shit from *you*."

"Go ahead, then—shoot me."

"I wish I could," he mumbled.

"But you can't because I'm your brother. Well, Richard was your brother, too, and you won't lift a finger to find out why he shot himself."

"I got *things* to do! I got a job. I can't just poke into stuff everybody else thinks wasn't a crime at all. I gotta run out tomorrow because we had a killing last night, and I got people to talk to—because I'm a lieutenant and that's what I do. I don't need to shoot you, for crysakes. I *love* you, Nicky. So quit bugging me."

We glared at each other for a long minute. I'd never seen him so angry. Then Alfonso's face crumbled slowly—first the eyes, then the cheeks, finally the mouth, making him look like one of those primitive dolls with faces made out of dried apples. He blinked hard, raising a hand to his temple and rubbing.

We shared filial love, but frankly, I didn't like Alfonso very much and never had. He was too arrogant, bossy, too much in love with himself. Now, however, I worried I'd pulled the rug out from under him. "Al, take it easy," I said softly.

"Goddamn it!" Alfonso whispered. He was moments away from actually crying. "*Nobody killed Richard!* I don't know where he got the gun or what happened to it afterward, but you gotta take my word. It was suicide—and you can knock your brains out tryin' to prove it wasn't, but you won't."

"Don't lie to me, Al," I said. "You can lie till you're blue in the face, but you can't lie to your brother."

He held up his right hand. "I swear I'm not lying."

"What was the deal? Was Richard on the mob's payroll?"

"You're bein' an ignoramus!" Alfonso hunched over, making himself even smaller, looking up at the ceiling. "Richard was on God's payroll."

I slumped back in my chair and drank the last few swallows of beer, which had gone warm and flat. "Don't make me laugh," I said.

It didn't make me laugh later that evening as I sat near the window of my hotel room, staring out into the night, watching lonely cars drive by. I occasionally sipped at single-malt scotch poured from a bottle I'd bought in a liquor store. I wish I'd known then what I know now—that hotel housekeepers rarely wash the glasses, just wipe them down with a towel and put them back, so they appear cleaner than they are. I'd added no ice, no chaser; there was just the soothing, almost medicinal taste that stayed on my tongue and got into my nose. Had I been heading out anywhere, I'd have worried that other people could detect the strong smell of alcohol on my breath and judge me for being a secret boozer.

Well, sometimes I was.

It was warmer the next morning, fifteen degrees toastier than the last three days, even though the sun tried without success to bang its way through the blanket of clouds. I parked halfway down the block from the police station, facing away from the front door so I could see in the rearview mirror who came in or out of the parking lot. I was looking for Alfonso, but I didn't want him to see me.

He arrived at work about ten minutes before nine, breezing into the parking lot and waving good morning to the attendant. He was known. He wore an unbuttoned trench coat over a brown suit and gold tie, looking casually elegant. The previous evening, in the little private room in his house where we growled and snarled at each other, had not ended happily.

I'd bought a newspaper in the lobby of my hotel and filled up my waiting time reading about the day's happenings, glancing into my mirror every fifteen seconds. There was national news on the front page, Browns and Steelers reports in the sports section, but what most interested me was the local stuff. Our Y-town big shots, judges, and politicians were in trouble almost every day, and even though their activities were different, eventually the stories all resembled one another. That was Youngstown for you.

Finally, just after ten, Alfonso came out of the building, this time in more of a hurry. He went directly to his car in the parking lot and pulled out onto the street. I waited until he was five minutes gone and then got out, fed more dimes into the parking meter on the street, and headed toward the station. I didn't want him to know I'd been here, that I'd gone over his head to get information he couldn't—or wouldn't—give me.

The sergeant at the desk recognized me the moment I walked in and smiled deferentially. I was, after all, the brother of a big shot. "Sorry, Mr. Candiotti, but you just missed the lieutenant. He probably won't be back until after lunchtime."

"That's okay," I said. "I actually came to see Captain Shemo."

That put the sergeant's eyebrows up. I said, "I'd just as soon Lieutenant Candiotti not know I was here. It's kind of awkward—but Captain Shemo's the boss."

He nodded. "Don't worry about a thing, sir," he said, picking up his phone to let Shemo know I was coming.

When he stood as I entered his office I realized once again what a big man Ed Shemo was. In slacks and shirt, he seemed even taller and heavier than when he had worn a dress uniform at Richard's funeral.

His tentative, unenthusiastic handshake took me by surprise. I didn't know if he was unhappy to see me or whether he passed out dead-fish handshakes to everyone.

"I'm surprised you're still in town," he said.

"I have reasons for staying awhile longer."

He indicated that I should take a chair opposite his desk. "You should work things out with Al."

"Al won't tell me much," I said. "I hoped you'd be more forthcoming."

Shemo's smile seemed pleasant, but it stopped below his eyes. "You know what everybody else knows. Al told you everything—he mentioned to me this morning that the two of you spent some time discussing it last night. I can't fill in any blanks that he didn't." He sighed. "I don't think you *have* any blanks."

"You took Alfonso off the case," I said.

"There was no *case*. It was a suicide, and it was Al's brother. I didn't want to put him through that, so I assigned someone else to the details."

"Who did you assign? I want to talk to him."

He leaned back in his chair and folded his hands across his stomach as if he were thirty years older. "Listen, Dominick— it *is* Dominick, isn't it? Well, listen to me. This is a police department—and you're not police. We do what we do for a reason, and we aren't open and transparent about anything. If we were, it'd make it that much harder to do our jobs. Say whatever you want to Al, because you're family, but you can't just march in here and demand answers from me to whatever wild-hair questions you want to ask."

"You mean you guys just huddle here behind closed doors, doing whatever the hell you do, and never talk to anybody?"

Now the fake smile disappeared altogether. "I'm talking to you, aren't I?"

"You're talking *at* me."

"Semantics."

"Is that another word for *bullshit*?"

He made a point of looking at his watch. "I don't have any more time. I got things to do. But I appreciate your coming in. I wish I could help you out, but there's nothing else to say."

"What if I told you I think Richard didn't kill himself at all—that he was murdered?"

Shemo frowned. "You're blowing smoke up my ass."

"And what if I said I think you know that's true and you're keeping it from me—for some reason of your own?"

He stood. "If you weren't Alfonso's brother, I'd throw you out the window myself."

I stood up, too, flexing my fists. I let my hands hang at my sides, ready to defend myself. "Might be fun if you tried."

He crossed his arms across his chest and glowered at me. "I'm the number-three guy in this whole department," he said. "I carry a gold captain's badge, which means I'm not some ordinary schmuck you think you can storm in here and push around. Are you threatening me? Are you actually *threatening* me?"

"Does 'Go fuck yourself' sound like a threat?"

I spun on my heel and walked out, opening the door so violently that it banged into the wall. The startled policewoman at the desk in his outer office jumped at the noise and stood up, her hand resting on the butt of the weapon at her hip.

"Don't shoot," I barked. "I'm leaving."

I almost bumped into Mike LeBlanc getting off the elevator. I didn't say hello.

"Hey, Mr. Candiotti, good to see you again," he said pleasantly. He was almost as tall as Shemo. I was starting to feel like a dwarf. "Can I help you with anything?"

"Fuck you, too," I said softly. Then I stepped into the elevator, hoping something untoward wouldn't happen to me in there and that I wouldn't end up bloodied like so many local criminals. I pushed the ground-floor button and watched the automatic door slide shut in LeBlanc's startled face.

CHAPTER TWELVE

I went back to my hotel room, where I shucked my jacket and shoes and sprawled out on the bed. I felt like one of those people who are desperate to learn the news but their TV set doesn't work. I'd asked questions of a lot of different people, all of whom had stonewalled me, including my own siblings, the heir apparent to the local mob, and the assistant district attorney.

Everybody in Youngstown kept secrets.

Why would the cops slam the door shut on Richard Candiotti's suicide? He'd been a much-beloved priest, "Father Candy" to so many, and he was my favorite brother. Why had it been so easy for Capt. Ed Shemo, supposedly in charge of the nonexistent investigation, to suggest that I shut up and go home?

It was three o'clock in the afternoon by the time I decided there was someone else to talk to, assuming I could wangle an audience with him. I showered and shaved again, then climbed into clean clothes. When I got where I was going, it would be important for me to look good—and show respect.

I'd never been to Franco's Italian Ristorante before, but I knew exactly where it was. I think everyone in Mahoning and Trumbull counties knew it—or knew of it. It was open to the public, but if you were connected in any way to the Severino family, you just didn't go there. "Franco" was Frank Mangione—the big boss of the rival mob on the east side of Youngstown. He'd owned the Italian eatery for at least thirty years, and now his son, Frank junior, managed it. The place where he presided over his other business interests was the sprawling apartment on the restaurant's second floor, although Mangione himself lived in a big house about six blocks away.

I wasn't sure exactly where Frank junior lived, and I didn't care. He was in his shirtsleeves behind the bar with another man, probably the bartender, when I walked in. They were going over what I assumed was liquor inventory.

"We're closed," Frank called out. The sign on the front door announced that they didn't open for business until five o'clock.

"Frank, it's Dominick Candiotti," I said. "Father Richard Candiotti's brother."

Frank and the bartender exchanged looks, and then Frank put down his clipboard and came out from behind the bar.

"I'm kind of surprised seeing you in here," he said.

"I live in Chicago. That's why I haven't been here for dinner before."

He folded thick arms across his chest. I remembered from a psych course in college all those years ago that arms akimbo over the chest is an unconscious statement of defense and protection. I wondered why Frank junior needed to protect himself from me. We hardly knew each other.

"I was touched you and your family came to Father Candy's funeral. I wanted to thank you."

He examined that from all angles. Finally, he said, "Awright—you're welcome."

"I was hoping I could pay my respects to the don while I'm here."

"Why you wanna do that?"

I gave him a weak smile. "Like I said—respect."

Frank pondered for a minute. Then he looked at the bartender and jerked his head toward the kitchen, and the bartender scurried off.

"We'll see if my father has some time for you."

"I hope so," I said.

We waited for three silent minutes until the bartender came back in. "It's okay, Frank," he reported. Then he came up to stand in front of me. "Lift 'em," he ordered.

"What?"

He made a motion that I should raise my arms.

"Are you kidding me?" I said. "I'm not carrying heat."

Frank's face turned unpleasant, the way it had at Richard's funeral, but then, I think he always looked like that.

The bartender said, "Lift 'em or pound sand, brother. Up to you."

I sighed and raised my arms, and the bartender frisked me thoroughly and efficiently. I bit down hard to keep from exploding in his face; I don't like to be touched by anyone unless I want them to. The bartender didn't look like anyone I'd want to touch me—and he had lousy breath.

Frank led me into the kitchen, where a head chef wearing a toque and several assistants all in white, their heads covered by hairnets, were busy stirring up red sauces and white ones, making salads, and putting together shrimp or calamari cocktails in medium-size liquor glasses. We headed toward a rear door made of heavy reinforced steel. Frank pushed it open and stood aside as I walked past him into the large backyard behind the restaurant.

There were several clubs around town where playing bocce was the main attraction, but some people had actually built regulation bocce courts in their backyards. As a matter of fact, there was a bocce court only a few yards from where my brother had been laid out for his funeral Mass. The bocce court steps led right up into Our Lady.

There was an elegant court constructed just behind Franco's, and eight men were milling around out there, playing the game.

Several others watched from the sidelines, but I spotted Frank Mangione, Sr. immediately. His red-and-blue argyle sweater almost covered an olive green shirt and an orange-and-blue-striped tie. He stood at one end of the bocce court, his hands in the pockets of his khaki slacks, intently studying the scattered balls. He was the most colorful of all the elderly men there, probably because no one dared tell him stripes look ridiculous with argyle.

When he saw me, he waved, then pointed to a bench.

"Siddown there and watch," he called.

I sat on one side of a bench, the coldness of the stone leaching through my pants and crawling up my legs. An older man was on the other end, huddled in a sports shirt and blazer with the collar up, wearing a black Borsalino hat pulled down low over his forehead, and smoking a cigar. He looked like a recently retired Parisian pimp in a French heist movie. He nodded at me, not smiling.

"You the brother of the priest, right?" His voice sounded as if he gargled with Drano. "I'm sorry for your loss."

"Thank you," I said. He didn't bother to introduce himself. I recognized the face, someone I saw or knew of a long time ago, but the name wouldn't come to me. Perhaps I'd met him through my father. Sticking his cigar into one side of his mouth, the old man folded his hands over his potbelly to watch the contest.

There are eight large balls in the game of bocce, all having different colors or designs so the players can tell them apart quickly, and one smaller ball, which the bocce cognoscenti call the pallino. The game is to toss your ball closer to the pallino than anyone else's. That means that you're considered "inside," while the other players' tossed balls are "outside." The inside player has to forfeit his turn, while everyone else in the game gets to take theirs. At the end of the frame, whoever is closest to the pallino wins a point. Then they start another frame, until one person has scored thirteen times. That's when the game is over and they can begin again.

It sounds boring as hell—the Italian alternative to shuffleboard or horseshoes—but when you're out there playing, it's actually fun. It's also *very* competitive. My father was pretty good at it, but I can't remember him winning too many times. The experts play all day—every day.

As I watched Don Mangione easily rack up thirteen points, I wondered whether everyone else was letting him win because of who he was, or if he was really skilled at a game he'd been playing all his life. Observing his surgical tosses, I decided his victory was legitimate. It's almost impossible to *try* being lousy at bocce.

While his guests gathered up the balls and the pallino and set them up again at one end of the court, the don came over to me, wiping his sweaty face with a handkerchief. The old man with the Borsalino hat jumped up from the bench and walked away, giving Mangione room to sit. Frank, the son, stood nearby, close enough to hear us but appearing to be out of the conversation. He kept putting his hands into his pants pockets nervously and then taking them out again.

A comfortable, relaxed sigh escaped Mangione's lips as he took his weight off his feet. "You come all the way over here to play with us, Dominick?" He was breathing medium hard, as if winning bocce had been more of a physical effort than it looked.

I shook my head. "I'm still in mourning."

"You out of practice?"

"I first played bocce when I was about five, Don Mangione. I got to be not too bad, until I left Youngstown and wound up in Vietnam. After that, I moved to Chicago."

"They got no bocce in Chicago?" He was chiding me, teasing me.

"Not when you're a stranger," I said.

He crossed his short arms across his chest, his eyes scanning the skies. "You wouldn't be a stranger here, but you *are* one. It was a choice you made. I understand that. Your papa always was closer to the Severino family than to us, so we never got to know any of you so good. Except Father Richard, of course. Now, with him gone . . ."

He shrugged rather elaborately and folded his hands on his thighs. "Your other brother, Alfonso—he's an asshole, if you don't mind me sayin' so. He's a cop an' he got his job to do, but he don' know the first thing about respect."

He lapsed into silence for half a minute. Then he said, "So, how about you? You dint come here to play bocce. You wanted to see me, no? So—what can I do for you, Dominick? Are you collectin' money for a headstone?"

"No, but thank you," I said. "The church is taking care of it."

"You think I don' know? I wrote them a check a couple a days ago. *That's* how they're takin' care of it. I did for him, for Father Candy." He inhaled deeply—we were outside, or else he'd have sucked all the oxygen out of the room.

I took a moment to compose my next sentence. "I'm here," I said, "because I don't believe my brother's death was suicide."

He closed his eyes, then reopened them. "Why you think that?"

"Killing himself was contrary to everything he ever thought or did in his life."

Softly: "You think somebody took him out?"

"I don't know. I wanted to ask you."

He turned his head sharply to stare at me—through me—and his voice grew hard and direct. "You think it was me that hurt him? Or one of my people?"

"No, sir. I can't imagine why you'd hurt Richard."

"Listen," he said, "priests an' bishops—nuns, even—they're sacred to me. Like the Pope, you understand?"

"I trust you, Don Mangione," I said, and added, "on that score."

That seemed to satisfy him, because he relaxed. Frank Mangione reminded me of a feral cat that was never more than half a pace from fear—he never completely let his guard down. He pursed his lips, his head nodding as his brain computed. Then he talked some more. "The last couple a years, the father come over here to play bocce—mostly in the summer. He'd shuck off his black jacket an' his priest collar an' he'd get into the game serious. He played pretty good."

"Did you talk with him?"

"About the game, mostly."

"You saw him almost every week at church, too."

Don Mangione put his right hand over his heart. "I'm a good Catholic," he said.

"Richard always heard your confession?"

"He was my priest—and Our Lady is my church."

"You confess every Sunday?"

He hitched his shoulders halfway up into a shrug. "Most Sundays, sure."

"Did he ever—when you'd talk together—did he ever confess to you, too?"

Mangione rubbed his hand over his face. "Do I look like a priest?" he said. "Besides, I don't repeat confessions, no matter what."

"There's got to be something."

"Not with me." He shifted his butt around so he half-faced me. "He wasn't close to my family. I don' know what he was doin'—or why. He hung with the Severinos."

"He wasn't your enemy, Don Mangione."

"Paolo Severino, that son of a bitch?"

"I mean Richard."

"Ah." Mangione nodded. "He wasn't nobody's enemy." He shrugged again. "Whatever he did with the Severinos, I don' know nothin' about. They don' talk to me, an' I don' talk to them." He reached out and tapped my forehead. "Wake up. This ain't no friendly town. You're either on one side or the other."

"Richard was on both sides."

"Priests are human, like the rest of us—and maybe when he

wasn' in no church, he was hangin' around, doin' shit for the Severinos."

I tilted my upper body toward him, my voice low. "What shit?"

"I got no spies in that family, so how the hell do I know?"

"I was hoping you'd know something. Anything."

"I know I'm gonna miss the father. I got nothin' good to say about Don Severino, but I think he's gonna miss him, too. Other than that . . ." He rubbed his hands together, as if he'd just crumbled up saltine crackers in his soup. "There's a lotta stuff goes on in this town that's family business. We don' talk about it outside the family. Only a dumb shit does that." He smiled almost kindly. "I'm not no dumb shit, Dominick."

"You might be the best bocce player in the world, Don Mangione."

He hung his head, sham-humble. "Nah. Maybe the best in Youngstown. Senior division." Then he lifted his chin and looked right at me. "If you need anythin', call me. Seriously. Richard was a big person in my life—I listened to him more'n anybody else I ever knew, practically. So if I can do anythin' now, all you gotta do is call." He poked me in the arm with a callused, arthritic finger—hard enough for it to hurt. "Call me at the restaurant here, day or night. I'm here to help." Then he shook that same finger—like a librarian warning rowdy kids to shush. "Don' lose my phone number, okay?"

CHAPTER THIRTEEN

"You pulled a fast one on me the other afternoon," I said. "When I was in the bathroom, you just took off without so much as a bye-bye."

Diane Burnham sat across from me in a small booth in the bar off the lobby of the Holiday Inn where I was staying, dressed more casually than she'd been at our last meeting, probably because it was early evening now—just after seven o'clock—and she'd changed from her daytime business attire to an outfit less stuffy and more sexy. More cleavage showed at the top of a "looking to meet a one-timer" blouse.

That was unusual; nobody local *ever* comes into a Holiday Inn cocktail lounge for a drink, not in Youngstown or anywhere else. It was a safe, secure venue for Diane because she wouldn't run into anyone she knew.

She was drinking bourbon on the rocks now, rocking the glass back and forth in her hand so the ice cubes tinkled. "I didn't have anything more to say."

"Maybe *I* did."

"You always have more to say, Nicky, and it's just as well you didn't. You live in the past—and this is the present, so there's nothing left to talk about."

"Why did you call me tonight, then?"

She raised one cynical eyebrow, as if my question were stupid. "Not to chat." Then she said, "Why didn't you call *me*?"

"I don't have your number. You're not listed in the phone book—just your husband's office."

"You could have asked around."

"Who was I supposed to ask?"

She twisted her mouth in a peculiar way, as if she were thinking it over, and it showed off her dimples. I remembered those dimples. A really adorable dimple on a woman's already-beautiful face was simply another delightful place, if so inclined, to put one's tongue.

"It doesn't matter," Diane said. "I'm here now, aren't I?" Her smile once more didn't make it to her eyes. "Happy?"

"I've been happier."

"You should take whatever happiness comes your way with a grain of salt."

"Should I take Richard's unexplained death with a grain of salt?"

She shook her head sadly. "People die. All the time."

"A kind, benevolent priest shoots himself, and I shouldn't worry about it?"

"I told you—it *was* a suicide."

"How do you know that, Diane? Who was mad at him?"

"Nobody." She looked right into my eyes when she said it.

"Nobody?"

"He never did anything to get anyone mad at him, not in his whole life. He was a good, decent man."

"Nobody was mad at him, according to you, so nobody shot him."

She nodded.

"And he was the best human being who ever lived, he was the best priest, and everybody loved him, so he had no reason to take his own life. But the police don't know where he got the gun," I said, "or bothered finding out—including my brother Al."

"Why ask me?" she said, and it came out somewhere between annoyance and whining. I couldn't remember Diane ever whining before.

"I'm running out of people to ask."

"Then stop asking," she said. "Go home—to Chicago."

"Is that what you want me to do? Go home?"

She knocked back the rest of her drink. "Frankly, my dear," she said. She didn't finish the *Gone With the Wind* sentence because she didn't have to.

"Then why did you call? Why are we meeting?"

"For fun. Wasn't the last time fun?"

I shook my head. "Jesus, Diane . . ."

"Jesus has nothing to do with it," she said, suddenly turning angry, "and He has nothing to do with what happened to Richard, either."

"But maybe you do."

Color fled her cheeks. "Are you insane?"

"You knew Richard better than any of us, but I can't get a word out of you."

"Richard was my priest, and an old friend, but others knew him better than I did."

"Who?"

"Lots of people."

"Yeah, but *who*? I know you're tight with the Severino family. . . ."

Whatever was behind her eyes changed, and an opaque curtain fell over the windowpane so no one could see in. "You don't know anything about that."

"Is there something I should know, then?"

Surly, defensive: "Whatever I want you to know, I'll tell you."

"Just tell me who it is who knew Richard better than you did."

Diane waved her empty glass at the waitress. "You're so smart, Nicky. Guess."

"I'm too old for guessing games—and too tired."

Her gaze swept the cocktail lounge then, as if she were searching out people to name. "Priests, monsignors, bishops, and old ladies who go to Mass every day of the week," she said. "Catholic businessmen with money. Italians. Irish."

"Let's start with who paid a million for the new rec center for kids?"

She waited a moment too long. "That was anonymous."

"Anonymous—a generous fellow," I said. "But somebody knows who it was. When a million dollars is moved around, somewhere there's a name on it. "My guess is that you know, Diane."

"Do I look like the bishop of Youngstown?"

"You look like somebody who knows everybody in town, and if you don't know them, your husband does—or your hairdresser."

She must have been clenching her teeth, because the muscles near the hinge of her jaw jumped. "You think somebody who gave the million also murdered Richard?"

"No," I said. "At the moment, I'd probably eliminate that person as a suspect."

She pursed her lips, thinking about it. Then she relaxed. "Well, what the hell. As long as it won't hurt anyone, I guess it's okay—as long as you keep it to yourself. That million came from Frank Mangione—senior."

"I should have known," I said, being sarcastic even though I hated myself for it. "Mangione senior has always been a wonderful human being."

"He's never been a wonderful human being, nor has Severino. They've both done plenty of rotten things, including blowing up each other's families. I quit counting them when I was nineteen. But for whatever it's worth, he paid for the rec center."

"Why?"

She lifted her shoulders, then dropped them again.

"How do you know anyway, Diane?"

"Call it a lucky guess."

That one threw me for a loop. "I thought you've been lined up with the Severinos all these years."

"That's me," she said. "Bob, too."

"Bob's not even Italian."

"It looks better for them if they have a lawyer with a good old American name. Trust me, though, the Mangiones have an Italian consigliere."

"Oh? And who's that?"

She bit at her drink again. "Leave it at that, okay?"

"Can't," I said.

More than a minute passed. The TV droned on, showing some sport, but neither of us looked at it, nor at each other. The only other noise came from two visiting salesman types chatting up the pretty bartender, and the clinking of the cubes in Diane's drink.

Ice cubes in a glass make a sensual sound; in certain places, it's a suggestive sound one can't ignore. Diane Burnham jiggled the glass again, drawing my eye to her cleavage. I raised my glance to her face—still beautiful but now grown hard and unyielding. She was only in her mid-thirties, but she'd lived a lot more years than that. I had, too, but my extra years were different.

On one hand, I wanted Diane as much as ever. I was hoping she'd follow me to my room, meet me on the high crest of sexuality, and stay with me until we were both satiated and exhausted—and then stay even longer than that. But she was different from when we were kids in love, which, in a strange way, repulsed me. I didn't know her anymore, even after the sex the other day. I didn't trust her anymore, either.

"Are you coming upstairs with me?" I finally said.

Diane looked directly into my eyes and through them, and the muscles around my heart fluttered and contracted as if they were cold.

"Can't," she said simply, and her voice was flat and dry.

I parked down the block on Hazel and made my way to the saloon on the corner of Hazel and Broadman. For reasons that escaped me, it was called the Purple Cow. It always had been, at least within my memory, and the usual clientele filling the place almost every night was diverse, although 100 percent male. Half the drinkers were low-rank mob guys overdressed to look like 1940s movie punks from post-Depression Hollywood, with diamond pinkie rings, pinstriped suits, slim cigars that smelled like spoiled candy, and black or purple dress shirts with plain white or yellow ties. Many of them wore hats in the style of George Raft or Humphrey Bogart, probably because no one told them men had stopped wearing dress hats in the fifties.

The other half of the customers were dressed more sloppily and less expensively, their wrinkled suits or sports jackets bought from Sears or JCPenney. That's how you could tell they were mid-level cops.

My brother was a gold-badge Youngstown police officer, and my other brother, lately deceased, had heard Mafia confessions every Sunday and passed out penance and forgiveness, but I couldn't make up my mind which group to join for a drink.

The bartender wiped the bar with a tired dishcloth and looked at me as if I'd wandered in from a different kind of movie. He didn't seem welcoming. "What's yours?"

"Scotch, rocks."

He cocked a cynical eyebrow. "What kind?"

"Whatever's on the top shelf," I said.

He turned around and surveyed the bottles on the top shelf, fists on his hips. Finally, he removed a bottle of Chivas Regal and poured my drink—a light scotch that ladies appreciate. Chivas wouldn't have been my first choice—but that was my fault.

He put a cocktail napkin in front of me and set the glass on it. "That's two-fifty," he said. Most cocktail lounges in Chicago would have charged more than that, except for the dirty-shirt neighborhood bars that wouldn't carry Chivas Regal in the first place. I gave him a five and told him to keep the change.

Jefferson Starship was blasting on the jukebox, "We Built This City," until it was replaced by several Bruce Springsteen hits in a row. I checked the customers. The ones nodding their heads or tapping their feet to the music were law enforcement. The others, the mob crew, were ignoring the sounds, probably waiting until some Sinatra or Tony Bennett tunes showed up.

Then I got bored, turned around to face the bar, and saw my reflection in the mirror. I didn't dress as sharp as the Italians or as shopworn as the police, so I guessed I didn't belong in the Purple Cow at all.

One of the cops came and stood by me, an empty beer pitcher in his hand, which he waved at the bartender. Then he turned to me. "I know you," he said. "I seen you at the funeral the other day. Your brother Alfonso is kind of my boss. Sorry about Father Candiotti."

He hadn't introduced himself, hadn't offered me his hand. He didn't continue the conversation, such as it was, but waited until the bartender brought him a new pitcher of Pabst Blue Ribbon on tap, and then went back to the corner table he shared with about four other allies. If I leaned a little to my left I could see them all in the mirror. The cop who'd fetched the pitcher was talking quietly to them as they all looked at me. They didn't smile. Youngstown—at least in this neighborhood and in this tavern—wasn't full of smilers.

I finished my drink and caught the bartender's eye. "Another one," I said, "but not Chivas Regal, okay?"

He shrugged. "Your deal, ace."

"Dewar's, then."

He looked confused.

"You carry Dewar's?"

"I think so."

"Good guy," I said.

This drink was poured to the brim, light on the ice cubes, and my first sip was executed carefully so I didn't spill any. Dewar's displays more character and packs more punch than Chivas Regal, but it still doesn't touch the single malts.

I was halfway through the drink when Mike LeBlanc walked into the bar, looked around, waved at a few on the police side of the room, and headed straight for me. "Hello, Mr. Candiotti," he said, and sat down on the stool next to me.

"Small world," I said.

"Not so small." The bartender was on his way over, and LeBlanc nodded to him, which was a regular customer's way of saying he'd have the usual. The bartender brought a PBR, in a bottle this time, glistening with frost. "Cheers," LeBlanc said. He tilted the bottle and gulped, then exhaled. "I'm glad I ran into you again."

"Why's that?"

"Last time I saw you, you told me to go fuck myself. I didn't know why, so I thought I'd ask."

"You stop into the Purple Cow every night, or are you here for a reason?" I didn't give him time to think about it. "My guess is one of your buddies recognized me sitting here and called you to give you the wake-up. True or false?"

"You don't miss much."

"I don't miss anything," I said. "That's the way I was trained."

"Trained? By who?"

"Whom," I said, correcting him. "The United States government, that's whom—the kindly travel agents who booked a long vacation for me just outside Saigon."

"Nam must have been rough," LeBlanc said.

"So are root canals, but we live though them. So here I am and here you are. Tell me what you want with me, and let me finish my drink in peace."

He lowered his voice. "I'd rather we talk outside."

I looked at him without malice. "You think you're going to

beat the crap out of me when we get outside? You and your buddies over there?" I drank some more, letting the Dewar's swish around on my tongue before I swallowed. "Take your best shot, but as big as you are, and no matter how many pals you bring along to help you, I'm going to count coup before I go down."

He tried to smile, but his heart wasn't in it. "No one wants to beat you up. As it happens, I want to be your friend."

"That'll make you the second-loneliest guy in town—next to me."

"I don't want anyone seeing us leave together," he said. "Finish your drink and go sit in your car outside. I'll be there within five minutes."

"How do you know my car?"

He tried not to patronize me. "How many cars parked within half a block of here have Illinois license plates?"

He got to his feet, taking his beer bottle with him, and joined the cops who'd been looking at me earlier, engaging them in idle conversation. Whatever he was saying made them laugh. I finished my drink and left. The creepy tingle of my skin told me everyone in the Purple Cow, police officer or outlaw, was watching my back.

I huddled in my car, the engine not running, and looked at my watch. LeBlanc's eventual appearance took more like ten minutes than five.

"Sorry," he said, and slid into the passenger seat. "Listen, this is just between the two of us, all right?"

"Why?"

He looked grim. "Because I'm putting my ass on the line for you."

"You don't even know me."

"I knew Father Candy. Let's just leave it that I'm talking to you for him."

It was stuffy in the car, and I cranked down my window an inch. "So talk."

"Dominick," he said, "your brother was more involved with the Severino family than you might imagine."

I didn't like the sound of that. "In what way? Richard wouldn't have stepped on an ant if it was raising hell in his kitchen."

"No, he never got anywhere near the rough stuff."

I waited, but LeBlanc seemed to want a reply. I finally snapped, "So he didn't beat up grocers and he didn't set up Youngstown Tune-Ups. So what?"

He frowned, worrying the corner of his lower lip with his teeth. "Sometimes," he said carefully, "the Severinos wanted errands run."

"Errands?"

"Pickups, deliveries, things like that, okay? Errands."

"And?"

LeBlanc turned his hands palms upward. "It was easy—always. Who'd worry what a priest was doing? So sometimes he carried certain . . . moneys, I guess, from one place to the other."

My mouth felt dry as cotton. I tried wetting my lips with my tongue, but it did little good. I'd heard the story, put more bluntly, from my uncle Carmine. "You're telling me shit I already know, LeBlanc."

"You probably haven't heard that a subpoena was in the works for Father Candy—to come in and testify to RICO."

"Who's Rico?" I said. "I don't know anybody named Rico."

"RICO's not a who. It's the Racketeering Influence and Corruption Organizations Act, from the federal government. R-I-C-O. And within the week, they were going to serve your brother with a subpoena to come to Cleveland and testify."

I sucked in deep drafts of stale air, not wanting to believe what I was hearing.

"That was the plan," LeBlanc said. "The government's plan."

"And Richard wasn't fighting it?"

"You can't fight a subpoena," he said, "no matter who you are."

"Jesus!" I said. I pressed my temples, where the pounding had magically appeared. I felt as if I'd just had a stroke that robbed me of my speech. "Is that why Richard was killed?"

"It's on the books as a suicide," LeBlanc said. "I wasn't anywhere near the case, so I'm in the dark."

"Does Alfonso know about this?"

"Lieutenant Candiotti? No, he doesn't know a thing."

I put my hand inside my jacket to feel my heart drumming. "He's a lieutenant and he knows nothing, but you're a sergeant and you're sitting here telling me . . ." Fighting to slow down my heart was harder than a punch-out in a military bar in Saigon when everyone had had too much cheap firewater. "How do *you* know so much about it—this RICO business and the federal subpoena?"

LeBlanc smiled, his eyes sympathetic as he just shook his head no.

"You're just pretending to be a local cop, aren't you? You're some kind of fed!"

"I'm on the Youngstown force and that's all you need to know." He touched my door handle and shifted his weight. "I'm just trying to clue you in. I want you to be safe. In the meantime, you and I never talked tonight."

"Sure," I said, my tongue dripping bitterness. "We're practically strangers."

With his other hand, he reached up and clicked the switch on my ceiling light so it wouldn't go on when he opened the car door. He nodded. "We *are* strangers," he said.

CHAPTER FOURTEEN

It was almost eleven o'clock when I parked in the driveway of Alfonso's house. There was no more rain, though the streets were shiny wet, and the temperature had plummeted throughout the evening. There was a chill in my chest that had nothing to do with the weather.

I hadn't grown up in a lovely house like this one. It wasn't a mansion, or even a mini-mansion, but it was elegant all the same, and advertised the comfort in which Alfonso and Dolores enjoyed themselves.

A light burned in one of the windows downstairs, and another one glowed upstairs, but I didn't know whether they'd gone to bed. I didn't care if I woke them up. Now it had become important.

I rang the bell three times, five seconds each time over the course of about a minute, waiting for someone to answer. Then I leaned on it.

Finally, there was a crackling noise in my ear—apparently, there was a speaker system inside—and Dolores's angry and half-asleep voice came from the small speaker below the doorbell. "What?" she barked. "Who is this?"

"It's Dominick, Dolores," I said. "I want to talk to my brother."

"It's late."

"No kidding," I said. "I'll have to wind my watch. Go wake him up."

"Kiss my ass."

"It's important."

"Kiss my *ass*!" Once more, with feeling.

I didn't respond this time, but leaned on the buzzer instead. She screamed the epithet several more times, and dusted off some new ones, until she realized I could ring the bell longer than she could shout obscenities into the speaker. Then she clicked off.

Finally, Alfonso yanked open the front door, his hair mussed, his cheeks puffy around the eyes, and his evening stubble showing. He was wearing pajama bottoms and a Cleveland Browns T-shirt, covered with a ratty bathrobe. His feet were bare and he looked madder than hell.

"Are you outta your goddamn mind?" he said. "What are you, *drunk*? Jesus, what's wrong with you?"

"Nothing—I'm just peachy keen." I pushed past him into the foyer.

His voice was thin with irritation. "Go back to the hotel and go to bed. You're on vacation here, Nicky, but I have to work in the morning."

Dolores had come halfway down the stairs, looking even more furious than her husband. She was wearing a silky nightgown with a sheer robe thrown over it, and her face was heavily made up, eyelashes blackened by kohl and her mouth painted into a thick clown's mouth with almost purple lipstick. She seemed to be waiting anxiously for Mr. DeMille's close-up. I thought only movie stars went to bed looking like that—movie stars or hookers. Or maybe she just hadn't cold-creamed her makeup off yet.

"Get the fuck out of my house," she said, her scratchy voice sounding like the Wicked Witch of the West's. "Nobody wants you here."

I ignored her, pleased that Alfonso didn't pay any attention to her, either. "Can we talk in your den?"

He automatically looked at his wrist, but he wasn't wearing a watch. Most people don't when they go to bed. Still, he shook his head. "It's late."

"This won't wait, Al."

"Throw him out!" Dolores screeched still only halfway down the staircase, leaning over the balustrade. "Throw his ass out of here!"

"Shut up and go to bed," Alfonso growled.

He took my arm and led me back into his little inner sanctum again. Her curses echoed off the paneled walls of the hallway and bounced into some hideaway for meanness and viciousness where they would never die but lie in wait until next time. I didn't know to which of us her use of the word *motherfucker* referred.

"I'm not offering you a drink," Al said, closing the door behind us.

"I don't want one. I want to talk about Richard again."

He ran fingers through his already-mussed hair. "You're really losing it, Nicky. I swear to God. You gotta let this go."

"I can't. Maybe you don't give a damn what happened to your brother, but I do."

"You're asking for trouble."

"It won't be the first time."

"Yeah," Alfonso said, "but you keep running your mouth off, it might be the last."

My eyes narrowed, focusing. My glare at Al could have peeled paint off a brick wall. "Are you threatening me?"

"No, no, no," he blithered. "I wouldn't threaten you. But guys in this town—no names or anything—get cheesed off at people who run their mouths."

"I'm running my mouth about how and why our brother

died. I'd think you'd be asking questions, too. Nothing stopping *you*—you've got a badge."

He sounded like he had to clear his throat. "Asking what?"

"Richard was into all sorts of shit he shouldn't have been in, wasn't he?"

The corner of his mouth twitched, and he rubbed his face as if to erase it.

"Don't lie right to my face, Al. You know it better than anybody."

"I *don't* know it!" he protested, but his expression was stricken.

"Al," I whispered. "Oh, Al . . ."

He sank into a chair as if he weighed six hundred pounds. "You're killin' me here."

"You're a cop, and I respect your loyalties," I said, sitting opposite him. "But this is family."

"You're makin' yourself crazy for no reason. Nicky, priests are human, like everybody else. We all take vows of one kind or another, and nobody ever keeps 'em forever. Not when you join the Boy Scouts, not on New Year's Eve, not when you get married, or elected, or accepted into the Knights of Columbus, or even pledge to make a donation. You believe your vows at the time, but eventually they don't mean shit. It was the same with Richard—and with all parsons and rabbis and Muslims and Buddhists, too." His chin was resting on his chest. "People who go to confession every week, they'd be shocked if they heard a priest broke some of those vows."

"Name one."

"It's not my place. . . ."

"Richard killed himself, Al. That makes it your place."

"I'm not gossiping about him over the back fence!"

"I'm not your next-door neighbor, either," I said, feeling myself grow angrier with every tick of the clock. "I've heard enough shit since I got here. Now I want the truth."

Between his thumb and his third finger, Alfonso massaged the bridge of his nose, up near his eyes, groaning softly from the headache that was forming there. When he finally spoke, his voice was old.

"Sit down, Nicky," he said.

I'd left Alfonso's house after midnight, but there were no liquor stores open, so I couldn't fortify myself with scotch, single malt or otherwise. I stopped into an all-night convenience store and bought three bottles of red wine—the only alcohol I could legally purchase at that hour—and an inexpensive corkscrew. By 2:00 A.M., I'd already finished one of the bottles, slugging it out of a hotel water glass, and was now working on the second one.

I knew what I knew. I'd heard it from my uncle Carmine, I heard more of it from Mike LeBlanc, and finally I heard almost all of it from Alfonso.

But the last little piece was missing, and nobody dared tell it, even if they knew it. I'd have to find it out myself, even if I had to shake a few trees.

Violently.

I fell asleep fully dressed. Two empty wine bottles in the trash basket and a third less than half-full on the night table were sad reminders of the long night. But waking the next morning with a headache, nausea, and a mouthful of fuzzy teeth, I was still too busy being mad at everyone—mad at the top of my lungs.

CHAPTER FIFTEEN

Everybody feels like a loner sometimes, but you're on your own, dealing with your own problems. When time runs out, as it does for everyone—whether slipping quietly away in your bed, surrounded by sorrowing family and loved ones, or swallowing a gun in the middle of the night—you die alone.

In our household, I was the lone wolf, the one who never shared with others—not inconsequential things like a candy bar or a bite of my french fries, and not important feelings or being scared. I gave up on fright when I was young; if I hadn't, fears would eventually have eaten me alive.

Richard had been a good listener, even as a child, and in his adolescence, women and girls were all over him, and boys his own age begged—or more accurately, negotiated—him to be on their team or on their side. Tall and lanky, he'd frequently extricate Alfonso from fights just by showing up and talking quietly to diffuse the situation—or when that didn't work, he could throw a pretty good punch. When he donned the clerical collar and foreswore punching forever, even more people cared for him, loved him, and wanted to be near him.

Alfonso always fought and bullied others, but he was a smooth operator, surrounding himself with other tough smart-asses who looked to him as a leader. Al made sure that when he engaged in fisticuffs, he'd be surrounded by his group.

My sister, Teresa, really didn't like her peers, and avoided them—but she ached for conversation and support nonetheless, and so she gravitated toward older people, like our parents' friends and neighbors. Because she was saintly and disgustingly sweet around them, baking cookies for sick people and running errands for old women, everyone expected Teresa to take the veil—until her first sexual misstep with her then boyfriend, Charlie, turned her into a bitter wife and mother, and turned Charlie into a wimp.

I hung out with no one. I loved my parents, naturally, but it was from afar. They weren't bad parents. They took care of their four children, especially Richard, whose entry into the priesthood fulfilled my mother's fondest dream. But they were undemonstrative and uncuddly—especially my father. He saved all his warmth for the Severinos, who took care of him. I can't remember ever getting a kiss from my mother; I never heard my father use the word *love* in any personal way. (He often bragged that he "loved" Mama's pasta sauce, and I guess that was enough.)

I was too young for the pals of my siblings, not sociable with my peers, and uneasy with the Severinos. My adolescent fistfights had nothing to do with Richard's support or Alfonso's stubborn loyalty; I fought them earnestly on my own, winning most, my motivation survival. I wasn't trying to kill anyone, just hurt my enemies enough so they couldn't get up again and hurt me—or want to. My reputation spread all over Brier Hill, and pretty soon nobody offered to fight me anymore.

The only person besides Richard I ever cared about was Diane, and when she decided to stay where she was born, to be a part of Youngstown, I couldn't wait to leave my hometown and the crowd who surrounded me from my earliest childhood—peers who grew up to be steelworkers like my dad, or the sinister mob families who seemed removed from me. When I pinned on the officer's insignia in the United States Army, I became what the government wanted me to be—and for whatever reason, I've spent much of my life being angry.

I grabbed a quick breakfast at a coffee shop downtown, and I headed to where I thought I could get as much information as possible about Father Richard Candiotti—the headquarters of the Diocese of Youngstown.

The diocese was created in 1943, built from spare parts left over from the Cleveland diocese. St. Columba Church, on the north side of town, was designated a cathedral, which, when you think about it, was a pretty impressive promotion for an ordinary church. I'd passed by St. Columba many times but had never gone inside. Unlike Richard's own parish, Our Lady of Perpetual Sorrows, St. Columba made all the Youngstown-Niles-Warren Catholics its business, not just the Italians.

Columba, the saint for whom the cathedral was named, had been a priest of sorts back in the sixth century, and was dubbed one of the "twelve Irish apostles." He died in his seventy-seventh year, closing his eyes for the last time while kneeling before the altar in his own monastery. His prayers, studying, and teaching every waking hour of his adult life got him elevated to sainthood. No one really knew what Columba looked like.

But northeast Ohio knew the face of Monsignor Danny Carbo because he got his picture in the newspaper or on TV almost as often as did the bishop. He was pushing sixty, but I remember when he'd just been promoted to monsignor, which is a position of respect but without authority, appointed by the Pope himself. I guess that's why he always found time to show up at ball games, parties, benefits, and anywhere else where he'd run into a reporter with a pencil, notebook, and camera.

Monsignor Carbo was a nice-looking man, small and slim, and when he moved toward me to shake my hand with both of his, I was reminded of Fred Astaire at his most graceful and elegant. Then he sat down behind his elaborate antique desk, his white clerical collar looking less than an hour out of the laundry, his blondish silver hair sprayed to motionless perfection. On a coat tree near the door, his black trench coat fit nicely over a wooden hanger. Next to it hung a black hat, naturally, and a black biretta with a small red tuft. That little red tuft was the real badge of his office.

Except for a framed photograph of the Pope and a large crucifix on the wall over the monsignor's head as he perched magisterially at his desk, it didn't look very sacred or holy in there. It looked like someone had spent a lot of money on interior decorating.

He hadn't expected my visit, and I doubted he remembered me from the funeral, but when I announced myself to a quiet elderly nun who pattered into Carbo's study to tell him I'd arrived, my last name gained me entrance without too much trouble.

"Let's see," Carbo said, stroking his chin like some Hollywood actor playing a wise and judicious old man in a movie. "It's Dominick, is it not?"

"That's right, Monsignor."

"If I didn't say it to you at the funeral, I deeply sympathize with your loss, my son. Father Richard was a dear friend. We spoke weekly, if not more, and he was often a dinner guest in my dining room—and the bishop's, as well." Having dropped an important name to me, he delicately wet his lips. "You're living in New York now?"

"Chicago," I said.

"Yes, it's a fine city—the Cubs notwithstanding. An Irish city, from my recollection." He smiled, pleased with his own little joke. "Which is your church?"

"I don't go to church, Monsignor."

He delicately crossed his small hands and rested them on the desktop. "That surprises me. The Candiottis were, and are, devout—and Richard most of all. Are you the family desperado? The rebel?"

"I'm not rebelling against anything." I lied.

He raised his fist to his mouth and cleared his throat discreetly. "So what brings you here, then?"

"I'm gathering the pieces of the end of my brother's life. Can you help me?"

"Everyone thinks I know absolutely everything," Monsignor Carbo said with a flare of arrogance. "The whole diocese mourns Father Richard, but I don't know what I can do to assist you."

"I know you were his mentor—or one of them anyway."

Carbo closed his eyes gently. "That's a big word—*mentor*. When Richard came to me and said he wanted to become a priest, I counseled him, naturally, and gave him advice whenever he asked for it. After he left the seminary, I helped him find his first parish over in New Philadelphia. When Youngstown was looking for a new priest for Our Lady—an Italian priest is what all the parishioners wanted—I did what I could to get him transferred here. I was hardly a mentor, though."

"Just a friend?"

He opened his eyes and nodded. "I *was* his friend as well as a colleague. That's why I'm so especially saddened."

"May I ask a personal question, Monsignor?"

He cleared his throat again. "That depends," he said, "on how personal."

"Fair enough. Do you own a gun?"

Carbo looked shocked. He unclasped his hands and put one on either side of the desktop, trying not to squeeze them into fists. "Good Lord, no! We are men of peace, not violence. What a strange question for you to ask."

"Did Father Richard own a gun, then?"

He drew himself up straight. His tone had grown annoyed. "I have no idea what he owned and what he didn't. We are servants of God and employees, if you will, of the Catholic Church, but we are human, as well, and we all are entitled to privacy." He attempted a smile to take the sting out of his voice. "I have several golf outfits, which I wear whenever I play—usually on Saturday afternoons. But Richard didn't know about them because he never played golf with me. So I have no idea what he wore when he wasn't 'on duty' in church—or what toys he owned, either."

"'Toys'?"

The smile died a-borning. "Guns. That's what I mean by toys—guns."

"He took his own life with a gun. If he didn't own it, where did he get it?"

Now Carbo's voice snapped as if he were scolding an altar boy. "How in hell would I know that?"

He actually leaned hard on the word *hell,* but I ignored such a mild swearword from a monsignor. "Nobody knows. There was a gun beside Richard's body, but somehow it disappeared. My brother Alfonso doesn't know where the gun came from or where it's gone. And even though there was a bullet in Richard's brain, nobody bothered doing an autopsy. Everyone is keeping very quiet...."

He corrected me softly. "Discreet."

"Secretive."

"There are some things that should remain police business."

"No one has a right to keep anything from me."

He closed his eyes again before he spoke. "Stop talking about rights. You're not from here anymore; you've turned your back on this city and your family—and on the Church, too. The fact is, you're a stranger, wandering around Youngstown demanding your *rights.*" His eyes opened quickly, squinting into a disapproving frown. "I resent your demanding them from me. I don't talk to the police about crimes, I haven't a clue when it comes to guns, and frankly, I don't know anything about suicide—not that of a Catholic and especially not that of a priest—and I don't accept it, either."

"I'm not blaming you," I said. "You find it easier to hide, don't you?"

"I don't hide from anything, Mr. Candiotti."

No more "my son," I thought, but I didn't verbalize this. "Is it okay," I wondered aloud, "to say *bullshit* when you're not in the cathedral? When you're just in somebody's fancy study?"

"It's not the first time I've heard the word." He cocked his head. "But the first time in my study, yes."

"It's not the first time I've used it, either. Father Richard was moonlighting for the Severino family, wasn't he?"

He tore his eyes from mine and looked around the room for a secret escape hatch into which he could disappear. Finally, he said, "I don't know what he did outside the church. He has his own time to do whatever he wanted. I'm certain he extended himself as much as he could. Favors, I suppose, for the Severinos, just as he did favors for many of his parishioners. That's part of the job."

"Is it? Does that mean monsignors do favors for the Severinos, too?"

Monsignor Carbo's head snapped back as if I'd slapped him. "No, we don't," he said, then added with all the authority he could muster, "When it's called for, though, I do favors for the bishop."

"Gee, that impresses the heck out of me. But you're in charge around here. You must know Richard was running errands for Paolo Severino and his son."

"I *don't* know anything of the kind! I was Richard's monsignor, not his mother."

"Cute."

"Whatever he did for, or with, the Severinos or the Mangiones on his own personal time is no business of mine."

That slowed me down. "Richard did favors for the Mangiones, too?"

"They go to Mass every Sunday—the whole family. And Mrs. Mangione—Frank senior's wife—attends early Mass at Our Lady at least four other days a week. Father Candiotti knew them as well as he knew the Severinos."

"I'll bet all their confessions were pretty fascinating for Richard."

"Priests are not fascinated by confessions." He sniffed. "They forgive—and heal."

"Did you hear Richard's confessions yourself, Monsignor?"

He rotated his head around as if his neck was stiff, but he was finally in comfortable territory. "Even you aren't so stupid as to ask that question. Confessions are sacrosanct. Inviolable—out of bounds for discussion."

"Are subpoenas inviolable, too?"

"Wh-what?" he stammered.

"Father Richard was days away from being slapped with a federal subpoena to go to Cleveland and tell the court all he knew about the Severino family."

Carbo leaned forward, worried again. "How do you know this?"

I shrugged my shoulders up around my ears. "I don't have to confess to you, Monsignor. I quit being Catholic a long time ago."

Carbo rubbed his hands together as if he'd just anointed them with moisturizing cream. "You think Richard . . . took his own life . . . so he wouldn't have to testify?"

"The timing was right, but . . ." I stared down at my knees for too long a moment. Then I said, "I don't even know if he *did* take his own life."

The monsignor actually gasped. "Are you saying someone killed him?"

"That's why I'm asking questions," I said. "To find out."

"Then why ask me?"

"Because, Monsignor, as you put it so succinctly a few minutes ago, everyone thinks you know everything."

CHAPTER SIXTEEN

I sat quietly, breathing deeply and getting myself together for at least fifteen minutes in my car in the parking lot of St. Columba. The meeting with Monsignor Carbo had scared the hell out of me. Monsignors are supposed to be more holy than ordinary priests, but Carbo didn't make me want to fall on my knees and pray. The saving grace of that brief fists and elbows go-round was that I think I scared him, too.

Once I caught my breath again, and after stopping off in a drugstore to buy a few tablets of yellow lined legal paper and at a filling station where they served very strong coffee in cardboard cups, I found my way to the Youngstown–Mahoning Valley Public Library on Wick Street, just a few blocks from downtown.

It took me all day to skim microfiches of the last four years of the *Vindicator,* looking for references to the Severino and Mangione families. The newspaper reported the mob stories carefully, but almost always when they *had* to. During that most recent four-year period, there were nine mentions of organized-crime killings—seven of them Youngstown Tune-Up assassinations and only three on the front page—in which one or both Italian clans were mentioned.

A few of the victims' names were familiar to me. Vincent Mazzi was a second-level field captain for Paolo Severino during the 1960s; I'd actually met him a few times. In his fifties and for all intents and purposes unmarried, he seemed to like kids, and usually carried a pocketful of Tootsie Pops to hand out at Italian festivals and street parties, although at that early-teen stage of my life, I wasn't interested in Tootsie Pops.

The other name that jumped out at me was Santino Ricciardi. Seeing his photo—actually a police mug shot on the front page of the *Vindicator*, reporting his automobile execution—I realized how big and rugged-looking he was. Almost everyone in town knew his name as one of the foremost muscle guys in the Mangione family. He never killed anyone—at least not to my knowledge—but he busted up many people for welshing on a bet or not making their usual loan payment on time, including a Severino scumbag named Angelo Cardamone, who used to peddle marijuana, porn, and slips for the bug out of the deep, hidden pockets of his overcoat to Brier Hill teens on their way home from high school every afternoon.

Ricciardi apparently knocked out most of his teeth and ripped off part of an ear before he broke both Cardamone's arms. He was arrested, but neither the police nor the district attorney ever charged him. I suppose the Supreme Being had decided that selling drugs and porn to schoolkids was a bad idea and sent Ricciardi in to right those wrongs, if one could truly believe Ricciardi was a licensed messenger of God. I'd heard tales about him when I was a kid, too, including that he slept in every morning and awakened at noon in time for a late breakfast. His demise occurred a few months after the Cardamone attack, when his 1964 two-door Pontiac went up in a sudden roar. Flames reached the third floor of the building where he lived, just east of downtown. He was heading out for breakfast at about one o'clock in the afternoon.

I couldn't locate a newspaper story linking my brother Richard to anything illegal regarding the Severinos or the Mangiones.

I did find several mentions of him, and several photographs, as well, when he was attending some benefit or other and had posed for a smiley photo with some big-shot businessmen and their wives, or appearing for empty occasions like the celebratory opening of a supermarket down near Boardman. He was frequently mentioned on the social page as officiating at Catholic weddings—and almost all the names of both brides and grooms were Italian—or at christenings of babies for the same family a year or so later.

He was also named often in press coverage of funerals. He'd been a busy priest—but he'd left me nowhere else to turn.

I flipped back over the news stories and checked the bylines. Seven of the nine assassinations over the past four years had been reported by the same *Vindicator* reporter. His name was Merle Leak—not Italian and therefore probably not tied in with either mob family—and since his stories had been written well, he'd probably done a certain amount of research. I wondered if I could get him to talk to me honestly.

Then I thought about the reputation of the large group of city reporters who got out and dug up interesting stories for the *Tribune* and the *Sun-Times* in Chicago. Irv Kupcinet and Mike Royko were journalistic superstars, but the rest of the ink-stained wretches who covered the news were like reporters everywhere. It's said that no matter what they were writing about, they'd happily crawl across the Rocky Mountains on their hands and knees if there were a free meal at the end of it.

I found the public phone in the library, dug a quarter from my pocket to call the *Vindicator* newsroom, and invited Merle Leak to lunch.

The MVR restaurant was just a few downhill blocks from the library, but Smoky Hollow, the neighborhood it anchored, was a world away. Both homes and commercial buildings were old and mostly well kept, but across the street from the restaurant the parking lot, such as it was, sprouted weeds and potholes from its broken asphalt. That didn't stop the businessmen and politicians from eating there. Not elegant, MVR was a no-frills restaurant with a definite Italian feel to it, including many of the customers, who worked low-level jobs for the courts and the city and county government and found their way there for lunch every day. The barroom, through which everyone entered, was festooned with football paraphernalia, and the bar itself was solid and comfortable, polished by thousands of elbows. The food served in the dining rooms was always good. Pasta came with almost everything.

I sipped a Pabst Blue Ribbon at the bar, waiting for Merle Leak, as he'd asked me to, my coat folded up on the bar stool next to me. I didn't even move it when newly arrived strangers demanded I couldn't save a seat for someone who wasn't there. Leak had told me on the phone that he ate lunch at MVR almost every weekday and never sat at a table, holding journalistic court at the bar—an excellent spot from which to observe who came and went, and, more important, who had lunch with whom.

When I told the bartender who my expected lunch partner was, he nodded knowingly and set a large diet Coke on the bar next to me. Leak, I was later to learn, never drank alcohol, at least not anymore. I envied him that.

When he came in, I saw he was younger than I'd thought—just a few years older than I, and not much taller than five six. He wore a tweed jacket, no overcoat, and a nondescript, ugly brown tie under the collar of a baby-shit green sport shirt that was never designed to support any sort of neckwear. He moved my trench coat from the adjoining stool to my lap and climbed up, reaching for the diet Coke he knew would always be there, taking a hefty swallow before he introduced himself.

"I know both your brothers," he said in a high-pitched, gravelly voice. "Tough deal for Father Candy. Sorry."

He sipped again at the soft drink, smacking his lips and

enjoying it the way a wine connoisseur might judge a superb Cabernet. "You told me on the phone you live in Chicago now. Matter of fact, I saw you outside the church, although I was shunted off to the annex to watch the funeral Mass on closed-circuit TV with the rest of the unwashed and uninvited. But I don't know why you asked me here for lunch. You're not one of those newspaper groupies, are you?"

"Only when the reporter might know something I want to know, too," I said.

"Ah. Well, let's order lunch first." Leak handed me a menu from the bar, but he didn't open his. Anyone who eats in the same restaurant five days a week for several years running never has to check the menu. He told the bartender he wanted the Italian baked fish. I asked for lasagna—and another beer to go with the one I was drinking.

"You've got an interesting job," I said. "What made you become a crime reporter?"

"Because the women's fashion job was taken," he snapped. "Writing a book?"

"Not really."

"Well, if all you've got is more dumb questions, I can pay for my own lunch."

"I'll try to do better," I said, meaning it. "You've reported a lot of stories connected with the Italian mobs in Mahoning County—mostly the Severino and Mangione families."

"So?"

"I've heard rumors that my late brother was involved with the Severinos. True?"

"'Involved'?" Leak was staring straight ahead, and it took me half a minute to catch on that he wasn't ignoring me, but studying me in the mirror behind the bar. "Father said Mass for them, he heard their confessions, and he married their children and baptized *their* children—like every other family on his end of town. This surprises you?"

"You know what I'm talking about," I said.

"A hit man priest?" He shook his head with disgust. "Get real, okay?"

"Christ, that's not what I'm saying. It never crossed my mind!"

"What then?"

"Was he Don Paolo's messenger boy? His consigliere? You tell me."

"If you want to know what I know," Leak said, "read the paper."

"You keep secrets?"

"We all keep secrets—or else we'd all end up paying alimony."

"Or on the unemployment line," I said.

"Or cleaning out toilets in some city mission." He chuckled.

"Or in prison."

His chuckle turned off, as if someone had shorted out the electrical circuit. He turned his body around on the stool so he was looking straight at me, measuring my suit. "Okay, pal, is this a quiz show? What kind of badge do you really carry?"

"No badge," I said. "I don't need no stinkin' badges."

"I saw that old movie, too," Leak said. "I didn't think it was funny the first time. You invited me to lunch, so I'm here. You wanna ask questions, ask. No rule says I have to answer them. And I for damn sure don't have to listen to your accusations."

"I didn't accuse you of anything."

"You didn't have to."

"My brother committed suicide. I can't think of a reason a man like him would do anything like that, so I'm trying to find one." I drew a line in the condensation on the outside of my beer glass. "Do you know about subpoenas?"

"I know what they are."

"Do you know about them before they're even served?"

Irritation made Leak's mouth look like a slash. "Think the feds call me up every day and tell me what they're doing?"

I looked hard at him. "How do you know I'm talking about the feds?"

He drained his glass, as if the meter were running. Then he turned his attention back to me, not looking in the mirror this time. "You're pushing me too hard."

"When a loved one dies young, and for no reason, there's no such thing as pushing too hard, is there?"

Our lunches arrived. My lasagna looked and smelled good, but I was rapidly losing my appetite. Merle Leak put his napkin in his lap and picked up his fork. "Have your lunch first, Mr. Candiotti. You'll feel better."

"Just call me Dominick."

"Sure," he said. "Dominick. On the off chance we'll ever have another conversation." He twirled his fork into his spaghetti. "Eat hearty."

When we finished our lunches, he pointed to some of the Cleveland Browns posters on the MVR wall and asked if I was a Browns fan or a Steelers rooter.

"I live in Chicago," I said. "I'm a Bears fan—when I think about it at all."

He raised one eyebrow. "Cubs, then? Or White Sox? Bulls?"

"Whenever I bother reading the sports pages. Otherwise . . ."

"What *is* your passion, then, if not sports? Movies, books, food, booze, women, or men? Politics? Collecting stamps? Or is there one I forgot?"

"I can't really say I have a passion for anything."

Leak wiped his mouth with his napkin and shook his head sadly. "That's the saddest fucking thing I ever heard."

"Maybe justice, then."

"Justice, is it? Your passion is for an abstraction."

"Justice isn't an abstraction," I said, "if someone killed my brother."

He quietly folded his napkin and pushed his plate away, asking for more diet Coke and waiting until it was served before looking at me again.

"I hear scuttlebutt," he said, "here and there. I listen more than I write. I run down the rumors and verify them, but I don't write them for the world to read unless news actually happens." He lowered his voice a decibel or two. "Nothing happened in terms of your late brother getting a subpoena."

"No," I said. "He died first." I leaned closer to him. "But you knew the subpoena was already drawn up."

"I *heard* it was, but I can't prove it one way or the other."

"What was it about?"

"I know the rumor that he did favors for both mob families. But they were just favors—like friend to friend, priest to parishioner, not like an employee."

"Why did he do favors for mob guys?"

Leak shrugged. "Everybody does favors for them. That's how we get along."

"Do you do favors for them, too?"

He didn't speak for a moment. Then he repeated, "That's how we get along."

"You're afraid of them," I said.

"No. When they make big news, I write about it. When they're being quiet and do what they do, I stay quiet, too."

"But Father Candiotti is dead," I said. "Maybe somebody out there didn't respect him so much after all. That's what I want to find out."

"For what?"

"For whatever reason he died."

"That was last week," Leak said. "Let it go—if you're smart."

"I won't let that happen."

"For what, your own curiosity? Is it just for the hell of it, or is it for justice with a capital *J*?"

I gritted my teeth, and my words forced their way through them. "You're goddamn right it's for justice."

Merle Leak sighed. "In this town, then," he said, "you'd better get yourself a gun."

CHAPTER SEVENTEEN

Hillman Street, running parallel with Market Street south of downtown, looked more sinister in the light of day than it had in the middle of the night. The creatures of crime and destruction—the dark souls—lurked in shadows at one o'clock in the morning, and nervous shoppers might not even notice them through their car window unless they were actually looking for them. But in daylight, the bad guys had nowhere to hide, so they simply prowled like feral cats near street corners. From what I could see, drivers—mostly men—were leaning forward, swiveling their heads from one side of the street to the other, hoping to spot a source to supply what they were looking for. I doubted anyone drove on Hillman for the fun of it.

It was right after my lunch with Merle Leak. I cruised Hillman slowly, checking out the characters doing business on the street, trying to decide which would be most amenable to my questions. None of them looked welcoming, but one, standing on a southeast corner, seemed as though he wasn't paying attention to anything. He looked at the sky, his head cocked, studying the overhanging gray clouds. He was a small black man with a mustache and beard, a bright red beret perched just off center in the spread of his oversized Afro. His coffee brown leather jacket, obviously expensive, nearly covered a tie-dyed T-shirt from the 1960s bearing the wild figure of Jimi Hendrix. I estimated he was about twenty-two years old.

I drove all the way down to Indianola Avenue, where I could turn around and head back north. When I reached the red beret again, I stopped and rolled down my passenger-side window.

"Whassup, my man?" I said. It sounded stupid and patronizing as soon as it escaped my mouth. I'd served in Vietnam with many black soldiers and had spoken easily with them without imitating what I took to be "blackspeak." Now I'd apparently forgotten how. The beret wearer wrenched his eyes away from the sky to look at me as if I were a rat that had just scurried out from the bushes behind him. Then he laughed a nasty laugh. "You don' sound like no nigger, so give it up."

"Sorry," I said.

"So, I'm spose to know you?"

"Not yet, but the day's young."

He didn't even bother a shrug, just examined the heavens again, hoping that when he lowered his head once more, I'd be gone.

"I was looking to do a little business," I said.

"I'm standin' here gettin' some fresh air. I don't do no bidness. You got me mixed up with the First National Bank."

I pulled a wad of cash from my jacket pocket. There were lots of singles in there to make it look fat, but it was a hundred bucks no matter which way you counted it. I waved it at him. "I was hoping to make a purchase."

"Sure. I'll pour you a cuppa coffee, get you a doughnut."

"I was looking for some tina," I said.

"Say what?" He screwed up his face. "Tina? Who be Tina? She some black honey pussy you after? I don't know no Tina."

"No. Tina—it's what they call crystal meth."

He half-turned his body from me, breaking eye contact, thinking about it. Then: "Never hear it called tina before. Forget about it—I don' know nothin' 'bout that shit."

"I bet you do."

"Get out my face, man. Don' walk up."

"I'm not a cop," I told him. "I got no badge, no weapon, no wire, and I'm not looking to bust your balls. I'm just a civilian—from Chicago—looking for some fun."

"Can't have no fun in Chicago, huh?"

"I'm here for a few days, and I need somebody to take care of me." I tried to sound embarrassed and forced out a weak chuckle. "I need to feel better."

"Take you a Tylenol," he said. "They sell it at Walgreen's."

"Come on, my man. I've got cash right here. Help me out. Have a heart, okay?"

He bent down to talk directly through the passenger-side window. "You look cross the street there, kitty-corner, you see a man wearin' a Steelers jacket?" I looked. The Steelers jacket was black, the same color in which the Pittsburgh Steelers play, and made the man wearing it practically disappear into the shadows beneath a tree. "You go over an' see him—drive slow an' don't roar up to him in your car—an' tell him Sonny Boy said to take care o' you."

"Is that you? Sonny Boy?"

"What you care? Gonna write me a postcard?"

"Just trying to be friendly."

"Be friendly cross the street," Sonny Boy said. "Take that cash with you."

I drove up two streets, then made a right-hand turn and went around the block. In a minute, I was confronting the guy in the Steelers jacket, who had moved out from under the tree and stood at the edge of the sidewalk.

"Sonny Boy says you should take care of me," I said.

His face showed no expression at all. "Don' know no Sonny Boy."

"Sure you do," I said. "He's right across the street."

"Don' know the man."

"That's funny. He just told me to come over here and talk to you."

He didn't look troubled, but he let me hang for about half a minute before he answered. "Well, Sonny Boy's just my advance guy. *I* do the deciding, know what I'm sayin'? Who are you anyhow?"

"I'm a civilian—from Chicago."

"What you doin' in Youngstown?"

"Visiting."

"Visitin' who?"

"Just family."

"Show me," he said. "And reach for your wallet double slow."

I carefully opened my jacket wide, showing him I carried no weapon in my armpit or tucked into my waistband. I removed my wallet, flipped it open to my driver's license, and handed it to him.

"Dominick Candiotti." He read it aloud as if it were a Shakespearean sonnet, pronouncing both my names properly. "So you a dago, then, huh?" He checked my photo again. "You *are* from Chicago, too."

"I told you that."

"You surely did."

"Ever been to Chicago?"

"I been everywhere," he said, handing me back my license. "So what you want, Candy-otti?"

I took the wad of money from my other inside jacket pocket. "Looking to make a purchase. I need some crystal."

He didn't seem to believe me. "You don' look like you use no crystal."

"What do you mean?"

"You too handsome, honky man. Methheads, they all look like shit. After while, they skin breaks out like they fifteen, they faces start comin' apart, an all they teeth break off an' fall outta their mouf like Chiclets. You, though—you too healthy-lookin'."

I tried to look apologetic. "I've only been into it for about a month."

"Into crystal?"

I nodded.

"That make you a dumbass."

I ducked my head as though I were embarrassed. "Things happen—you know how that is. So, can you help me? Please?"

He thought it over for a while. Then he said, "Lessee the money."

I handed him the roll. He stepped back under a leafy tree and turned his back to count it. When he returned to the car, the money was gone, but he had a packet in his hand, appearing magically from his jacket. I reached, but he held it away from me.

"If you wanna spend your money, I be here to take it from you," he said. "But if you run your mouf off 'bout where you bought crystal, firstly it's your word against mine, which ain't much. Second, I know where you live—even in Chicago—an' you blow a whistle on me or my homeboys, I promise you won' see the sun come up the next mornin'. Unnerstan' what I'm sayin' to you?"

"I gotcha," I said. "Hey, I might come back. Maybe even tomorrow."

"I kin hardly wait."

"Thanks, Mr.—uh, what's your name again? Your first name?"

"None a your beeswax," he said.

"Right. Well, thanks anyway. Thanks a lot."

He tossed the packet onto the seat of my car and turned to walk back into the darkness. "Don' say good-bye nor thanks nor nothin'," he tossed over his shoulder. "Jus' drive away—dago."

I got out of there, burning rubber as I peeled away. I didn't want to overstay my welcome. Not this time anyway.

Back in my hotel room, I ripped open the pack. There wasn't

a lot of crystal meth inside—more like a twenty-dollar bag. So what? I thought. He'd ripped me off royally for a hundred bucks, but I wasn't planning on using it anyway. I poured the drug into the toilet, flushing it three times before it was all gone.

Sonny Boy knew me now. The guy in the Steelers jacket knew me, too—even better. That's just the way I wanted it, because the next night when it was dark, I'd remember where I saw him and track him down again—and attempt to buy a gun. At least Steelers Jacket would be easier to talk to next time than a perfect stranger.

Merle Leak had been right. I did need a weapon—for my own safety, if nothing more. Why not? Everyone else in town was probably carrying one, too.

CHAPTER EIGHTEEN

I had a day and evening to kill, and nowhere to go. Visiting my remaining siblings was out of the question. Teresa hated my guts, and as for brother Alfonso—well, I think he was too afraid to talk any more openly than he already had. Besides, I had no desire to see dear sister-in-law Dolores again. Uncle Carmine, reporter Merle Leak, Police Capt. Ed Shemo, and Sgt. Mike LeBlanc had all said whatever they had to say. Even Monsignor Carbo would probably manage to be away, or busy, or even hiding from me in the confessional if I tried approaching him again.

I'd driven around Brier Hill, slowing down to stare at the house where my family had once lived, but although the neighborhood had changed very little—it was still Italian and still a nesting place for the hundreds of steelworkers who traveled each day to the smelting floor at the bottom of the hill—it didn't tug at my nostalgia, nor did a quick cruise around the campus of Youngstown State, which brought back a few crazy reminiscences about my college days, mostly involving alcohol.

There was another place, about ten miles out of town, one I remembered with sorrow—Meander Lake. It lives up to its name, an oxbow-shaped lake meandering on both sides of the Ohio Turnpike. It's quiet, surrounded on all sides by beautiful oak, chestnut, and pine trees, bathed in sunlight on many days when the rest of Ohio sulks under a blanket of clouds, and disturbed only by the splash of trout as they leap from the water to catch dragonflies in flight.

The Severinos owned a sprawling acreage bordering the lake, and sometimes we Candiottis were invited there to join in a family picnic, where the kids could ride horses and motorcycles. I was too young for the motorcycles, but Richard and Alfonso zipped around when they weren't swimming, rowing, or fishing. Those picnics were attended by many who worked for the Severinos, either full-time or as outside consultants, and they looked terrifying when I was ten years old or so. I wouldn't have been surprised if they still looked pretty scary, even though some of them had grown old. Some others, I was sure, had died young.

Meander Lake was also where the state police had found the bodies of my mother and father when their car slid across a patch of ice one freezing February night and plunged off the highway into the deep water. A shiver ran down my back just thinking about it. By the time I got to see my parents, the undertaker had attended to them, applying makeup to their dead faces. He had done the best he could. Mom and Dad looked decent-enough, but they also no longer looked like my parents.

Theirs were not the first bodies discovered in that area. More than one mob enemy had been murdered in the dead of winter—usually by gunshot or garotte—and discreetly dumped into Meander Lake. Nobody knew what happened to them until spring melted the ice and they floated to the surface, well preserved from a winter's worth of freezing.

I wanted to see the lake again after almost twenty years. Maybe I could forget about that tragic night and recapture those fun memories from when I was a kid and the wealthy and all-powerful Severino family took care of my family and invited them to Sunday picnics. Then maybe I wouldn't be so angry with them.

I hadn't brought much in the way of casual clothes with me, but I did have a pair of jeans and some athletic shoes and a kind of satin-black Ike jacket. I donned them all and headed west. I wasn't sure how to get there—it was my father who'd driven to Meander Lake when I was ten, and kids don't bother memorizing road and street names. So I aimed for the only hotel I knew about in the area and hoped I could get some information.

The inn looked like every other hotel just off the highway in America: two stories, a theater-type marquee to welcome tourists or conventioneers—the sign completely blank at the moment—a kidney-shaped swimming pool already drained for the cold months to come, and a shabby lobby with one wall built of faux stones. I felt as if I'd been inside it a thousand times before in a thousand different towns all across America. The restaurant was empty in the middle of the afternoon, and there were few cars in the parking lot, most of last night's occupants having checked out before noon.

I went into the lobby, my footsteps squeaking on the marble-type floor, approached the unmanned desk, ostentatiously cleared my throat in hopes someone would notice me, and waited. The sound system played soothing, insufferably boring Mantovani with strings music from twenty years earlier, when all we Youngstown State students thought it new.

It felt like ten minutes before a woman appeared at the end of the lobby and almost skipped up to me. She was a cute blonde at least twenty years my junior, wearing black slacks and a Pittsburgh Steelers T-shirt. Over her left breast she sported a pin with the hotel's name on it and a printed badge announcing HI, I'M JUDY.

Then she said "Hi, I'm Judy," unaware it was redundant. "Can I help you?"

"I hope so," I said. "What's the best way to hike from here to Meander Lake?"

Her eyes widened. "Oooh," she said. "I don't think you're supposed to go there."

"I'm not?"

"No. Nobody's supposed to except—um, nobody, really. Are you a guest at the hotel, sir?"

"No," I said, "just passing through."

"Well, it's all fenced up now. Meander Preserve, I think they call it."

"And what does that mean?"

Her clear brow furrowed. "Um, do you have a gun with you, sir?"

I made a show of patting my jeans pockets. "No."

"I meant a hunting gun—a rifle or a shotgun or something."

"No. I left my shotgun in my other suit."

She seemed to accept that without laughing. "Fishing rod?"

I shook my head.

"How about a camera?"

"No camera, no binoculars, not even a notebook so I can jot down my feelings. I swear I won't kill anything, even a spider that bites me. I came here when I was a kid—before you were born. I don't live in the area anymore. I'm visiting for a few days, and I thought I'd relive some old memories by the lake. I won't even pick a flower."

She thought it over. "I can't tell you what to do. I make schedules for our employees—housekeepers and maintenance men and restaurant workers." She tried to suppress a giggle. "I'm not in charge of anything around here."

"Good," I said. "That means you're a nice person. Nice people are never in charge. Now, if you could tell me which way I can get down to the shore of the lake . . ."

"I can't do that, sir," she said mournfully. "I'd get in trouble if I did. And also . . ." She cast down her eyes. "I'm not sure which way to get there from here anyway."

"You've never been down to the lake?"

She shook her head. "I've only worked here about eight months—and the first four of them were part-time." She chewed over another decision and then looked around furtively to make sure no one was listening, as if she were preparing to say words that were obscene or illegal. "I think it's that way, though," she whispered, and discreetly, without raising her arm so anyone might see, pointed out the lobby window to her left with one slender thumb.

I also lowered my voice to a whisper. "Thanks, Judy. Now we share a secret."

I went back outside, crossed the parking lot, and headed out into the trees. October is the zenith of autumn colors in Ohio, and ahead of me loomed a high, thick Technicolor wall of reds, oranges, browns, and yellows that took my breath away. I've always loved the fall best.

It had been raining off and on for several days, and I found myself in mud as soon as I left the asphalt. Quickly, my athletic shoes and socks were soaked through. I had no pressing reason to explore Meander Lake and no expectation of learning anything. But memories of my childhood—and of the night I lost my parents—dragged me farther into the woods.

I hoped that maybe the lake would help heal me. The smells of autumn certainly did, and I found myself looking up, searching branches for the Ohio state bird, the cardinal, or some other winged creatures that made the Meander Preserve their home. I knew the woods were full of owls, but they hunted at night, scoping out their territory with their huge round eyes. I wondered if there were any great blue herons about. I knew they nested near water, building their nests high in the trees, but I hadn't actually seen one in thirty years. I saw plenty of squirrels, though, and chipmunks, rabbits, and even some raccoons. I managed to startle a groundhog as I crashed through the underbrush. I tripped over a fallen tree limb he was hiding beneath, and he leaped about a foot off the ground in momentary panic and then scooted away from me. I deserved the annoyed look he gave me over his shoulder. He belonged here, and I didn't.

It was only about twenty minutes from downtown to Meander Lake, but I felt as if I were deep in the country. Most Americans know about the bigger Ohio cities—the muscular working-class Cleveland; the Buckeye-crazed state capital, Columbus; quiet Toledo and Dayton at the north and south ends of the state; and the almost sleepy major city of Cincinnati, which boasts the Procter & Gamble headquarters and major-league football and baseball teams. What's in between are farms, and long stretches of wilderness and woods that look almost virginal.

I found a path through the trees and followed it, my soggy shoes squishing with every step, leaving a trail of footprints in the damp mud. I didn't imagine anyone chasing after me. Maybe it was just what Judy had said back at the hotel about the fact no one was supposed to be here, or perhaps the woods just *felt* intimidating. So I walked as carefully as I could and tried not to make any noise.

It took another five minutes to get to the chain-link fence. I remembered no fence from my childhood, and the newness of the links proved it. It was about nine feet high, and the gate at the end of the path was padlocked—twice—with heavy-duty locks. A metal sign had been affixed to the fence with several twists of piano wire: MEANDER PRESERVE. NO TRESPASSING. NO ADMITTANCE. Below it, in smaller letters, it warned that trespassers will be prosecuted.

My eyes followed the path on the other side of the fence for about seventy-five yards until it ended at the shore of the lake.

The surface was still as glass except for the gentle lapping of the water against the bank. The sky over the lake was filled with the birds I'd been looking for earlier, traveling from tree to tree in pairs and communicating with their fellow birds. I still didn't spot any great blue herons, though. Then I recalled that they made their appearance in February, monogamously mated for the season, and stuck around until June or July.

I flashed backward to being out on the lake, sharing a rowboat with Alfonso or with my father, who'd doggedly dragged his fish bait through the dark blue water in the fruitless hopes of catching anything and pretended he wasn't aggravated with waiting. I hadn't been much of a fisherman, either, but I'd stayed out of his face, enjoying the quiet time. Just being afloat and moving had been a major kick for me, hanging my hand over the bow.

I remembered how my parents had been found in the lake on that terrible winter night, along with the twisted and broken remnants of their 1964 two-tone Pontiac. I wasn't there then, of course. I didn't see it, didn't see them until they'd been laid out in their coffins, dressed in their finest clothes and repaired by the mortician. My mother's hair had been well-coiffed and her lipstick looked soft and sweet. My father seemed too made up, too much powder rendering him almost effeminate-looking.

I squatted now, taking my weight off my legs while I considered continuing. I wasn't sure whether I wanted to go anywhere near Meander Lake.

But I was there, after all, so I stood up and jiggled the gate. The padlocks held.

To my right, the fence curved in toward the lake, and I followed it until I was about a 150 yards from the gate, walking in tall grass. Now that it was October, the insects had more or less disappeared, so my feet and ankles wouldn't be eaten alive. I stopped and shook the fence again to see if it would hold my weight without collapsing. Then I took a breath and hiked myself over.

Most city-dwelling men wouldn't have landed so lightly on their feet. I was used to climbing fences, though, and jumping down from high places. Now I was getting too old for such shenanigans, but I didn't feel any twinges in my knees or ankles, and no wrench at the small of my back. I was on the other side of the chain link, unscathed.

I made my way down to the water. It was peaceful there, the sounds of the woods soothing. I bent down and put my hand in the lake, the water stinging cold, fresh, and clean.

I walked to my right, hugging the waterline. From what I could surmise, I was moving west, toward the brightest part of the sky, thin clouds masking the afternoon sun. After about five minutes, I saw a deck attached to a big gray boathouse that needed a coat of paint. Beyond that was the big house where the Severino clan had spent many of their summer days, the place that, for a few visiting hours anyway, had made me feel like a special and privileged kid.

That's when I felt, rather than saw or heard, someone coming up behind me.

I turned around, not surprised to find someone there. The revolver pointed at my stomach was, however, unforeseen.

"Put 'em up, pal," the man said, gesturing upward with the gun barrel. I think he'd seen too many TV shows about cops who approached villains with that silly opening remark. I doubted he knew how to fire a weapon, but I wasn't about to find out.

"Who the hell are you and what're you doin' in here?" The gun-pointer was a little shorter than I was. His craggy, lined face had a swarthy complexion, and his black hair was going aggressively gray. He wore a greenish brown uniform and cap with a gold badge that announced he was SECURITY. A thick ring of keys bobbed on his left hip.

"I grew up around here," I said. "I used to play in this lake."

"Guess nobody ever taught you to read, huh? Din you see the sign back there?"

"I saw it," I said, "and ignored it."

"Oh yeah? Well, go lean up against that tree over there while I frisk you."

"I'm not carrying. Let me get my wallet out and I'll show you who I am."

"You keep your hands where they are," he ordered, nudging me hard in the chest with the revolver. "Now move your ass over there and lean against that tree."

I sighed. "Mister, if you try running your hands all over me, I'm going to take that gun away from you—and your doctor will have to remove it surgically."

"Try it," he said. "Just come on an' try it." He attempted a display of bravado, but his telltale voice wavered. He wouldn't last twenty seconds playing a tough guy. "I get paid . . ." He coughed, clearing the frog out of his throat. "I get paid to enforce the rules and to keep strangers the hell out of here."

"I'm not a stranger," I said. "My name is Dominick Candiotti. My brother—who just died—was the priest at Our Lady. Father Candiotti."

That didn't impress him. "Makes no difference to me."

"My other brother is Alfonso Candiotti. *Lieutenant* Candiotti, Youngstown PD."

Security's lip curled. "I don't care whose brother's a cop."

"Me, neither. But I'm also a good friend of Paolo Severino."

Now he was impressed, but then most Youngstowners are by the Severino name. He gulped hard and blinked his eyes, but he was determined to stick to the badass role he was playing. "Well, I didn't know that, did I?"

"That's why I'm telling you. When I was a kid, my whole family came to the lake to play and fish and have a good time, invited by Don Severino. I came back to town to bury my brother—and I had a long talk with the don. He invited me to his casino. I had a meeting there with Polly, too."

My invoking the names of the leader and the heir apparent of the Severino family shook him. His gun trembled visibly, but he wasn't ready to put it away just yet. "Polly said it was okay for you to come here?"

"No, it was my idea—but I don't think he'll mind. You probably should ask him."

He shook his head almost violently. "I don't wanna bother him."

"You want me to write down his phone number for you?"

Another negative head shake.

"The Severinos own a house here—like they used to?"

"Yes, sir," he said, finally remembering it might be a good idea to call me that.

"They own the lake, too, don't they? The whole lake?"

He pushed back the bill of his cap and scratched his head with his free hand. "Listen, sir," he said, his voice more of a whine than anything else. "I won't run you in or write you out a citation or anything. But I gotta ask you to leave." He smiled weakly, offering an apology. "It's my job."

"Tell you what. You stop pointing that thing at me, and I'll go away quietly. Sound like a deal to you?"

"Well," Security drawled, "I gotta make sure you're gone."

"Walk along with me, then." I headed back the way I'd come, and he holstered his weapon and trotted along beside me.

"How'd you get in here anyhow?" he said, wiping his hand on his pants to remove some of the gun oil. "To the reserve."

"I climbed over the fence back there."

He rubbed his nose with a knuckle. "If you can do that, so can anybody else. Maybe we should put razor wire on top. That'll slow people down—people like you."

He was inept, clumsy, and helpless, but Security was still one of the most annoying individuals I'd ever met. I wished he was intimidating so I could smack him down, but no such luck. Instead, I tried not to laugh when I said, "Just FYI—when we really, *really* want to go somewhere, there's no slowing down . . . people like me."

CHAPTER NINETEEN

Rainstorms and the chill that came with them had departed Youngstown, at least temporarily, so there were more pedestrians on Hillman Street later that night than there had been the afternoon before, although they weren't out enjoying the Indian summer weather. More pedestrians meant more cars, too, because the walkers and loungers on the sidewalk were still selling one thing or another—and a vibrant market like this one attracted many buyers.

I was a customer myself that night—a real buyer and not the phony one I'd been the day before. In my pocket was a fat roll of twenty-five twenties, wrapped once in a rubber band. I'd removed the cash from two different ATM machines that accessed two different accounts I kept back in Chicago. Five hundred dollars, half a G, as they'd call it on the street, meant I was serious.

My search this time was for Steelers Jacket, but he wasn't on the corner where I'd met him earlier. For that matter, Sonny Boy wasn't in sight, either. Maybe they were members of some sort of union and this was their day off. I drove the entire length of the street, then turned around and came back the other way. The vendors were looking at me—some eager, some flirtatious, some hungry, and a few hateful. I knew—felt—I didn't belong.

Everyone had said Richard had comfortably fit in wherever he went, and that his genuine goodness drew perfect strangers to him and made them love him, but I doubted he'd ever walked Hillman Street with that holy aura around him, or someone would have clocked him on the head and lifted his wallet.

I watched as one of the street hookers, short, skinny, wearing big glasses, and dressed like a twelve-year-old—though I could tell even at a distance that she was in her late forties—stopped and talked to a skinny man with a 1960s Afro lounging against a lamppost. He looked angry and threatening as he snarled at her, and she cringed away, hunching her shoulders and trying to look small. Some errant DNA strand of gallantry pulsed inside me, but I wouldn't stop to help. I doubt I'd have lived more than ten minutes if I had. I was glad the incident between them ended without violence.

On the next block, a young man with a coffee-and-cream complexion, wearing tight jeans and a T-shirt that wouldn't keep him warm, looked directly at me, smiled, and winked, raising his tweezed eyebrows. I shook my head and drove on.

I wondered who was actually running the many businesses on Hillman Street. It might have been an African-American operation, considering there were no Caucasians on the stroll at night, but I didn't think so. The black underworld community in northeast Ohio had the muscle to take over any local illegal operation, but apparently not the organizational skills. The muckety-mucks out of the Hillman Street spotlight had to be one of the arms of either the Severino family or the Mangione family—or possibly both. Their ongoing rivalry was bitter, but both capos could easily spot a successful enterprise and would share it, albeit reluctantly.

Business is business.

Worrisome. If I eventually made the investment I was there

for, it might get back to the mob guys, and then I'd be in more trouble than I could imagine. I figured anyone wearing a Steelers jacket on this street was aligned with the Mangiones, connected with the Pittsburgh families, and not the Severinos.

Either way, it was too late for me to worry about it.

I checked my watch—not quite midnight. I veered off, turned left on Market Street, and found a bar that catered neither to cops nor criminals, but to Youngstown State undergraduates. Most students were either studying in their quarters or sleeping the night away. The few inside paid no attention to me when I walked in—and they'd never recognize me as an alumnus of the university they now attended. I didn't look like the college grad type—too old, and too mean-looking.

I killed the better part of forty-five minutes drinking two beers at the bar. Then I drove my car back onto Hillman.

I was in luck. Sonny Boy had staked out the same corner where I'd found him the day before, this time wearing a bright yellow anorak, its hood shadowing most of his face.

I braked to a halt in front of him and rolled down the passenger-side window. "Whassup?" I said.

He didn't move, didn't even look my way.

"Hey, Sonny Boy," I said, louder.

That got his attention. He shoved his hands into the pockets of the anorak and strolled over. "We know each other?"

"We met yesterday," I said. "Around lunchtime—right here. Remember? I asked you for crystal, and you sent me across the street to negotiate with your pal."

His eyes clicked almost audibly as he rapidly checked out the cars driving past. "I got a pal across the street?"

"Yesterday he was wearing a Steelers jacket."

He nodded. "So?"

"I want to see him again and make another buy."

Sonny Boy shook his head disapprovingly. "Man! You done gone through a whole dime bag since yesterday?"

I was perversely impressed—Sonny Boy and his buddy must have discussed me. "Different kind of buy this time."

"Different kind?"

I nodded.

"What kind is that?"

"I'd rather tell *him*."

"What you got to tell him *about*?"

I pulled the rubber-banded five hundred dollars out of my pocket and waved it under Sonny Boy's nose. It took him more than a moment to consider it—not because he was too stupid to figure it out, but because he considered issuing a warning.

Finally, he did so. "If you cheese him off," he said, "you be a step an' a half away from never wakin' up again. An' no matter what goes down from here on in, that roll you be flashin' gonna be in *his* pocket, not yours."

"I brought it here to spend, not to tease with it."

He laughed aloud. "'Tease'? *Tease!* Goddamn, you talk funny an' shit."

"I want your friend to laugh, too," I said. "Where do I find him?"

Sonny Boy shuffled his feet, thinking about it. Then he bent to talk to me directly through the opened window. "Drive up there a ways to Breaden Street. Hang a left. The third house on the right—look like it all boarded up, but it ain't. Knock once, wait, then three times more. Whoever opens, tell 'em Sonny Boy sent you."

"Thanks," I said, and started rolling the window up.

"Hey! Don' I get a tip? For personal service?"

"A tip?" I said. "Sure. Stand up straight, keep your shoulders back—and be proud." And I gunned the car away from him.

Turning onto Breaden Street felt like sailing off the edge of the world into the unknown.

There were no streetlights on the block. The houses there were mostly dark at this time of night—really dark, with no lightbulbs burning anywhere on the main floors. The house to which Sonny Boy had directed me seemed buttoned up tight. Low-grade plywood sheets, complete with cracks and knotholes, were nailed over the windows, and even the door had been replaced, or maybe the old one had just been covered with plywood—I couldn't tell which. I made a U-turn and parked at the curb across the street.

The prickling needles at the back of my neck made me leave the driver's door unlocked in case I had to get out of there quickly. I walked through sodden fallen leaves up the front walk, and when I climbed the three stairs to the small porch, I heard rap music playing inside, tinny, as if it came from a cheap radio. I tapped smartly on the plywood with my car key—once, then three more times.

Feet shuffled around inside, there were sharp whispers, and the radio was turned off. Silence. But I sensed someone standing just inside the front door, breathing, listening. I waited for half a minute and then knocked again.

I heard the door—the real one behind the plywood—swing open, and through one of the knotholes a bloodshot brown eye stared out at me.

"What?" The voice was low, guttural. The single word dripped with suspicion.

"Sonny Boy said to come here. I'm looking for the guy who wears the Steelers jacket," I said, moving as close to the plywood as I could and keeping my voice down. "I know him from yesterday."

The eye blinked, and I could hear him mumbling. I couldn't make out the words, but I would have bet the farm obscenities were sprinkled throughout. Then the eye disappeared, there was more low talking, and then the footsteps came back. The plywood slid open, so I could see my welcomer in the entry hall—a skinny black man with a grizzled beard. He was wearing baggy khaki pants, work boots, and a bulky shawl-collared sweater that reminded me of young men's fashions in the 1960s.

His hair was wrapped up in a bright blue do-rag, over which he'd plopped a battered New York Yankees ball cap.

He was also pointing a gun at me—a 9mm automatic. He didn't hold it the way a cop would, out in front of him, and he used only one hand, held as high as his face and turned over so the barrel did not waver but looked as if it were on its side. "Hands on your head, mofuckah," he growled. He frisked me down expertly, running his hand over the pocket where I kept my roll of bills but not investigating. He was looking for something deadly instead.

Finished with his search, he nudged me none too gently in the ribs and I lowered my hands. I walked in front of him through a wide arch into what used to be the living room. There was Steelers Jacket, looking surprised and a little amused to see me again. This time, his jacket was unzipped, and I couldn't help noticing his military-surplus green khakis worn tight, probably a size small. He was skinny as a refugee—hardly any hips or ass.

"Man," he said, "you musta burnt up that crystal in a hell of a hurry. Want more?"

"I'm not interested in crystal tonight."

He leaned forward, studying my face carefully. "You ain' high."

"No," I said.

"I c'd tell by your eyes. You straight an' sober." He shook his head. "You sure you ain' no cop?"

"Not a cop."

"'Cuz iffen you a cop come knockin' on my door, man, the only way you get outta here is in a box."

"He ain' heeled," the other man said.

"That's my problem," I said.

"Huh?"

"I'm not carrying. I need a weapon."

Steelers Jacket uncoiled himself and stood up. "Why?"

I shrugged.

"Gonna rob a bank?"

"Maybe."

"Or maybe what else?"

"That's my business," I said.

Jacket put his hands on his hips and studied me some more. Finally, he said, "You even know howta use one?"

That called for another shrug from me. "You stick your finger in the trigger guard and squeeze."

He nodded, then grinned. Two of his bottom front teeth were gold. "You got a plan to waste your ol' lady—sump'n like that?" It made Do-Rag laugh, and Jacket laughed, too. "Tell you what, man—I take her off your hands. You never see her again, an' in the meantime, I hook her on crack. Then I make me some good money peddlin' her skanky white ass. That way, nobody gonna knock on your door, askin' you about killin' her." Then he frowned. "Unless she a dog. Is she a dog, man? You jus' an ol' fart an' shit—you hooked up with an' ol' fart, too? Gah-damn, then I bet I gotta sell her pussy for quarters!"

"I don't have an old lady. I want to buy a piece for my business, not yours."

"Lissen up," he said. "I took care a you 'fore cuz that be *my* job. Why you come scratchin' aroun' lookin' for firepower?"

"I don't know anyone in Youngstown," I said. "I know *you*—from yesterday. So if you don't sell what I'm buying tonight, send me to somebody who does."

"Uh-huh."

"But I don't think so. You're a pretty big man around here. I think you can get me whatever I want. I wouldn't be surprised if you have something I could buy from you right here in the house."

Jacket licked his lips. "What kinda bread you got?"

I pulled out the roll and slipped the rubber band off. "Here you go."

He stuck out his hand, palm up, demanding. "Give it over."

I handed it to him and watched while he counted it. "Half a

yard," he mumbled. He slipped it into the pocket of his khakis. "What you want?"

"An automatic would be my first choice."

"Yeah? What's your second choice?"

"Beggars can't be choosers," I said.

He thought it over, or at least pretended to do so. "Can't help you there."

"What?"

"I can't sell you no piece."

"Why's that?"

He shrugged. "Le's jus' say I don' wanna."

"Send me where I can, then."

"Can't do that, neither." He turned both his hands over, palms up, and wiggled his eyebrows.

"Okay," I said. "Then give me the five hundred back."

He folded his arms across his chest. "Wha' the fuck are you anyway, some kinda dumbass?"

"Are you robbing me? Is that it?"

"Oh, no, man," Jacket said, and the "no" came out sounding like *noooo*. He tried not to laugh. "You come here without no invitation, so the five hunderd is the—how you say?—price of admission. You got in to see me. I got your money. We's even."

"You're a thief," I said. "And a Steelers fan to boot."

"I been called worse 'n that."

"I want the five hundred back. Even better, I want a weapon, which is what I came here for."

He looked over at Do-Rag. "You gonna get a weapon up your white ass, 'less you move outta here quick." The friend stood a little taller and started waving the gun in front of his own face again.

"It's not fair," I said without anger.

"Life ain' fair. Now move out, sucka."

Do-Rag shoved the automatic into my side and steered me into the entry hall and toward the door. Jacket called, "Don' come back no more—'less you wanna die."

I felt the flush heating my cheeks, and I hoped it was too dim in there for anyone to notice. I didn't like being cheated—or treated as a chump.

Do-Rag opened the door and unbarred the plywood, standing aside for me to step out. "You a lucky fuckin' man," he said softly, " 'cuz I just as soon waste your ass right now." And with the muzzle of the 9mm, he shoved me over the threshold.

The plywood was swinging shut behind me. I spun around, moving fast, the way I used to when I was in-country and working for Delta Force, and kicked the plywood inward—hard. Then I followed it back inside.

Do-Rag was caught unawares, stumbling backward, the automatic waving impotently as he flailed his arms for balance. I drove my fist hard into his unprotected ribs, feeling one shatter against my knuckles. He went down hard, dropping his hardware. As he rolled over to reach for it, I grabbed his right wrist, straightened out his arm, and snapped it against my shoe. That crack was even louder.

So was his scream.

I scooped up the weapon and had it pointed toward the archway even before Steelers Jacket came running out from the living room. When he saw me armed, he skidded to a halt. His suddenly amazed eyes got big and round.

"Sumbitch," he said with a kind of wonder.

Then I shot him in the left kneecap, and he made the kind of noise I was certain he'd never made before in his life.

My hands didn't even shake, even when I returned to my hotel and locked myself in my room. I'd gotten what I wanted—a weapon—but the cost had been high. Do-Rag was on the floor with a savagely broken arm, and Steelers Jacket now had a knee he'd never properly walk on again. I'd also left a lot of rubber on the tarmac outside the Breaden Street house, certain everyone else on the block heard the tires screech. But it wasn't the kind of neighborhood where residents rushed to the window and stuck their noses out to see who was making all the fuss. Stuck-out noses were often shot off.

My years of experience in the jungles and alleyways of Vietnam had served me well that night. My reflexes were as sharp as ever, even though more than a decade as a civilian might have slowed me down half a step. But my ethics might have changed some since my black op duty—my values, maybe—because in Vietnam I'd first come to the realization that I liked to hurt people.

Not regular people, of course—not nice ones—and I'd never in my life raised my hand to hurt a woman. But killers, rapists, traitors, child abusers, animal torturers, and general all-around sadists—well, they deserved it.

CHAPTER TWENTY

Shopping was to be the first order of the day.

There was a small shop dealing exclusively with firearms and hunting bows and arrows not too far from Brier Hill. Its address gave me a few moments' pause before I went inside. I didn't want to be recognized by the clerk, and I didn't want my buying habits gossiped about to the mob guys, either.

The clerk didn't look or sound Italian, though. His face had that cheery reddish glow, puffy cheeks, and a jutting-out chin that telegraphed his willingness to mix it up if necessary, despite the pleasant smile. Probably his only interest was making a few bucks on the items he had for sale, and he wasn't concerned with the identity of his customers. He didn't even attempt to push any of the upscale bullets that fragment on impact and bounce around inside your body, destroying everything they touch. He just asked what I wanted and supplied me with a box of 9mm shells for the automatic I'd taken away from Do-Rag the night before. He also packaged together a kit with gun oil, patches, a rod, and rags, along with a product called Break-Free.

It felt strange to strip, clean, and load a weapon I'd stolen from someone else. The hotel maids would have a strange feeling, too, when they came in to change the sheets and towels and recognized the smell of gun oil in the room.

Before leaving the gun shop, I spent another forty bucks plus change on a gravity knife. Although not nearly as effective as a handgun, it would be a hell of a lot more quiet.

In the hotel lobby, I bought a copy of the *Youngstown Vindicator* and read it from cover to cover, although I didn't notice any names that captured my attention. I even napped off and on all afternoon. When I woke up, the TV was on and I found myself watching dreadful daytime television like *Donahue*, and Sally Jessy Raphael with her silly red-framed glasses. I couldn't remember the last time I'd *ever* watched TV on a weekday.

The ringing of the phone made me jump. I wasn't expecting a call. Not from my sister, Teresa, who didn't like the best part of me. Not from my brother Al, who resented me for questioning him and trying to make me shut up about it. Not from Captain Shemo, who hadn't the vaguest idea where I was coming from. And not from the Severino or the Mangione families, who were probably hoping I'd gone quietly back to Chicago.

Well, I thought, what the hell. I picked up the receiver.

"You're still in town," Diane Burnham said. Her voice was low, cool, sexy—the way I'd always remembered it.

"I lost my road map, and now I don't know how to get back to Chicago." I waited for her to laugh. It wasn't drop-dead funny, but a polite chuckle would have been nice. It didn't come.

"I'm surprised you're calling," I said. "I got the idea you were fed up with me."

"I was," she said. "Everybody gets fed up sometimes. But eventually you get hungry again."

"I guess that's a good thing, then. Want to get some dinner?"

She took a two-beat pause. "No, Nicky," she said, sighing deeply. "I do not want to get some dinner."

Diane had brought a pint bottle of Stolichnaya vodka in her big purse, but she didn't present it to me until she was securely in my hotel room. I poured drinks for us, which we hardly touched, so anxious were we to get into bed. After a solid ninety minutes or so in various stages of nakedness, rolling around on the sheets—the top one of which was now crumpled on the floor, along with the blanket and bedspread and most of our clothes—we lay there quietly, taking our first time-out, with the only illumination in the room a spillover from the overhead bulb in the hallway, drinking the stuff straight, no ice, out of bathroom water glasses.

Unadulterated vodka always has a bite to it. No matter how gently you sip it, the burning catches you off guard, making you blink, inhale quickly, or sometimes gasp.

Relationships between people can be that way, too.

Diane Burnham certainly took me by surprise. This erotic encounter was one to write home about. Our sex was hard, rough, down and dirty. She did things with her mouth that shocked even a fallen-away Catholic like me. She growled and whispered things into my ear that made my hair stand on end. It also excited the hell out of me. After more than an hour and a half without even stopping to take an extra breath, almost every part of my body was sore, especially my cock. The reddened outlines of her front teeth were embedded on both my shoulders, and my back tingled from her digging into me and scratching. Her own ass was red, bearing imprints of my spanking palm—her request, not mine.

Part of me wanted to stay in bed with her for the rest of my life, but I'd been making plans, and now, at nearly nine o'clock, my real day hadn't even begun. I had another drink and tried to look discreetly at the face of my watch on the night table so she wouldn't notice.

It didn't work. Her lip curled the way a mature woman might regard a too-eager adolescent. "You're bare-ass naked, guzzling vodka, you've been fucking my brains out, and now you're checking what time it is? Jesus!" She shook her head, less a negative than an attempt to rattle something out of her mind. "Do you have somewhere to go, Nicky?"

"Eventually, we both have somewhere to go."

She rolled over on her back, her eyes half-closed and her mouth sulky. A line of perspiration glistened between her breasts, and all I wanted to do at that moment was to lick it and taste it. Instead, I ran the tip of my index finger softly through the dampness, then cupped her right breast with my palm.

She didn't seem to notice. "You know what I think?"

"No, I don't know what you think."

"I think it's time for you to go home."

"I am home—this is my room."

"I mean back to Chicago. There's nothing for you here anymore."

"*You're* here."

"You can get laid anywhere."

"Sure, but not by you. You're the important one, Diane. You always have been."

"I'm just one in a long line for you."

I took my hand away. "The first in a long line," I reminded her.

"Everyone's got to be first at something."

"We were first for each other."

Her lips pressed together, and she thought quietly. Then she took a breath, as if to begin another sentence, then changed her mind and looked away, toward the wall. Finally, she said, "That was another epoch—the start of the Ice Age. But things change—invariably. Things turn to shit."

"That's pretty cold."

"Go back home, Nicky. You're wasting your time. Your

siblings are sick of the sight of you, and so is Youngstown—and you can't tiptoe around here too carefully, or you'll step somewhere you shouldn't."

"How do you know Youngstown is tired of me, Diane? Or my family, either?"

"I . . . I know, that's all. I hear things."

"Where?"

"Around."

"More pillow talk?" I said.

She flipped over onto her side, threw one arm across my chest and one leg across my thighs, squeezing tight. Her crotch was still wet—and warm—but the arm embracing me trembled. "Give it up." She ground her face into my neck, and I felt her teeth nipping at me—not gently. "If you don't, you're going to get hurt."

"I'm hurting right now," I said. "Are you going to suck my blood like Dracula?"

"I'm not talking about Dracula."

Affection and passion flew out the window like a canary suddenly released from its cage. My whole body grew rigid, and I turned my head away from her. "What do you know about that, Diane?"

She rolled over on her back again. "Forget it. I don't know anything." Her words were clipped, as if she were answering the questions of a U.S. census taker.

"The Severinos? Is that who you're talking about?"

"Just people in general."

"How do you know old man Severino?" I said. "Your husband isn't even Italian."

"Everybody in the world isn't Italian." Not looking, Diane reached out blindly for a cigarette, feeling around on the nightstand until she found one. "My parents knew Don Severino, and I met him when I was a kid—just like you did." She clicked her lighter, inhaled deeply, then exhaled, the smoke curling around her before rising toward the ceiling. "Besides, I get around pretty good on my own."

"You're impressing me again."

"I hope I am. I hope you're impressed enough to get out of town."

"That sounds like an old line from *Gunsmoke*."

She puffed irritably on the cigarette. "Do you make everything serious into a punch line? This isn't a playground, some make-believe Bogart movie. They play for keeps around here."

"They played for keeps in Vietnam," I reminded her, "but I'm still walking around."

She glared at me, her face set on Angry. Then something happened inside that face. It collapsed, and Diane started crying. I tried to recall if I had *ever* seen her cry before, even back when we were little more than kids.

She rolled out of bed, groping on the floor for something to wrap around herself, finally grabbing the blanket. She staggered over to sit at the table near the window, huddling under the blanket, which concealed every part of her except for her head and one hand, which still held the cigarette. Her shoulders quivered, and she ducked her head, trying to suppress the sobs.

I felt like a fool. Tears were a new wrinkle to our relationship. I finally got up, slipped on my Jockey shorts and shirt, and went to her. Her tears had slowed, but she hugged the wrap tightly around her. I knelt and put my arm around her.

"Don't touch me!" she said. "Goddamn it, don't put your hands on me."

I took the cigarette from her hand and put it out in the ashtray. "I'm not going to touch you."

I took the chair opposite her and we sat quietly. It seemed like hours, but it was less than five minutes before she said, "Do you still think you were my first, Nicky? The first man I ever went to bed with?" Her voice was low and she spoke very calmly. A chill spread over me like a sudden gust of cold wind out of a bank of fog.

I didn't say anything.

"You were the second," Diane said. "You were inexperienced. You wouldn't have known a virgin if one had fallen on you."

My throat felt filled up with school glue. All I could manage to say was, "All right."

Her voice went up into coloratura soprano. Finally, I'd surprised *her*. "'All right'?" She turned to look straight at me. "Is that all you have to say? 'All right'?"

I tried clearing my throat. "Like you said, a different epoch. It doesn't matter."

"It matters a lot, Nicky—because it was with your brother. Richard."

Suddenly, I was dizzy, stumbling, crashing around, bouncing off walls, my vision blurred, my brain swelling and threatening to explode—and yet I hadn't left my chair. I managed to say, "I don't believe you."

"I'm not *that* good at making up lies."

"Richard was probably at the seminary—if he wasn't already a priest."

"That didn't matter to me at the time—and it sure didn't matter to him."

"You're concocting this story to get me to give up, leave Youngstown, and never come back. Is that it?"

"You don't believe me? Well, Richard had a bigger dick than you do."

The air rushed out of me like I were a punctured tire.

"You're pretty well hung yourself, so I wouldn't make up such a lie unless I was certain." Diane's laugh was more like a snort. "So much for his holy priesthood."

"He always liked girls," I said, sounding like I was whining, "before he went to the seminary."

"He didn't stop liking them. He was a player, Nicky, almost right to the very end." She picked up my glass and drained whatever was left of the vodka. "It wasn't a big thing—it wasn't to me anyway. We only slept together twice, and then he said I was too young and he didn't want to get involved, so we became friends instead of lovers. Then I started going out with you instead, and I never mentioned anything about Richard and me because I didn't want to hurt you." She put the glass on the table, a little too hard. "It *was* love with you, Nicky. Not with him. You knew it was love." She sighed, sounding sad. "Why did you run away and leave me behind? Why the hell was that?"

I got up and walked back over to the bed, found my pants on the floor, and stepped into them, creating a scene in my imagination that I couldn't bear. "When I came home for two weeks to see you, I knew things had changed."

"Nothing had changed!" she protested. "I loved you like I always had."

"But you slept with somebody else when I was away." I zipped up my trousers and went back over to her, but I didn't sit down this time. "I was too naïve to know you weren't a virgin when we were together for the first time—but I could tell after so many years together that you knew things to do in bed that you never learned with me."

"You were no saint then, either—after a year in Saigon."

"You think I was messing around with pathetic Vietnamese whores while I was thinking about you?" I shook my head. "You weren't as smart as I thought you were."

"Fine, then," she said. "I apologize." She stood up and, dragging the blanket around her, walked to the side of the bed, where she'd thrown most of her clothes. She bent down and picked up her panties, then threw me a demanding look. She wanted me to turn away while she got dressed.

I looked out the window, seeing not much of anything in the dark. I knew in my gut that somehow we'd both be embarrassed if I saw her naked.

I wasn't finished talking, though.

"Was it Bob back then?" I asked her. "Is that who you were

fucking all the time I was playing John Wayne in the jungle and little people in pajamas shot at my ass?"

"What's the difference?" I heard her clothes rustling.

"Just wondering if you two crazy kids were practicing for your honeymoon."

"Well, it wasn't Bob."

"Ah. Not until after I left—after we broke up."

She didn't answer.

"So when I asked you to go with me to Chicago," I said, "when I asked you to spend your life with me, was it this other guy you were hanging around Youngstown for? Is that why you said no?"

"It wasn't about any other guy. This is my hometown, Nicky. My family's here, my friends and my career."

"You didn't have a career."

"As it turned out. But my parents knew the Severinos just the way yours did, and I hoped they'd help make my dreams come true."

"We all had dreams. I still have mine. I dream about walking through the jungle in the middle of the night—not a sliver of a moon and it's dark as the inside of a coffin. I walk, but I don't make any noise. I learned to do that. Neat, right?"

"Nicky . . ."

"And then I dream of seeing one of those little guys in pajamas walking around in the jungle at midnight, just like me. You know what I do then? In my dreams? I kill him, quick as you please. I kill him with a knife, so my gun doesn't make any noise. I kill him and then go back the way I came, not making a sound stepping on the leaves and the twigs, not even stopping to wash the other guy's warm blood off my hands. I have that dream all the time, Diane—because I lived through it."

I went over to her. She was completely dressed from the waist down—skirt, stockings, shoes—but she hadn't put her blouse on yet. Her bra was similar to the one she'd worn last time, only this one was blue.

"So that's why I wanted to get out of Youngstown," I said. "Everybody I knew here was part of the war—the Severino-Mangione war, or the war between the people on the street and the people who run this town, or whatever war's being fought at the moment. Everybody here feasts on war and can't wait to read about the next attack. They secretly *love* the war, no matter who's fighting."

"No wars in Chicago?"

"There are wars everywhere—but here they're fought in your front yard." I sat down on the edge of the bed. "Your husband knows about us?"

"It was common knowledge back then," Diane said. "And after a while, he didn't really give a damn, either."

"Did he know about you and Richard?"

She looked angry again. "*Nobody* knows about Richard. Except now you know, and it throws you for a loop. You thought I was pure?"

"We're talking degrees of purity."

Her laugh was nasty as she slipped on her blouse and began buttoning. "I have no more degrees of purity. I told you that my marriage is now sharing a nice home with a mildly friendly roommate, didn't I? And that Bob is banging one of his law associates."

I nodded.

"You don't think I've become a nun, do you? Well, I have a lover too, Nicky. Besides you, I mean."

"You kind of indicated that at lunch. Thanks, but I don't have to hear about it."

She picked up her cigarettes again. "You're asking so damn many questions of everybody, and you'll eventually ask me. It's in your blood, isn't it?" She shook one out of the pack and lit it with aggression. "Well, I'll tell you anyway; it'll save you the trouble of digging for it later."

"I asked you if it's someone I knew. You said it was none of my business."

"I changed my mind," she said. "It's Polly Severino."

I reached out for the dresser and leaned against it. It was either that or fall over on my face. The name of *any* current lover of Diane Burnham would have bothered me greatly, but Polly Severino was just about all I could take.

"We see each other once a week or so," Diane continued, most of the emotion gone from her tone, "at a nice quiet hotel in Boardman where we won't run into anyone we know. Sometimes we do, of course—because they're cheating too, just like we are. But mostly, it's a private affair."

"I see," I said, not seeing.

"It's not so private anymore. The Severinos have kept their business to themselves—until you showed up. Now you're pushing everybody. You even got Alfonso running his mouth to you. That pisses Polly off."

"How does Polly know that?"

"He didn't share his chain of information with me. He's not stupid, okay? He's not his father, but he's not stupid."

"Did he tell you all this in bed?"

She ran a hand through her hair, brushing it back from her forehead. "That's right, Nicky. He told me all this in bed. Yesterday."

Diane, hearing it all in bed, Polly on top of her, whispering in her ear while he played between her legs. I was perilously close to upchucking.

Diane blew out a lungful of smoke, the jet streaking toward the ceiling. Her hand shook, and so did her voice. She tossed her head again, slapping at the bangs drooping over her forehead. "So save yourself the trouble. Stop poking your nose where it doesn't belong, stop asking questions, and haul your sorry ass out of town."

CHAPTER TWENTY-ONE

Another tossing, no-sleep night, grinding my teeth and trying to ignore that almost piercing ache that went through my chest, and by the time I finally got out of bed the next morning—the bed that still smelled of Diane Burnham, her perfume, her bodily fluids, her natural scent—I'd finally reached a conclusion.

I'd had it—too much pain and confusion, and too much hatred for the people I'd turned my back on in Youngstown, the hatred springing alive and well from where I thought I'd buried it in the past. I was finished.

So without shaving or showering, I packed my suitcase. I stuck Do-Rag's gun into the waistband at the back of my pants, planning to dump it somewhere along the road. I checked out of the hotel early and got into my car. It was probably an eight-hour drive to Chicago. I thought about stopping in Cleveland and making inquiries with the FBI about a summons for Richard to talk to the RICO investigators, then decided against it. It had nothing to do with me anyway.

But I figured I should say good-bye to my siblings. It was the only decent thing to do.

I'd see Alfonso first. Despite his being a gold-star goof-off of a cop, Lieutenant Candiotti did have to show up at work early, so I'd catch him before he left his house. I didn't want to see my sister-in-law, Dolores, one more time, so I decided to wait outside Al's house and say good-bye to him at the curb. I was leaving and not coming back, ever, so I could ignore Alfonso's foulmouthed wife without going to the trouble of telling her what I thought of her.

My sister, Teresa, was a stay-at-home wife and mother, so I could swing by for a few moments after I saw Alfonso, just to say "Ta-ta" and "See you soon." There was little love between us—there never had been. But I didn't think she'd start a fight with me again. She'd be too delighted to see the back of me as I tootled off home.

It was twenty past seven when I pulled up in front of Alfonso's house. He was, I knew, due to arrive at work at eight o'clock, so he'd have only a few minutes to say good-bye. His car was parked in the driveway, nose out, so I pulled up across the street, cut my ignition, and settled back to wait for him.

It was a cool, sunny morning; the leaves on the trees had turned October yellow and orange, and two bushes that lined the sidewalk from the street to his front door were a rich, dark red. I leaned back in my seat, one elbow out the opened window, and tried breathing in the snapping chill of autumn.

Alfonso came out the front door five minutes later, carrying an uneaten Pop-Tart in one hand and struggling into his trench coat. He slowed down as he saw me, then stopped and waited as I got out of my car and crossed the street.

"For you, it's the crack of sparrows," he said. "What's up?"

"I'm leaving, Al—leaving town, I mean. I stopped off to say good-bye."

He took a bite of his tart and licked a few crumbs off his lips. "Well, ya know, that's a good thing, Nicky, when you get right down to it. I don't wanna make myself crazy for the rest of my life. You don't, either. Look it straight in the eye and then forget about it and move on."

"I am."

"I know you're not happy in Youngstown. I don't know why, but you are the way you are." He took another bite. "You wanna come in, say good-bye to Dolores?"

My chuckle was short and sweet. "Not a good idea."

"I guess not." He shrugged. "She's not the easiest broad to live with, but things tend to work out in the end. She's okay—at least for me anyway—and sometimes when nobody else is around and she hasn't had too much to drink, she can be a lot of fun."

"Al . . ."

He lifted one eyebrow. Alfonso was shorter than every other man in the family, but he wasn't really a bad-looking guy. He had that kind of arrogant, half-amused Italian face, which, for some reason, made lots of people like him.

"Al, that stuff you told me before—about Richard, about the Severino family . . ."

His pleasant demeanor disappeared behind a cloud, and he glanced around furtively to see if anyone was listening. "Forget it," he said. "I never told you nothing."

"The word's . . . around—that you talked to me. Polly knows. He's torqued off about you."

"How do you know Polly knows?"

"I just do."

"Hey," Al said. "He knows on account of I told him myself."

A breeze kicked up, rustling my hair. I'd never learned how to tame it. Maybe it was all those months wearing a helmet or an army beret, but it had bequeathed me a permanent bed head. "What the hell possessed you to tell him?"

He hiked both shoulders up around his ears and then let them drop. "He knew we talked. We're brothers, after all. So, yeah, he was pissed. But he'll get over it."

"You think?"

He shoved the rest of the tart into his mouth. "He's got one of those Severino family tempers. But he scratches my back and I scratch his, so we get along. Look, he won't fuck with me. Not for just having a conversation with my own brother."

"*About* your other brother."

"Half the people in two counties are talking about Richard. Crying 'cause they miss him, 'cause they all loved him. But me and you—and maybe even Teresa a little bit—we loved him more'n anybody. Right, Nicky?"

"Right, Alfonso."

"So don't worry about Polly. Him and me, we're like this." He looked at his watch. I couldn't help noticing it was a Rolex.

"I gotta get crackin'," he said. "I goof off on the job a lot, but every once in a while Shemo expects me to walk into the office on time and hang up my hat. Just so's I *look* like I'm gonna work." He opened his arms for a hug, and I moved between them.

"Listen, Nicky," he continued, speaking into my ear now, "maybe one of these days I'll make it to Chicago. I travel for seminars or police stuff, so if I'm in that direction, I'll call you, and we can spend some real time. Just the two of us—no Dolores, no Teresa, no mourners. Not like this week, because everything's up in the air, but we'll really hang out together—go out, have a good Chicago steak, and get shit-faced in one of those Near North Side clubs." He squeezed harder. "I miss you, Nicky," he said. "I miss you all a time." He coughed out of nervousness; this wasn't like Alfonso. "I love you, ya know."

I pressed my face to his. "Me, too." We pounded each other's backs for a few moments, and then we let go. I moved away from him, walked down the driveway, and crossed the street to my own car. Unlocking it, I turned around for one more wave.

Alfonso waved back, grinning, and pride inside me welled up and filled my chest. Damn, he *was* pretty good-looking for a brother. Other than Teresa, he was all I had left. I watched him slide behind the wheel, shut the door, and turn on the ignition.

The explosion lifted the front of his car about six feet off the ground, the roar like a sonic boom on the quiet morning street. The hood and the windshield flew into the air, but I couldn't see them through the towering jet of fire and the thick black smoke—and I couldn't see or identify what was left of my brother Alfonso. I was frozen to the spot, paralyzed with shock and fear. And grief, too—another double dose of grief and another empty hole where once my family used to be.

I had been an eyewitness to a local specialty—the Youngstown Tune-Up.

A few seconds after the explosion, the front door of the house flew open and Dolores came running out, wrapped in what must have been the first thing she'd reached for—her husband's bathrobe. It was the one Al had been wearing the last time I saw him, and it tore my guts out. She stood on the front step for about five seconds, clutching the robe around her neck, coughing at the smoke and the horrific smell—part explosive, part fire, and part cooking meat—and staring at the flaming wreck in her driveway as if she couldn't quite understand it.

Then she opened her mouth wider than any operatic soprano and started screaming.

CHAPTER TWENTY-TWO

Alfonso Candiotti's funeral wasn't as big and crowded as our brother Richard's the week before. Teresa and her husband were there, of course. Teresa had taken charge of all the formal arrangements, and now she sat in the front row at Our Lady once again, straight-backed and stone-faced like the carved woman on the prow of an old-time pirate ship. My uncle Carmine's wheelchair was again stationed at the far end of the front pew. He wheezed, sucking oxygen through his nose from the little tubes that met on his upper lip. I wondered if he were carrying a gun again.

Dolores, the grieving widow, sat between Teresa and me. She wore a medium-short black dress that would have startled anyone sitting opposite her if she'd crossed or uncrossed her legs, but the heavy black veil over her face, cascading down from a brand-new black hat, ruined the glamorous effect. She was crying too loudly to convince anyone of the extent of her sorrow, but they were crocodile tears. She should have won an Emmy.

She was taking a time-out from hating me because I'd been there when Alfonso died. It had been a quick death, and I had to be grateful for that. It had also been a surprise to Al—at least for those two seconds before the explosives wired under his driver's seat blew him into pieces. Dolores really hadn't seen his body, because she'd gone completely hysterical as soon as she ran outside—and a good thing for her, too. I'd put my arms around her and quickly led her inside, away from the smoldering ruin that was her husband, and patted her back and let her bury her face in my neck, and I spoke softly and gently to her and took care of her until the police arrived to take charge.

There were more grim-looking policemen in uniform at the church to bid good-bye to Al, led once again by Captain Shemo, distinguished in his formal brass-bedecked uniform, and almost as many reporters scribbling madly in their notebooks, but the only TV camera assigned to cover the funeral was stationed outside Our Lady of Perpetual Sorrow to videotape the mourners entering and leaving. As high-ranking a police officer as Alfonso Candiotti had been, he didn't feed the frenzies of faith, belief, and television drama the way Father Richard had.

On the left side of the sanctuary, the Mangione family was there en masse once again. Old man Mangione looked tired, almost defeated. Behind me on the right side, Paolo Severino, Sr., avoiding meeting anyone's eyes but staring down at his knees and breathing quietly through his open mouth, was wedged between his elderly wife and his mistress, Lucy Waldman. Lucy gave me a sorrowful smile and shook her head. The old man's two ever-present bodyguards sat behind him, watchfully guarding him from anyone who might harass or hurt him, and paying little attention to the eulogy.

Polly Severino was apparently busy that morning, though, and was elsewhere. So, apparently, was Diane Burnham. I wondered whether they were busy together.

The mayor did not attend the funeral, but he sent a gigantic wreath, which was installed at the head of Alfonso's closed coffin, next to two larger and more garish floral displays donated by the mob families. Except for the police commissioner, Youngstown politicians were also missing. So were the multitudes who'd spent the last decade kneeling in the confessionals, baring their souls to Richard, the ones who'd cried and blubbered through his funeral Mass and leaned over to sobbingly kiss the lid of his casket as it passed up the aisle. They loved their young priest enough to give up an entire day to attend his services, but apparently they didn't care about a cop, even a Candiotti cop, because most of them had not shown up.

I cared, though, about my brother. Unlike Richard, who'd supposedly put a gun in his mouth and pulled the trigger, Alfonso hadn't blown up his own car in his own driveway. That was no suicide, no matter how hard anyone would spin it. He'd been murdered.

The bishop didn't conduct the service this time. Saying high Mass and eulogizing a priest was one thing, especially given the relentless press and TV coverage. Saying words over the broken pieces of a Youngstown cop was another—the bishop normally didn't involve himself in the births or deaths of the little people. This time, Monsignor Danny Carbo had been appointed to run the funeral Mass. He was going through the motions and giving less heart and meaning to Alfonso's eulogy than when he rooted for the Pittsburgh Steelers on Sunday afternoons.

I wasn't listening. I was boiling.

The afternoon was déjà vu. The rites of the Church, the interment up on the hill, and the so-called party afterward at Alfonso's house were similar to the farewell for Richard—same mass, same burial, same postritual eating and drinking, and, for me, the same kind of grief. Nobody blubbered, though—there weren't that many women in attendance. The men, especially those in blue, looked mean and angry. Being on the take to racketeers was one thing, but the killing of a fellow cop was something else altogether.

I approached Ed Shemo, who was standing in the corner of Dolores's living room, sipping red wine and talking to someone

I didn't know. He turned away to avoid me, but I firmly touched his arm.

He turned to me, frowning. "Once again, I'm very sorry. More than I can possibly express to you. My heart aches for your family."

"How much does it ache?" I said. "Enough for you to find out who set that bomb—and who ordered it—and bring them to justice?"

Shemo sighed. If he hadn't been genuinely upset over Alfonso's death, he might have looked pissed off. "Jesus—we're police officers. That's what we do. We kicked off an investigation that same morning."

"And?"

"And we're working on it." He didn't meet my eyes. Instead, he looked over my shoulder—searching for escape, maybe?

"'Working on it'? Tsk, tsk," I said. I didn't cluck my tongue at him; I actually said the words, making it sound like *Tisk, tisk*.

It pushed him toward anger, but he kept his voice down in the crowded living room. "I know what you think of the Youngstown PD," he said through clenched teeth. "I know you think we're all connected in some way, that we're on the mob payroll." Now he threw a glance over his shoulder to make sure no one else could hear. "Well, that shit goes by the board when an officer is killed. There's no such thing as fair or no fair now. Somebody took out a *cop*! That trumps everything." He made his point by poking me in the chest, once for each of his last three words. Then he continued: "We'll find out who did it, and make sure he pays for it."

"And I sit around scratching my ass in the meantime?"

"No," Shemo said. "Scratch your ass in Chicago; leave policing to the police."

"Sure, Captain," I said. "You just take a nice deep breath in—and hold it until I'm back in Chicago."

I tried not to spin around on my heel and stalk away from him, but I did it anyway.

Eventually, everyone stopped looking at me as though I didn't belong there, no matter that my surname was the same as the deceased's. Teresa stood by the fireplace, greeting everyone as if this were *her* house. Her husband, Charlie, was out in the kitchen, replenishing serving trays—sent around, apparently, by Glenn Keeney's staff—with deli meat and finger-food veggies. Dolores was on the big sofa, lounging, almost reclining, her fist firmly at her mouth, accepting more condolences from her guests. I wandered down the hallway, heading for the bathroom, but I passed by the door—closed because some other guest was using it—and moved on to Alfonso's little getaway room, where we had talked. Inside, I could smell the cigars he'd smoked in there because Dolores wouldn't allow him to puff on them anywhere else in the house. The pungent smell of high-priced cigars had always clung to him. Better than expensive men's cologne, it had announced to everyone that he was a man of substance and taste and was not to be trifled with. A man of importance.

A man who'd died instantly in the shattering, deliberate explosion of his car on a brisk autumn morning. I would exact familial revenge for it, or die trying.

I looked around carefully in Alfonso's hideaway, wondering where he'd stashed all his personal items, things he wouldn't have wanted Dolores to stumble on by accident if he'd left them in the dresser drawer in their bedroom. I opened the only other door in the room and found myself in a sort of walk-in closet, its temperature controlled by a thermostat set at about seventy degrees. On one side was an entire wall of wine racks, and I took only a moment to check a few of the labels and see that Alfonso was semiseriously collecting wines. I even found a 1968 Château Palmer, which, the last I'd heard in Chicago, was selling for about three hundred dollars. On the other wall was a rack for humidors. I screwed off one of the lids, dipped my nose almost inside, and inhaled. I don't know whether they were Havanas, but they smelled superb.

I went back out into the sitting room and began opening drawers and cabinets. It didn't take me long to find a rubber-banded stack of bank statements. The bank's address was in Kansas City, Missouri. I knew that for years, probably through the end of the Eisenhower era, Kansas City had been comfortable under a political machine, run by the Prendergast gang—and the Italian mob wasn't that far removed from them.

The statements showed a savings account in the name of A. Robert Candiotti. Alfonso's middle name was Roberto. Mine was Francis, by the way, Teresa's was, naturally, Maria, and Richard's middle name was Anthony. I never knew why my parents tagged Alfonso with two very Italian given names when he was born. Maybe they had assumed *he* was the one who'd eventually don the cassock and clerical collar.

Al's using his middle name for that bank account wouldn't fool anyone, but it might make it more difficult to find if anyone searched for it. Looking through all the statements, I saw he'd opened the account nine years earlier. The statements showed nothing but deposits—first three hundred dollars a month, then six hundred, a raise that coincided with his promotion to sergeant. Four years later, when he'd become a detective, the monthly deposits had been increased again, this time to one thousand dollars. Finally, corresponding to his earning his gold lieutenant's badge, the deposits had been kicked up to two thousand dollars on the fifteenth of every month. All the deposits had been electronic transfers—no cash and no personal checks. I looked at the final deposit total on the most recent statement, including the interest gained each year—and didn't even want to think about it. I tried to put the statements in my inside jacket pocket, but they wouldn't fit. I finally undid my belt one notch and slipped them into the waistband at the small of my back. I knew they made a bulge, but I didn't imagine any postfuneral guest would check out my ass. I figured I could get away with it.

Dolores's name wasn't on those bank records. I was sure she and Alfonso maintained a joint bank account locally, so this account was something else again. I didn't even have to wonder where the deposits came from. I knew for certain they'd not been issued by the Youngstown Police Department.

The rest of the papers disclosed no further secrets. There were medical records for both Al and Dolores, and a list of charities, mostly Catholic and/or law enforcement. Alfonso's name would eventually show up on one of those law-enforcement charity organizations as that of an officer who had fallen in the line of duty. I was sure Richard's name would start appearing all over those Catholic charities, too, and mourners with empty aches in their chests would fork over even more money to the church in memory of Father Candy.

It took me less than a minute to discover what else I was looking for. Reaching to the far rear of one of the drawers, I found Al's "throwaway." It was a small pistol, a .22—not the standard-issue piece a police officer would carry. Its aim wasn't effective at long distances, and it was considered a ladies' weapon in most circles, but I knew it didn't belong to Dolores, since it was secreted in Al's little private room. The .22 also had an infamous reputation among mobsters of every ethnicity as a close-up assassination weapon. Press the muzzle against someone's skull, or aim well within five feet of the target, and pull the trigger. While there wouldn't be much more noise than a staccato *pop*, the accuracy would be deadly effective.

I flipped the gun open. It wasn't loaded, and there was a shiny spot on the metal where the serial number had been filed off cleanly. That didn't surprise me, either. Most cops carry anonymous weapons in case they have to shoot a criminal down on the street. Later, they often find out the person was reaching for a handkerchief or a ballpoint pen instead of a gun. The cop would then carefully place the throwaway—wiped clean of prints—into the dead outlaw's hand, thereby justifying opening fire on him.

It would be easy leaving Dolores's mourners' party with what I found next to the throwaway. It was a set of handcuffs, and from the keyhole sprouted a tiny key. I removed it and put it on my own key ring so I wouldn't lose it, then pocketed the cuffs. I also commandeered a strange little metal doohickey I knew was a tool designed to unlock any door.

I spent another five minutes poking around for anything else that would tell me who'd arranged Al's death. I was sure the hands-on guy had probably taken a car mechanic's course somewhere and then did all the dirty work, attaching the dynamite under the hood and wiring it to explode when the engine was turned on, but I was less interested in him than in the guy with all the power who'd given the order.

I wandered back out into the living room, the party still in full swing. I'd been out of circulation for more than fifteen minutes.

My sister, Teresa, was hissing angrily into her husband's ear, but she came toward me when she saw I was back in the living room. Charlie's face was registering grateful relief that his wife was finally leaving him alone for a moment. Then he looked around desperately for something more to drink and almost fled back into the kitchen.

"You've been gone for hours!" Teresa lived half her life with exaggerations. "Where the hell have you been?"

"In the bathroom."

"My God, you got the runs or something?"

I couldn't quite hide my sigh. "And I haven't been gone for hours, either."

Her half grin was ugly and insincere. "What? Were you actually timing it?"

"Teresa," I said quietly, "I'm going back to Chicago in a day or two. I won't bother you anymore."

"Thank you, Jesus," she said to the ceiling.

"Let's keep it even, then. Don't you bother me, either."

She poked my chest. It was annoying having two people do

that to me within the course of a few minutes. "Just remember this, Nicky. Like you or lump you, and you won't be shocked to learn that I mostly lump you"—her eyes filled with tears so suddenly that it surprised her—"you're the only goddamn brother I've got left!"

She spun around smartly, like a trained soldier executing a to-the-rear-march, and headed back toward where she'd left Charlie. She slowed down when she didn't see him, so she elbowed her way through the mourners staking out their semipermanent stations at the buffet table and the portable bar. God protect poor old Charlie when she finally runs him to ground, I thought.

I found my sister-in-law in deep conversation with two high-ranking police officers, their dress uniforms sporting a plethora of gold stripes and braid. Her eyes were red, naturally—partly from crying and partly because she'd already had too much to drink.

"Dolores," I said, putting my hand on her arm.

She turned and looked at me, and instead of the scorn with which she used to regard me, her eyes grew bigger and her lower lip began quivering again. "Nicky," she whispered. "Oh God, what would I have done without you?" She threw her arms around my neck, pressing her body against me, grinding her cheek into mine. The smell of bourbon was almost—but not quite—disguised by the perfume she'd splashed all over herself. When she finally disengaged herself from me, she hastened to introduce me to the two police officers—also lieutenants—as Alfonso's kid brother. They shook my hand, one clapped me on the upper arm as he shook, and they both murmured their sympathies. I returned my attention to Dolores as soon as it became polite to do so.

"I'm going to go, Dolores," I said.

"No . . ."

"I have to."

"Why?"

"I'll call you."

"Nicky..." Her voice got higher, and I feared she'd go to pieces right there in front of everyone.

"Be strong, Dolores. You're the only Candiotti in town. Get tough like they did."

She sucked in a ragged breath, but it seemed as though she were actually batting her eyelashes at me. "You mean," she said, "tough like *you* are."

"You have no idea," I said.

I stood on the sidewalk in front of Alfonso's house, trying to remember where I'd parked my car. When I did so, I turned right and started down the street. I heard footsteps behind me, though—I was far too used to hearing all the little sounds most normal people take for granted. Unarmed, I wrapped my gloved fist around the handcuffs in my pocket so I could use them as a striking weapon, then whirled around to face my pursuer. Mike LeBlanc was chugging down the sidewalk behind me.

"Wait up, Dominick," he called. I guessed he was no immediate danger to me, so I let go of the cuffs and took my hand from my pocket.

He caught up with me, then bestowed upon me a pitying smile. "Sorry again," he said, "for your loss. This is turning into a rough time for you, these last two weeks."

I just nodded. I was sick of thanking people for feeling bad about my brothers.

"You still figure to hang out here in Youngstown awhile longer?" he asked.

"What's the difference, Mr. Fed?"

He didn't smile. "You don't even know what I am."

"I don't *care* who you are. So should I tuck my tail between my legs and scoot back to where I came from?"

"I'm not warning you to leave town."

"Why's that?"

LeBlanc wrapped his overcoat around him. "Let's walk a little, okay?"

"You want to hold hands, too?"

He started strolling in the direction in which I was heading, toward my car. "You're always a smart guy."

I nodded. "As opposed to a dumb guy."

"You want revenge, right? For both your brothers."

I widened my eyes, trying to look like a vestal virgin. "Oh my stars, no, Officer. And I'll drive the speed limit, wear my seat belt, and I won't even spit on the sidewalk."

"Are you planning to kill somebody? To get even for Richard or Alfonso?"

"You should say Richard *and* Alfonso."

"If they were my brothers who'd died, I'd feel just the way you do."

I looked over at him. "Are you joking?"

"No. I believe American justice works. It just doesn't work all the time." Then he stopped walking and held up a hand. "Hey, I'm not out to kill anybody—at least not without a warrant."

"Federal warrant?"

He waited half a beat too long before he said, "Just talking—that's all I'm doing."

"So," I said, "if you had a warrant—not that you do, of course—but if you had a warrant to ice the motherfuckers who killed my brothers, who might they be?"

"I told you already; I don't know for sure. But Father Richard was on call whenever they needed him, to run errands. Nonviolent errands, naturally—but . . ." He shrugged. "As for Alfonso . . ." He looked down, watching feet go one in front of the other as we moved.

"Alfonso was on the Severino payroll, wasn't he?"

"I don't know that for sure, either. All I know's that he got that gold badge mostly for taking good care of the Severinos.

Just like you got your gold oak leaf for erasing highly placed Vietcong."

That stung, worse than I'd imagined. "Sucker punch, wasn't it? How do you know I was a major in Vietnam?"

LeBlanc shrugged. "I hear things."

"Apparently, you hear lots of things. So the Severinos took Al out?"

"Somebody took him out, Dominick. It wasn't an accident."

"Maybe," I said, "but it could have been the Mangiones, too. They've been feuding with the Severinos for most of this century. Maybe they got mad at Alfonso...."

"If the Mangiones were going to fiddle with a car, they wouldn't mess with a high-ranking police officer. It'd cause too much trouble."

"They'd take it to old man Severino, then."

"Or somebody almost as high up. But they didn't, so I don't think the Mangiones had anything to do with it."

"Polly Severino—Paolo junior—ordered the hit on my brother Alfonso?"

He shrugged again. We'd reached my car. "If I knew—*really* knew—whoever did it would be in custody."

"All right, then," I said. "Did the same person who blew up Alfonso also kill my brother Richard?"

LeBlanc held his hands palms up. "I already told you there was a subpoena to be served on Father Candy by RICO, but I don't know what it was about—or who was behind it. I'd tell you if I knew."

I mulled this over in my head for a while. Too many names, too many incidents. Finally, I took out my car keys. "Don't bother," I said. "I'll find out myself."

LeBlanc started to say something, then rapidly shut his mouth. He watched as I walked around the front end of my car, unlocked it, and slid in behind the wheel. When I turned the key in the ignition, nothing happened. I wasn't blown to kingdom come. Maybe the bombers didn't know my car—or maybe they just didn't give a shit.

They will give a shit, I thought, and drove away. Glancing in the rearview mirror, I could see Mike LeBlanc standing where I'd left him. Almost timidly, he was waving at me.

They will.

CHAPTER TWENTY-THREE

I'd decided to move back into the Holiday Inn for a few days, long enough to get through Alfonso's funeral. Now done with it, I stowed in various pockets all I might need for later in the evening and checked out again. The Holiday Inn bastards charged me an extra day because I didn't bid them good-bye before noon. I could have taken advantage and spent another night anyway, but I wanted out—out of Youngstown, out of the tattered remains of my family, out of the trouble into which I'd somehow gotten sucked.

Besides, if my name was next on the Youngstown Tune-Up list, there were too damn many people who knew at what hotel I was staying.

But I had things to do before I left town.

I stopped at a Woolworth and purchased things I thought I might need. I'd spent time hanging out in that five-and-ten when I was a kid, mostly at the lunch counter or, on occasion, boosting a toy or a baseball and walking out with my loot stuffed underneath my jacket. But this time, I actually paid for a box of clinging latex gloves, a roll of duct tape, and some strong rope. Then I headed out of town. I didn't know where

I was going—I had a lot yet to do, but not until much later that night—but my car somehow pointed its nose west.

I found a small motel off the highway in Lordstown. The clerk behind the desk was East Indian, his voice pattern that musical singsong. He didn't ask questions, though, nor did he offer me any information unless I asked, probably because I didn't strike him as the kind of guy who was looking for the Lordstown tourist attractions. It wasn't much of a town at all except for the gigantic General Motors plant, which kept almost everyone in that area who was not toiling in the steel mills the way my father had alive and working. I couldn't figure out why anyone would build a motel there anyway, except for people driving on the nation's interconnected highways; when it got to be a certain time of the evening and they couldn't sit behind the wheel, struggling with the deadening effect of white line fever a minute longer, they had to stay *somewhere*.

The room, overlooking the parking lot, was small but, under the circumstances, pleasant enough, and everything *looked* clean. I couldn't nap, I was too bored to watch TV, and I'd brought nothing with me to read. I went out and drove around for a while, looking at nothing. I stopped for dinner at a T.G.I. Friday's joint. Being a chain restaurant, it boasted the same menu in Lordstown, Ohio as those in every other state in the union. And it looked the same as all the others, too. My chicken sandwich with fries was knotting up my stomach. I washed it down with a beer, then went back to the motel.

I slipped on a pair of khakis, a T-shirt, and a casual sports shirt, then tried not to doze off in front of the TV. When the clock hit 1:00 A.M., I started getting myself together. I put on a mid-length windbreaker and a pair of boots I'd bought in Chicago. They weren't exactly cowboy boots with elevated heels and pointed toes, but they were heavy and sturdy. I checked all the things in my pockets that I'd brought from the Holiday Inn and bought at Woolworth, grabbed my suitcase, checked the road map I'd acquired at a gas station, and headed out into an unknown chill.

Half an hour later, there were hardly any lights illuminating Youngstown's streets. There was never any arguing with the darkness of a dangerous night—not where I was going.

A headache was pounding behind my eyes, but by the time I drove slowly past Severino's casino—not *too* slowly, in case I attracted attention—the headache was gone and I was perfectly calm. During my Vietnam years, my pattern had been one of feeling fear, followed by quiet stillness. When I'd crept down the dark streets of Saigon, I'd been completely in control. There'd been no nerves left. It was afterward, on the way back to safety and the officers' quarters, when my gut had always wrenched, twisted, thrust itself into my throat, and bent me over with cramps and nausea as I thought about what I'd done. I couldn't have told you accurately how many men I'd killed—and how many times I'd bent from the waist in painful cramps immediately afterward. Now I wondered if that would happen again—because I wasn't hunting total strangers in the worst parts of Saigon. I was after people I knew. How badly I'd hurt them, I didn't yet know.

The bright yellow casino was closed—it always shut down promptly at 1:30 A.M. because the police had actually asked the Severinos not to run an all-night gambling joint. There were eight cars parked in the front. I knew the big black Lincoln Town Car one space away from the main door must belong to Polly. The spot nearest the door was empty, but there was a big RESERVED sign posted there for whenever the old man showed up. A wide guy in a leather coat wandered the parking lot; I was certain he carried a weapon. On my second drive-by, when he'd turned the corner and was checking out the side of the casino, I slowed down long enough to take a good look at the turrets, which were usually manned by well-trained snipers. They were empty; the shooters had evidently gone home.

I knew if I left my car on the street, I'd be noticed within minutes, and if an on-the-pad cop didn't come by and ask me what I was doing there, I was certain a casino employee would. Instead, I parked around the corner, in front of someone's house, and walked quietly back to the casino, taking up a spot right across the street, an oak tree and a stand of chest-high bushes affording me a reasonable hiding place.

I waited.

It was only October, but I wished I'd worn a heavier coat instead of my windbreaker. My hands were encased in latex gloves. They didn't keep me warm, but they would conceal any fingerprints I might leave wherever I went.

At a few minutes past 2:00 A.M., the front door of the casino opened and eight men walked out. They were all big, and from what I could see, they all had telltale bulges on the left side of their jackets. But four of them also carried what we used to call "tommy guns"—handheld machine guns named after some poor son of a bitch named Thompson, who'd probably preferred to remain anonymous. The other four guys, the ones not holding weapons, each toted two large canvas sacks, taking the night's profits to deposit. The other four with them would ride shotgun. It wasn't safe to leave huge amounts of money inside the casino at night, and the Severinos were reluctant to trust armored trucks and well-heeled guards, preferring to rely on guys they knew, people they'd grown up with. That's one of the reasons those well-organized criminal gangs are referred to as "families."

The sack carriers and the armed companions split up into four teams, all the teams getting into their cars and firing them up at the same moment. Then the small convoy began a slow drive around the lot. I stepped back and squatted down behind the bushes, staying quiet and still until they passed through the open gate and disappeared into the darkness, heading downtown.

Twenty minutes later, the front door opened again and a

young woman emerged, wrapping her coat around her against the wind. Her hair, however, was already messed up, and there was regret in how she held her shoulders. I didn't recognize her for a moment, but when she turned to head for her car, I was shocked to recognize her as Taya—the cocktail waitress who'd brought me my drink several nights earlier. I'd tipped her with a fistful of cash because I'd feared she needed it. It made me sick to think she was evidently one of those women who, from time to time, helped Polly "relax" after a long and stressful evening—whether they wanted to or not.

When she got to her car, the wide guy patrolling the lot on foot broke into a lazy run so he could be there to open her door for her. They talked for less than a minute, and then she slid behind the wheel and started her engine. The patrol guy waved at the rear window as her car exited the lot.

I was sure Polly was still up in his second-floor office. There was no more money to count—it had all been carted off to the bank. And Taya was gone. I wanted to confront him, but I feared the two gorillas who usually guarded the stairway would still be around. Maybe they were all having a drink together.

I waited another half hour or so, until the bodyguards exited the building, their coats and suit jackets loosely open in case there was trouble. They stood in the doorway, smoking cigarettes, until Polly Severino came through the door to join them, puffing on a cigar.

He wore a suit under his trench coat, but no tie. His top two shirt buttons were undone. He talked to his bodyguards until he finished the cigar and threw it down on the driveway, crushing the stub with the toe of his shoe. They waited until the guy patrolling the lot drove Polly's personal vehicle up to where he stood, then jumped out and held the door open so Polly could get in.

He slumped in the driver's seat, idly playing a make-believe piano on the steering wheel, waiting while his bodyguards moved to their own cars. Then the three of them left the parking lot, a small parade, with Polly in the middle. I loped around the corner to my own car and, not turning on my headlights, followed the convoy at a discreet distance.

It took me only about five minutes to figure out where they were going.

Mill Creek Park is one of the most beautiful sections of Youngstown, with its rolling hills and profusion of trees and trickling creeks. Now, in October, it was wearing its most colorful seasonal outfit, leaves of bright yellow and orange and lustrous red—so spectacular that I could even appreciate its brilliance in the middle of the night. The homes within the park, upscale and then some, were hidden behind the foliage and the tree sentries that kept nonbelongers from slowing down and staring, or, even worse, invading the very private property of doctors, attorneys, business mavens, and the rest of Mahoning County's richest and most powerful citizens.

The streetlights along the road in Mill Creek Park were few and far between, but it was easier and safer for me if I kept my headlights off.

Polly's house, perched on the side of a hill, was white brick and flagstone, with picture windows in the front. It had probably been built less than thirty years earlier; it had a modern feel to it. Two floodlights on the lawn were aimed brightly at the front of the house and at the garage door on the right side. Had the trees all been cut down, Polly could have boasted about his spectacular view of downtown Youngstown, and probably in winter, when the leaves were all gone, there would be reason to look out the windows. During spring, summer, and fall, though, the house nestled gracefully in what might be described as a small forest. It wasn't as big a house as some others in Mill Creek Park, but Polly was a swinging bachelor who valued his privacy. Otherwise, his entire life was a party, every night, held among important people, high-level employees, and a cadre of beautiful women like the one I'd just seen leaving his casino.

He'd put his car to bed for the night, but the two hoodlums who'd followed him home had left their rides in the driveway. They'd entered the house through the garage, and twenty seconds later the garage door had lowered itself shut.

I parked my own car about forty feet past the house, positioned so that it pointed downhill, and strolled back to where I could look through the front window, now illuminated from within. A tired-looking Polly had taken off his coat and jacket. He helped himself to a drink of whiskey with no ice, then plopped down on the larger part of the sectional sofa to enjoy it. For a few moments, he chatted with the other two men—he talked; they listened.

I wanted to listen, too, but I was about fifty feet from the window. Still, I waited.

About ten minutes later, the two hoods seemed to be saying good night to Polly. Then they left—through the front door this time. They walked around to the side of the house, each getting into his own vehicle, and backed out of the driveway. I knew if they drove up the hill, they'd notice my parked car and know something was amiss, but they headed down instead. I wasn't surprised. Bodyguards who spend their lives wiping the snotty nose of a mob boss rarely reside on the top of a rolling hill in an elegant neighborhood.

I waited another five minutes, then moved closer to the house, keeping Polly in sight through the window. He was slumped into the soft sofa cushions, staring off at nothing, deep in thought. I couldn't imagine what went on in his head.

I took a few minutes to circle the house, until I found the terminal, on the back wall, to which his phone system was connected. I pried the door open with my gravity knife and pulled out the plug, then cut the head off. Nobody would be making a phone call from this house for some time.

Then I swung back around to the front. I heard music when I neared the door—Verdi grand opera. Unmistakable was the voice of Luciano Pavarotti, playing loud and brave. Italians like

Polly, having grown up amid wealth and faux sophistication, all loved Italian opera, especially when the tenor was singing. Low-class dagos like me came as close as we could, having grown up listening to Italian warblers like Jerry Vale, Frankie Laine, Don Cornell, and Julius LaRosa on the radio. Tony Bennett and Frank Sinatra were also Italian, but far too hip and musically sophisticated for families that worked in Youngstown steel mills.

I was glad Polly blasted the music. It enabled me to fiddle around with the lock pick for a few minutes without his hearing me. Finally, the door swung open quietly, and I stepped into a vestibule. I was still blocked from Polly's sight, although he wasn't paying attention anyway.

I stepped into the living room and cleared my throat. Polly looked up, startled. By the time he was on his feet, Do-Rag's gun was in my hand, pointing at the widest part of him. He said something tired and resigned, and I crossed the room to him in four strides and jammed the muzzle of my weapon up underneath his chin.

"Don't get excited, Polly," I said, "or you'll get dead."

Then I whacked him on the side of the head with the barrel, which put him on the floor—not unconscious, exactly, but stunned and pretty much out of things and unable to run away or defend himself.

Which was just fine—exactly how I wanted it.

CHAPTER TWENTY-FOUR

In the kitchen, I immobilized Polly Severino at his butcher-block table with handcuffs, rope, and duct tape. He didn't argue about it. When he first saw me in the living room, he simply muttered, "Oh, for Christ's sake," and lifted his hands shoulder-high. He wasn't overwrought, but the corners of his mouth drooped.

Eventually, I finished. I made him sit in a heavy kitchen chair, his ankles duct-taped together. His cuffed hands were out in front of him, tied tightly with a rope that passed beneath the butcher block twice and knotted the way I'd been taught when I functioned as an army Ranger in Southeast Asia. He wasn't going to wiggle out of those knots. I'd wrapped more duct tape around his chest and abdomen, pinning him upright against the back of the chair. He could move his head—and, more important, his mouth—but not much else.

The kitchen was, naturally, in the rear of the house, but I'd left the opera playing on his stereo, blasting away in the living room. Passersby wouldn't hear a thing over the music.

I sat down opposite him. I felt no nerves, no apprehension, and no worry about what would happen later, even when he said to me, "You're not gonna survive this, Dominick. Whatever you do to me, they'll hunt you down. Here, Chicago, or Timbuktu—you're a fuckin' dead guy."

"Timbuktu doesn't sound all that bad."

"Your porch light is out," Polly said easily. "You're a cuckoo bird. You're in love with Diane—the one you walked away from years ago—and now it makes you nuts knowing I'm the one's fucking her instead of you. She told me she told you—she tells me everything. Is that why you're messing with a guy like me—who can have you blown away for a buck and a quarter—over some cunt who hardly remembers you anymore? Go somewhere and spend the next ten years talking to a shrink."

I didn't say anything.

"I got lotsa broads," he continued. "Because I'm rich and I got clout, they're standing in line to spread their legs for me—nice, fresh young ones, too. But who am I to say no to Diane? Listen, pussy is my thing, but she's different. She's hot, and kinky as hell—up for damn near anything that won't draw blood or leave scars. Every time I fuck her, it's a different surprise." He made a sound that could have been a cruel laugh. "Did you find that out? Did you start up a return engagement with her and notice what she likes to do now that she didn't used to?"

"Shut up."

He breathed deeply, enjoying this, a smile hiding behind his face but visible in his eyes. "You like it when she puts that pretty little tongue of hers in places where the sun don't shine? You love when she whispers obscene things into your ear while she rides your dick? You like her biting and scratching? Or do you dig pulling out at the last second and shooting jizz all over her face? She loves when you do that, man."

I stood up, leaned across the table, and backhanded him across the mouth. His head snapped back, then forward again. Blood from inside his cheek ran down his chin, and he licked at it as best he could. "Hit a guy who's all tied up, and you got a gun. All balls, aren't you? Cut me loose and put your gun somewhere you can't reach it, and we'll see which one of us's got the balls."

"You're the dumb one, Polly. I've iced more men than I can remember, and never blinked an eye. You think killing you will bother me?"

"You gotta kill twenty more, then, because Diane's a real whore." He laughed, then spit out a mouthful of blood. "I'm not even jealous she's doing you since you come back here. She's just a piece of ass for whenever I feel like it. I couldn't care less who else's dick she sucks—and her dumb-shit husband don't care, either."

I sat back down. "This has nothing to do with Diane. I came here to hurt *you*, Polly—for a completely different reason."

Worry crept across Polly's eyes, and he managed to press his lips closed despite the cut inside. I asked him, "Who killed Alfonso Candiotti?"

He looked shocked by the question, but only for a second. "How sh'd I know?"

"Don't insult my intelligence."

"I don't know everything goes on in this town. I'm a smart guy, but I'm no genius. Besides, I got an alibi for the morning he died."

"You've never pulled a trigger in your life. You said so at the casino. You don't carry because you don't have to. And you don't sneak around wiring somebody's car to blow up when they crank the engine. You pay people to do that, just like you pay 'em for everything else."

"You're full of shit," he said. The security in his voice had flown away to hide.

"Not going to tell me?"

"I got nothing to tell. You can ask questions all fucking night, but I still got nothing to tell."

"We'll see about that," I said.

I reached into my pocket, pulled out the gravity knife, and

flipped it open with a *snick*. Polly Severino's eyes grew wide when he saw it, but he had no time to say anything—not to beg or to plead—before I leaned forward and cut off the index finger of his left hand.

It took the removal of two more fingers before he told me what I wanted to know. I didn't enjoy the process, but, push come to shove, I would have chopped off all of them—and whatever else I had to remove—to make him more cooperative.

The scariest part of it for me was that it didn't bother me in the slightest.

I wasn't into torture. I didn't like reading about people like Vlad the Impaler doing it in the sixteenth century—and even less what we all know about Hitler and Stalin. I wanted to believe all Americans were against torture, but I'd put in my time in Southeast Asia. My two brothers were dead, though, and I had to do whatever it took to find out who'd put them away—so I did it.

Do I sound like a monster? Vietnam had turned me into what I was, what I'd been ever since I came back to the States, except that I'd learned to control my anger. I hadn't raised my hand to another human being since then, not until coming back to Youngstown, but that didn't mean that I couldn't anymore. I wouldn't brood about Richard's and Alfonso Candiotti's violent deaths within a week of each other without doing something about it. Now, whether I liked it or not, it was part of my DNA.

Polly, the heir apparent to the powerful Severino mob family, was blubbering like a baby, watching blood pumping out of the stubs where his fingers had been moments earlier, as he confessed to me that Alfonso had been on the Severino payroll for many years—as adviser or consultant or facilitator. Al had never been asked or ordered to hurt anybody physically, because, Polly said, he was the "brain" guy. He argued, schmoozed, negotiated, and eventually threatened better than anybody else, and the family's enemies took it from him because it was less deadly than if they had to face the Severino punks directly. Al was a highly placed cop in a police department almost as corrupt as he was, and he came in handy for the Severinos.

None of that surprised me, even when I asked Polly about Al's semisecret bank account in Kansas City and he told me it was pure Severino money, laundered out of town and deposited halfway across the country. It was the cost, Polly said as his sobbing eventually lessened, of doing business.

Then why, I wanted to know, wasn't Al still walking around?

He blabbed too much, Polly admitted, about things that should have stayed within the family. He talked to too many people, including me, and there was a worry he'd say something incriminating to somebody *not* in the Severino corner, someone who could put all of them away for a long time.

"Meaning somebody who's not on your side in the department? Like who?"

Polly didn't know. He suspected, but he didn't know.

"And that's why you set up a Youngstown Tune-Up," I said. "To keep Alfonso's mouth shut, permanently."

His eyes filled with more tears, but this time I suspected he was crying over the death of my brother—which he had ordered. "Alfonso and I was friends," he whimpered, "ever since grammar school. We played poker every week together."

I nodded. "But this time, you dealt to him from the bottom of the deck."

His chin hit his chest and stayed there.

"When you told somebody to wire up his car, did you think about that friendship?"

Polly turned his face up to regard me, and the look in his eyes begged for mercy. His voice quivered. "I thought about it—plenty. But my job is looking out for my family. Family comes first, and Al wasn't family. I didn't hate him; I even loved him. But you gotta understand—business is business."

I'd put my weapons away—my gun in my waistband and

the gravity knife in my jacket pocket—but now I tingled from wanting to grab one and finish the job. I took a big breath instead and sighed it into the air of the kitchen.

"Al was *my* family, Polly—and this business is *my* business. So's Richard."

He stifled a sob. "I didn't have nothing to do with Richard, so help me."

"He worked for you, too. Alfonso told me that. He was an errand runner—a bagman—because nobody'd ever suspect a priest."

Polly nodded. "Yeah, yeah, but I never done nothing to him—and nobody in our family done, neither." He shook his head. "I never woulda—he was my *confessor*!"

"He was about a week away from getting subpoenaed to talk to the RICO guys in Cleveland," I said.

He looked stunned. "I didn't know nothing about that—about the RICO guys."

"They've been after your family for years. Decades."

"Yeah, but Richard wouldn't a known about that. He never did nothing but run errands for us, and we never gave him nothing for it, either. We donated money to the church instead—to Our Lady."

I studied his face the way I would've studied a calculus formula back in college, but I couldn't see any signs of his lying. "Who else was Richard doing favors for—so they'd donate to the church?"

He stared at what remained of his left hand—the thumb and the little finger. "Coulda been anybody."

"Don't fuck with me, Polly, or I'll cut you again, except this time it'll be your nose."

"Wait!" His voice rose in pitch and decibel, so it was almost a scream. I took a step back to let him know I was waiting. "My lawyer worked with him, too," Polly said, more quietly. "Stuff that didn't have anything to do with us."

"Stuff like what?"

"I dunno, but may I die right here on the spot if I'm lying."

I considered it, his dying on the spot. "Who's your lawyer, Polly?"

He sniffled. "Bob Burnham."

My spine stiffened. Bob Burnham—Diane's husband. He was Frank Mangione's attorney, too. He must have been playing both ends against the middle.

"He's my personal lawyer," Polly went on hurriedly. "I got him on retainer, but he does things I don't know about—'cause I don't give a damn about 'em."

"And he used Father Richard to run errands for him, too?"

Polly worried the idea in his head, then finally admitted he knew it was so. "Most of what Burnham does is legit," he said. "For different people, different business. I don't know, but he used Richard sometimes as a go-between."

"Going between who and who?"

"He never told me and I never asked."

I stood up. "I'm going to stop and see him next," I said.

"Wait a minute, wait a minute!" Polly was close to getting hysterical again, white spots of spittle on his lips and mucus running out of his nose, and he struggled against his restraints. "Are you gonna just leave me to bleed to death?"

What *was* I going to do with him? He'd ordered Alfonso killed—admitted it after I relieved him of his fingers. And he'd sworn that whatever I did to him, the Severinos would hunt me down and pay me back—with interest. The pistol at my hip was hot against the skin beneath my shirt, and everything in me wanted to take it out and use it. But would I shoot Paolo Severino, Jr., while he was tied up and helpless?

I couldn't very well turn him over to the cops, because most of them were on the Severino side anyway. But he was no stranger to me, unlike the higher-up VCs I'd assassinated during the Vietnam conflict. Polly and I had grown up together—played together on those Sundays at Meander Lake, or at least I'd watched while he and Alfonso played. That made his execution unthinkable, even though I hated his guts.

I moved behind him, so he had to crane his head around to look at me. "I *should* let you bleed to death—or, better still, put a cap in your head."

His chin was quivering. "I won't say nothing, Dominick. I swear to God—"

"Leave God out of this." I ran through options in my head. "Suppose I let you get up out of your chair and I just leave. What then?"

"Nothing," he said, shaking his head earnestly. He *was* being earnest at the moment, but I doubted his sincerity would last for very long. His nose was running, and he snorted loudly. "Jesus, I gotta get to a hospital."

"Shut up. Let me think."

He was imprisoned there, sobbing like a three-year-old. Part of me wanted to cut him up into even smaller pieces—the rest of his fingers and toes, his nose, his dick—before I cut his throat.

But that was just part of me.

The other part was that I was overtrained and sick of killing. I'd left the army and left Youngstown and my brothers and sister—and Diane—because earning those oak-leaf clusters had turned me into a hand-of-God murderer, and I couldn't bear being around my family or the woman I loved. Had I turned coldblooded? Maybe—or maybe I didn't have any blood at all.

"I'm ready to make a deal with you," I said.

He sniffled but looked interested.

"I cut you loose and go about my business. You make sure nobody bothers me while I'm in Youngstown, and nobody comes looking for me in Chicago. Understood?"

He nodded.

"Because if they do, I'll kill them where they stand. You know I can do that."

He nodded again.

"And if they get me before I get them," I went on, "I have friends in Chicago. If they get mad at you, somebody'll have to pack you up in small parcels of butcher paper. Tonight was a day at the beach compared to what they'll do to you."

His breathing got louder and faster.

"You had Alfonso killed. I'll never forgive you for that," I said. "So count yourself lucky tonight—and forget everything, or your luck's gonna run out fast. *Capisce?*"

"Yeah," he said, his head bobbing earnestly, like that of a puppy who'd just been promised a treat. "*Capisce.*"

"Don't fuck with me, Polly," I said. I walked around next to him and flipped the gravity knife open again, its blade now stained with his blood. His eyes were wide as saucers, and deep in his chest he made a whimpering sound over which he had no control.

I began cutting away the ropes and duct tape that immobilized him, starting with the strands around his neck and then working at his feet and ankles. The top of the butcher-block table was a mess, though, and neither one of us wanted to look at it. I was glad I'd worn my latex gloves all evening. They'd prevented my leaving fingerprints and saved me from touching anything gruesome with my bare hands.

When I'd finally finished, he had nothing to hold him except the cuffs binding his wrists together in front of him. "I'm leaving those on," I said.

"How do I explain wearing handcuffs when I get to the hospital?" he whined.

"Lie. Make something up. Be inventive."

His shudder was involuntary. He rose shakily to his feet and stumbled across the room to lean against the refrigerator. Shock had set in and his whole body trembled. "How could you do—*this*—to me?"

"How could you order Alfonso killed?" He didn't answer me. "Alfonso was corrupt, and I knew it," I said. "He was on your old man's payroll, and whatever else he did, that made him a dishonest cop. But he was my brother and I loved him, no matter what. And that makes you one lucky son of a bitch—because if you'd killed my other brother, Richard, you'd already be dead."

"I didn't do nothing to him...."

I put the roll of duct tape and the rope in the pocket of my jacket and picked up the gravity knife. Then I turned back to him. "Hope real hard, Polly, that I believe you."

And then I saw his face change. Behind the torture that had turned his mouth into a mask of tragedy, there was suddenly hope and even joy. "You shit-eating bastard!" he roared for the first time all evening, waving his cuffed hands in front of him, "You cut off my fucking fingers!"

I'd been in the killing business too long not to recognize an announcement when I heard it—which meant Polly was communicating with someone else. I spun around quickly and saw one of his bodyguards—the one named Chet—in the kitchen doorway. He was pulling his weapon from its shoulder harness. I knew I had only seconds to live if I didn't move even faster.

With one wrist snap, I freed the blade of the gravity knife and threw it backhand at Chet. It lodged perfectly at the front of his throat. He made a horrible gurgle, a noise rarely heard from another human being, and he dropped his weapon on the tile floor, raising both hands to stave off the blood shooting from his jugular. He stared at me, shocked for a second or two before the spark behind his eyes went out. He pitched forward, dead before he hit the floor, his blood spreading rapidly across the tiles.

Polly called me a dirty name. I think he'd hoped Chet would cap me before I even saw him. His enraged cursing didn't distract me from the idea that wherever Chet went, Vinny—his bodyguard partner—wouldn't be far behind.

"Get down, Polly," I said, "or you'll get hurt."

He crouched down under the butcher block with his head low; Polly Severino didn't want to die. I waited for Vinny to come through the door just like Chet had, but he surprised me. He was standing outside the kitchen window, just over the sink, and he smashed the glass in with the barrel of his gun and fired at the same time. The slug passed so close to my head, I actually felt the breeze.

I threw myself onto the floor, too, rolling onto my back to see where Vinny was. He'd disappeared from outside the window, which meant he could pop up anywhere. I pulled out my weapon—the one stolen from Do-Rag—flicked off the safety, and waited.

Under the butcher-block table, Polly whimpered. My glance at him was nanoseconds long. He'd put his mangled hand between his thighs as if to hide it, rocking back and forth, muttering obscenities under his breath. The blood from Chet's throat was advancing slowly across the floor.

Polly stopped moaning long enough to say, "You're dead, Dominick."

We're all dead. *When* depends on whose turn it is.

I didn't pay any attention to him. He was a wuss now—a chickenshit. I'd removed more than his fingers.

Vinny wasn't going to come in the same way Chet had. If he did, he'd have to step over Chet's body, and probably into his blood. Vinny wouldn't want to do that—and he'd blown his surprise by shooting at me through the window. That left the dumbass just one way to get into the kitchen and kill me. I changed my position a bit, ready for him, and zeroed in on my target.

It wasn't a shock. The door leading to the garage exploded open, and I knew Vinny was behind it, taking a second to look around. I wouldn't give him a second. I blasted three more bullets through the opened door, approximately at chest level, and heard the grunt of pain and the sucked-in gasp of panic. Then Vinny stumbled forward a few steps, clutching his bleeding chest with one hand, the other still holding his own automatic. He moaned, his finger tightening around the trigger. He fired one shot into the wall above the kitchen sink, then sank to his knees. He struggled there, trying to remain conscious, but didn't make it, slumping onto his side instead. His weapon trickled from his hand.

I thought he was dead, but I wasn't sure. I stood and went over to him, nudging him with my foot. There was no response. His eyes were half-open, staring up at nothing. Then I bent down and picked up his gun.

My fault, I guess, because with all the shooting and killing, I'd nearly forgotten about Paolo Severino, Jr. He reminded me when he launched himself out from under the table and with his good hand grabbed the late Chet's gun where he'd dropped it, spun around on his knees, and got off a clean shot at me.

Polly didn't have much of an aim, probably because he rarely held a weapon. The best he could do was send a searing fire through the fleshy part of my left thigh.

I'd never been shot before. Son of a bitch, it *hurt*. I fell back against the wall with gritted teeth while Polly, cursing at himself now instead of at me, took his time to make the next shot a good one. I didn't need that much time—I was a better shot than he was. I leveled Vinny's gun at Polly and drilled him right through the forehead.

The quiet was absolute, and I stood with one hand pressing down to stanch the flow of blood from my thigh, looking at the three men I'd just killed. I felt nothing about Vinny and Chet because to me, they weren't real people—just like the high-level Vietcong I'd assassinated. Polly, however, was another story.

For some reason—I've never figured out what—I'd wanted to spare him after he talked to me. He deserved to die, but I'd decided to walk away and let him live—until his bodyguards came back to the house and screwed everything up.

Those bodyguards cost Polly Severino his life.

I don't know if anyone nearby heard the shots, or even heard the sound system in the living room blasting Pavarotti singing Verdi in the middle of the night. Gunshots, especially from handguns, don't sound the way you hear them in the movies. They are more like staccato pops, like Fourth of July firecrackers. Still, I had to get out in case any of Polly's neighbors had identified gunshots and alerted the police.

I wadded up a kitchen towel, unzipped my fly, and slipped it into my pants, covering the entrance and exit wounds in my thigh as best I could. I wasn't seriously hurt, but I didn't want to bleed all over my car, either. I picked up all the guns, pulled the gravity knife from Chet's throat, and stashed the weapons in my pockets. I'd left no fingerprints, so there was nothing for me to clean up or wipe down. I took one last look in the kitchen, at the hellacious mess I was leaving.

"Sorry, Polly," I said. Looking back, I'm not certain that I spoke it aloud, but I was thinking it.

CHAPTER TWENTY-FIVE

At 5:30 in the morning, the sun had not yet made an appearance, but a smudge of light in the eastern sky allowed me to see the house—not nearly as elegant as Polly's in Mill Creek Park, but more affluent-looking than Alfonso's place. The style was Georgian, the brick facing a rich rust red color. The front windows overlooked the front lawn and a gently rolling incline to the road below. Al had made a good living as a police lieutenant, and raked in an extra hunk of change from the Severino mob every month, but his income wasn't even close to the pay of a corporation lawyer, so this particular home had been purchased with financial ease.

There weren't any lights on in the house—at that hour, practically no one was awake. I didn't care. This was to be my last stop in Youngstown. The place where the bullet had passed through my thigh was throbbing and pulsating, even though the bleeding had dwindled down to a slow seep. I couldn't hang around in this city any longer, but I had one more job. What might happen afterward, when either the police department or the Severinos figured out what I'd done, was a mystery on which I chose not to dwell.

I marched up the driveway to the covered porch and pounded

on the front door. It would have been easier to ring the doorbell, but I didn't want it to be easy. I didn't want the people inside gentled into thinking a friend was visiting too early for coffee.

My anger had peaked once again by the time the door opened. Bob Burnham stood there in his T-shirt and sweatpants beneath a dark blue robe hastily donned. He wasn't wearing bedroom slippers, and his eyes were still swollen from interrupted sleep. He had to stare at me for a moment before it dawned on him who I was.

"What the hell . . ." he said, but it was all he got out before my fist crashed into his nose. The blow was hard, my hand traveling no farther than eight inches, and to poor Bob Burnham, it was a surprise sucker punch. The United States Army had taught me all about guns and knives, but it was my growing up on Brier Hill that had trained me in how to fight hand-to-hand. I was surprised at how much pleasure his delicate nasal bones crushing against my knuckles gave me.

Burnham's eyes rolled up in his head, and for a moment all he could see was the ceiling. Crying out with shock, he stumbled backward into his entry hall and fell, sitting down hard. I stepped in and slammed the door behind me. Then I took out my gun and pressed the muzzle into his right eye.

"Say your prayers, Bob." It wasn't a suggestion. I meant it.

Diane came halfway down the stairs. She was wearing pajamas. Pajamas, for God's sake—not a nightgown or a teddy or anything remotely sexy. *Pink flannel* pajamas, topped by a terrycloth robe.

"Nicky!" she almost screamed. "What the hell are you doing?"

"Stay out of this, Diane. It's none of your business."

Bob was sitting up now, one hand trying to cover his face, and he made a funny sound that might have been "Aaaack!" His broken nose was bleeding a lot, red running down his upper lip and into his mouth.

Diane came all the way down and rushed to me, digging her

fingers into my shoulder, pulling at me. "Are you crazy? Don't hurt him, Nicky."

"It has nothing to do with you."

"It has everything to do with me," she said. "He's my husband."

"For maybe five minutes more."

Burnham mumbled something through his fingers.

"Don't be a sucker, Bob," I said through my teeth. "I guarantee I can make you tell me anything I want to hear within two minutes, so you'd better start singing like a canary." I wasn't feeling at all sorry for him. "You killed my brother—or had him killed. Didn't you?" And I ground the muzzle a little harder into his eye.

"Bob didn't kill Richard." Diane's voice was shrill, quivering, close to hysterical. "He wouldn't do anything like that. He *couldn't*."

Bob nodded enthusiastically.

"Don't either one of you bullshit me." I took the gun out of his eye but kept it pointed at his head. "Then who *did* kill him?"

"Richard killed *himself*," she said, pulling hard on my arm. "Everybody says so."

"Bob is bleeding all over your living room."

She stared at the bloodstain on my pants, and the entrance and exit holes where Polly's bullet had found me. "Nicky, you're hurt."

"You have no idea what hurt is." I lifted Bob off the floor and onto his feet.

Diane entreated with me awhile longer. I finally gave in reluctantly, and we all moved into the living room—but I never let go of the back of Bob Burnham's neck until I plopped him down in a chair and once more pointed the gun in his face.

"Talk to me now, Bob—or die."

Bob could do little more than hold his breath for about half a minute, his terrified stare moving from my face to the gun I pointed at him. He didn't find relief in either place. Eventually, he slumped back in the chair and wiped his nose blood on the sleeve of his robe. "What is it you want me to say?"

"You had my brother Richard on your payroll, didn't you?"

"I don't have a payroll," he said. "I work for a law firm."

"You're a partner."

"One of many partners. And none of us had Richard on a . . . payroll."

"He did work for you—personally." It wasn't a question.

Bob nodded.

"And you paid him for it."

"No! You think he had a seven-figure bank account in Switzerland?"

"He wouldn't work for nothing."

Bob's mouth had gone dry, and he tried licking his lips. "Every time he did me a favor, I dropped a couple hundred dollars into the basket they passed around on Sunday. He knew that—we set it up right from the start."

"Define 'favor.'"

"He—he moved money around from time to time, when we asked him to. Nobody would suspect a priest—and they had no reason to. Richard didn't know what the fuck he was doing for us."

"'Us'?"

Now not only scared to death and in pain, Bob looked very nervous, glancing around at nothing, finally locking eyes with his wife. Diane was leaning against the wall, arms crossed over her chest in a defensive pose, her mouth set and grim.

"Who's *us*?" I said, my voice louder.

"I—I do some legal work on the side. It has nothing to do with my law firm."

"'On the side'?"

"Favors," Bob Burnham said. "Don't you understand, Nicky? The world operates on favors. Especially Youngstown."

With my free hand, I slapped his face. Not that hard, but enough to sting—and the sound of it was like a rifle shot. "Don't call me Nicky, you little prick. My name's Dominick—assuming I let you live long enough to use it again. Who are you working for—on the side—that you got Father Richard involved with?"

"Friends, businessmen," he said vaguely.

I slapped him again.

"Don't play coy with me, or I'll emasculate you right here while your wife watches me do it. *What* friends and businessmen?"

He looked even more miserable. "Well, uh, I personally represent Don Severino sometimes. For stuff that doesn't go through my law firm."

"What did he have to do with my brother's death?"

"Nothing. He loved Richard like a son. Richard would never accept money on his own, but the don gives a fortune to that church every year. I thought you knew that."

"Who else do you represent—on the side?"

Diane said, "Nicky, you can't ask Bob things like that. He's an attorney. Didn't you ever hear of lawyer-client privilege?"

"Didn't you ever hear of getting tortured to death?" I snapped. "I'll cut off little pieces of your hubby here, one by one, until he gives up the idea of lawyer-client privilege." I turned my head to look at Diane. "Don't think I'm just trying to scare you," I said. "I've done it before."

"My God," Diane said, and covered her face with her hands.

"Who else, Bob?"

"Could I have a drink of water?" he asked, sounding like he really needed one.

"I'm not your fucking headwaiter. Who else do you work for—off the books?"

"Uh, every so often for the Mangiones."

"Frank Mangione? You're playing both mobs against each other. I've heard of slimeballs before, but they should frame you. Did Mangione put out a hit on Richard?"

"God no! The old man, he wouldn't hurt a fly anymore. He loved Father Richard, too."

"So what are you doing with him?"

He couldn't stifle a sob, which started his nose bleeding again. "Oh God, Dominick, I can't tell you that. . . ."

I switched my gun to my left hand and dug my gravity knife out of my jacket pocket and flipped it open. Bob immediately noticed the recent bloodstains. "Don't say what you can and can't tell me."

He moaned, writhed in the chair. A wet spot appeared in the crotch of his sweatpants and began to spread. How humiliating it must have been for him to piss his pants in front of his wife. "Don't make me ask you again," I said.

"Okay okay *okay!*" His hands fluttered like hummingbirds in front of his face. I gave him another half minute to marshal his thoughts. Finally, he said, "Have you ever heard of a pyramid game?"

"I haven't been living at the bottom of a coal mine, stupid. In Chicago, we call it a 'Ponzi scheme.' They pay off the initial investors with money they're stealing from the Johnny-come-latelys investors, the little guys with a few thousand to spare to make themselves new-rich. The Ponzi geniuses screw over people with big money who are trying to make even more big money without getting off their asses—not the nickel-and-dime guys who shoot fifty cents on the bug with the Mangione family—or with the Severinos, either. So you're the front guy, the one who knows all the rich people."

He didn't answer.

"Richard found out about it," I said. "And you knew the feds were within minutes of handing Richard a subpoena to come to Cleveland and talk to the RICO commission. So you killed him to keep him from blabbing, from naming names."

"I didn't," Burnham said, and started to cry this time—real tears. "I'm not the front guy anyway. I'm a lawyer, for God's sake. I wouldn't put my name on something like that. I was only doing legal work, like any other lawyer, and getting paid commensurate with my job. I wasn't selling shares that weren't worth a goddamn thing."

"Then who was?" I said. "Who knows even more big shots in Mahoning and Trumbull counties than you do?"

He looked imploringly at Diane, but she was chewing on her bottom lip and didn't even meet his eyes.

Then he told me. There'd been a lot of surprises since I'd arrived in Youngstown for Father Candy's funeral, but this one really took me unawares. It meant I had one more errand to run.

I put the gun away. I even pocketed the gravity knife. Then I tied both of them up, their hands behind them and their ankles duct-taped tightly together, and left them comfortably trussed up in the living room—Diane on the sofa and Bob where he'd been perched ever since I put him there. If he had to spend time sitting in his own urine, it was his problem.

Then I warned them both that if they moved a muscle for the next two hours, I'd be back to finish the job—on both of them.

I was heading for the front door when Diane said, "You wouldn't hurt *me*, Nicky. You'd never hurt me." The tone of her voice had dropped to a low purr. It would have been sexy under other circumstances. Not this time.

I turned toward her. "I'd hurt you in a second if I had to."

She looked shocked. "You don't mean it. My God, we have a history," she said.

"History is the Battle of Gettysburg. It's the Duke of Windsor's copping out on being king of England, giving up the throne for the woman he loved. It's Babe Ruth and his sixty home runs. It's Joe Louis and Johnny Unitas, and FDR's getting elected president four times. But you and I? We're not history. We're just something that happened to each other when we were very young."

"And since you've been back in Youngstown?"

"Jesus!" Bob said. I knew he and Diane weren't sleeping together anymore, that they'd both moved on to other people and functioned in this make-believe marriage for the hell of it, but it still rattled him to hear about Diane and me again.

"A blink of an eyelid out of time. It's over. We're over."

"We don't have to be." She leaned forward as far as she could without falling off the sofa.

"You're over already, Diane. I'm over, too," I said as I walked out the door. The sun was all the way up when I stepped outside, but it was hidden behind the clouds. As soon as the light and fresh air hit me, I knew that what I'd said to Diane, I meant.

It was to be another gray northeast Ohio day. I glanced at my watch involuntarily. I'd have to hurry to take care of my last self-assigned mission. But before I got back into my car, I went around to the back of the Burnham house and sliced the telephone connections so that on the outside chance they got loose, they wouldn't be able to call and warn anyone.

That's why I'd tied them up so tight.

It was about twenty minutes before eight. I hadn't slept, but I wasn't a bit tired. After I left the Burnham house, my thigh had stopped bleeding. I drove clear to the other side of town, pulled up beside what used to be a warehouse near Crab Creek, and changed my pants. I threw them behind a rock pile, fairly certain no one would discover them for days, or even weeks.

I got downtown just after eight, parked my car several blocks away on a side street, and strolled almost casually toward the building I'd only visited once before. I'd hoped fervently I'd not have to go there again.

I didn't go inside. I found the parking lot where the important officials left their cars every morning, crouched down comfortably beside a Mahoning County GM van, and waited. I didn't have to wait long.

A Cadillac that looked brand-new—burgundy-colored, newly waxed and polished, with tinted windshield and side windows—pulled into the lot and eased into a numbered reserved spot. I couldn't help noticing the personalized Ohio license plate. It contained three numbers—I didn't know what they meant—followed by the letters *ADA*. The driver—an assistant district attorney—got out, locked his car with a remote control, and started toward the exit, heading for the county building with a jaunty step. He was startled when I stepped out from behind the truck and confronted him.

"Good morning, David," I said.

David Ratner stopped dead in his tracks. "Dominick?" he said. "What brings you here at . . ." He looked at his watch, but I didn't give him time to answer, because I didn't give a damn what time it was.

"I'll tell you all about it," I said, and quickly moved behind him, standing far too close for his comfort, "while we take a little ride in your car. What do you say?"

"I can't go anywhere with you," he said, like someone who considered himself important. "I have a busy schedule this morning. What's all this about?"

He couldn't see over his shoulder, but I jammed my gun hard against his back. That got his attention. "It's all about whether I shoot out a big chunk of your spinal cord," I said. "On the off chance it won't kill you, you'll never walk into Severino's casino with another one of your bimbos ever again. Get back in your car and sit in the passenger seat. If you make the smallest fuss, I'll kill you right here. Have I made myself clear?"

I slid in quickly behind the wheel, taking the keys from him and starting the car.

"Where the hell are we going?"

"Sightseeing," I said. "Don't worry—I'll wake you when we get there." Then I reached over and smacked him as hard as I could with the gun, on the side of his head, just above the left ear. His eyes practically crossed, then closed, and his chin dropped down against his chest. Scalps, I'd read somewhere, bleed easily and copiously, so it wasn't thirty seconds until the left side of his face was red with his own blood.

In order to keep him out cold so he wouldn't cause me any further trouble, I had to hit him twice more as I drove out of the downtown lot, out of Youngstown proper, and into another world.

CHAPTER TWENTY-SIX

Frog Alley isn't a place most Youngstowners know. I vaguely remembered going there with my old man to fish—I must have been about eight. Otherwise, I wasn't even sure where it was, and not until now did I have a reason to care. Even locals who are vaguely familiar with the name consider it terra incognito, a place of mystery. But I'd found it—or at least its roads and coordinates—on the local map in my car before I'd parked it and hijacked David Ratner's Cadillac.

Frog Alley is more than rural—it's practically primitive, tucked away in the northwest corner of Mahoning County, between Bloomfield and Mesopotamia. The rumor says that during the Prohibition era, several saloons, casinos, and sleazy brothels operated in Frog Alley for the benefit of two counties, but I have no proof. Today, it's not much more than a swamp, running east to west on State Route 87, between SR 534 and SR 46—a real gone-to-hell Dumpster of an area noted for huge dead trees, copperhead snakes, stagnant backwater, a pervasive rotten smell that hangs in the air like eternal fog, and a host of slithery, creepy swamp creatures—including noisy ubiquitous frogs, which probably gave the neighborhood its nickname. On SR 87, I noticed a tiny run-down general store and a few pockets of falling-down houses close to being condemned and then destroyed. Hardly anyone ever goes to Frog Alley, unless they're looking for privacy and secrecy.

It's not a jungle—there is no jungle in Ohio—but the stories, myths, and legends about Frog Alley, like the fearful imaginings about an old haunted house on the next block, reminded me of Vietnam in-country, where anybody could do anything they damn well wanted to and get away with it.

That's why I'd picked Frog Alley—so I could visit quietly and privately with David Ratner. I'd come home to Youngstown to grieve and to bury a brother. I'd wound up mourning and burying a second brother, and that made me want to get answers. I'd find them in Frog Alley, or else I'd never get them anywhere.

I wasn't certain of the spot I was looking for—only the general type, hidden from view of the rest of the world. Finally, after cruising around for fifteen minutes without seeing a car, house, or another soul, I spotted a grove of willow trees abutting what looked like a tiny lake but was really a stretch of bad-smelling backwater. I figured if I pulled Ratner's Cadillac around behind the trees, no one would see it from the road. No one would hear him yell, either.

I hauled him out of the car—he was still out cold—stretched him out on the damp grass, and removed his shoes and socks. I duct-taped his hands together behind him, then his ankles. The willow limbs overhead were so thick that the rays of the sun never reached the ground. Most of Frog Alley was a nightmare of perpetual twilight.

I slapped his cheeks lightly, trying to wake him up, but the last time I'd banged his head in the car, I think I'd hit him too hard. I took the elegantly ironed handkerchief from the breast pocket of his suit—assistant district attorneys always wear elegant decorative hankies—dipped it into the muddy backwater, and squeezed it over his head. He woke up sputtering, coughing, and gagging. When he spit most of it from his mouth, he sucked in a ragged breath. I took rough hold of the lapels of his raincoat and suit and pulled him into an upright position, then dragged him about six feet and propped him up, his back against a tree.

He battled manfully to get his deep breathing under control before he could talk. I waited, in no hurry.

Eventually, he summoned from within all the arrogance and self-important dignity he had left. "I don't know what you think you're doing, but you're out of your mind. I'm the assistant district attorney."

"I'm shivering with fear," I said quietly.

"What is it you want? Money? I'm not rich, but maybe I can help you out a little."

I laughed aloud. That made him annoyed. "Well, what is it, then?"

"You knew my brother Richard."

"Of course I knew him. I told you that. I didn't know him well, because I'm not a Catholic and never went to his church. But he was an important man in town—like me. So we ran into each other often—at meetings and things. That was it, though."

Ratner could keep his cool, and mentally I awarded him a few extra points for it. Not enough points, though. "He didn't work for you?"

"Why the hell would a priest work for an attorney?"

"That's what you're going to tell me."

"There's nothing to tell."

I moved closer to him, standing over him. "There's a lot to tell. You'll talk eventually—I guarantee that."

His eyes narrowed and he drew himself up as much as he could, considering he was trussed up and sitting in the damp grass against a tree trunk. "Are you stupid?"

"Tell me about Richard's subpoena."

That got to him, but he was acting his heart out, shooting for an Oscar, and made a grand try at not understanding. "There was no subpoena I knew about. And I would know, because I'm—"

"Yeah, yeah—you're the assistant district attorney. Don't bullshit me. You're in no position to bullshit."

His put-upon sigh crackled in the cold morning air. "Read my lips." Slowly, enunciating each syllable, he said, "There—is—nothing—to—tell."

I tried not to let this get to me, but I was feeling a big hole of nothing where my stomach used to be. I shook my head sadly at him, and then I stamped the heel of my boot hard on the shoeless toes of his right foot. In the preternatural silence of Frog Alley, his scream of pain echoed and resounded like someone in the Alps shouting hello into a vast canyon. His upper body rocked from side to side, he tossed his head back and forth as he screamed, and he managed to raise both his knees close to his chest. I gave him all the time he needed; I wasn't going anywhere.

When his howls and squeals faded away to hoarse groans, I said, "That was one foot, Mr. Ratner. Want to try for two?"

"You broke my fucking toes!" he whined.

"That was only the first inning."

He snarled through teeth clenched in agony, "What do you want from me, then?"

"What was my brother Richard doing for you?"

"I keep telling you . . ." His eyes grew wide as saucers as I moved toward him, my eye on his undamaged foot, and he changed his mind in one hell of a hurry. "No, no!" he pleaded. It must have been difficult, hurting so badly, completely terrified, and stammering over a simple word like *no*.

"Don't lie to me, then. There are so many interesting parts of your body I can cripple, one by one, until I hear the truth."

"What truth?"

"Let's start," I said, "with the Ponzi scheme."

Ratner flirted with the idea of more resistance, until he realized it would be futile. It took him almost a minute before he bowed his head and his shoulders began to shake. He was weeping, quietly and softly. When he was all cried out, he sniffled, shook his head to clear his brain, and told me what I wanted to know.

Initiating the pyramid game had been David Ratner's idea to begin with. He'd talked one of his superwealthy clients, a rock-ribbed ultraconservative named Rogan Smythe, who owned some of the larger and more profitable coal mines in eastern Ohio and western Pennsylvania, into contributing his name and prestige to the initiation of a hedge fund, being "out front" for a piece of the package without doing a damn thing, so that Ratner, a well-known and relatively powerful but not-too-rich assistant district attorney in Mahoning County, would never be involved. This was his personal deal, a simple and effective con in which he'd steal from Peter to pay Paul for as long as he could, taking a big portion for himself with every transaction.

To keep his name out of it, naturally, he wanted someone everyone in the world could trust to handle the day-to-day business, someone who had nothing to do with Wall Street or with the Securities Exchange Commission, a government watchdog that might get too interested and launch an investigation. And who was more trusted—more loved and admired, even—than Father Richard Candiotti?

Ratner assured me, when I pressed him, that Richard had never pocketed a nickel, because Ratner had made sure that every time he made a handsome deposit in his own Cayman Island savings account, he contributed 5 percent to several different local Catholic charities Father Richard recommended, like the ones emanating from the Diocesan office in Youngstown. Ratner never missed bestowing a generous gift on the do-good fund at Our Lady of Perpetual Sorrows.

He also told me that neither Frank Mangione nor Paolo Severino had any knowledge of my brother Richard being an unwitting bagman for the Ponzi scheme.

Poor Richard. Poor vague, clueless, honest-to-Jesus Richard, who never had a glimmer that what Ratner was doing was illegal. He thought the rich people who were buying shares were being allowed to "get in on the ground floor" of an idea that couldn't miss making money. David Ratner went through the motions of being an assistant DA, but he was much more interested in raking in cash on the side, hand over fist, until, he swore, he'd have twenty million dollars in the bank—other people's money. He'd created the hedge fund three years earlier, and figured it would take another four or five years until he'd discreetly reached his monetary goal. Then he'd quietly slip out of the country to someplace in Central America, a sovereign country like Costa Rica that didn't maintain an extradition treaty with the United States, and live like a king for the rest of his life. Even if the Youngstown mobs did find out where he was, they wouldn't care, as none of them was being bilked by Ratner's phony game. They might be irritated that someone made a ton of money and didn't let them in on it, but they wouldn't care enough to bother about it in some faraway country.

I wanted to know how Ratner knew about the impending subpoena that would blow the roof off his illegal scam.

"Rogan Smythe told me," he said. "The man who fronts the hedge fund."

"And how did *he* know?"

Ratner shrugged helplessly. "It's a mystery to me. He delivers coal, which keeps this country moving along. Because of that, he has connections in every department in Washington, so somebody tipped him off—but he didn't tell me who."

"Smythe was to be subpoenaed?"

He shook his head. "Richard was the only name I know of that the feds got hold of. Smythe had his ways—and his lawyers and his wealth. So he figured he'd be clean—unless Richard blew the whistle on him."

"And Richard?"

"Richard didn't know anything about testifying to the SEC and the FBI in Cleveland about the . . . help he was giving me. Not until about three weeks ago."

"Who told him?"

David Ratner turned his bleeding, tear-streaked face away from me in what I perceived as shame. "*I* did," he said.

He admitted that he'd talked things over with Richard at Our Lady. He'd confessed—not a Catholic confession, because Ratner was a nonpracticing Jew, but a confession nonetheless—that he and Smythe were running the pyramid scheme, and that if it ever got out, both of them would go to prison. Smythe owned more coal mines than anyone knew about, Ratner said. He sold the hell out of the idea to Richard, telling him that if Smythe were forced to give up his CEO perks for a gray canvas jumpsuit and an eight-by-ten cell, everyone in the entire Ohio-Pennsylvania area would suffer all winter long for years to come because there'd be no one left to mine, sell, and ship the coal. The miners who worked his mines would lose their jobs. Kids would go hungry.

He laid it on even thicker—the people who'd invested to begin with, the few honest rich ones who wouldn't be screwed when all their money disappeared, would go to prison, too—and they were *really* innocent.

I think Ratner was trying to convince me, too.

"And what about you?" I said. "You'd go down, too."

He tried not to grimace from the pains shooting up his leg from his broken toes. "Only if Richard testified against me. I told him the truth—that I had a boy graduating from high school next spring, and a daughter who's a sophomore at Temple, and they'd be destroyed and their lives ruined if I wound up taking the fall."

"Richard's life would be destroyed, too."

Ratner paused before answering. "Maybe not," he said, "if he could convince the SEC that he didn't know a goddamn thing about the Ponzi scheme."

"But you didn't tell him *that*, did you?"

Ratner shook his head—not a negative shake, but as if he was trying to clear the ringing in his brain from the three times I'd knocked him unconscious. "I told him he'd go to jail and be kicked out of Our Lady forver—and that every Catholic in the Midwest would hear about it, be disappointed in their beloved Father Candy, and maybe turn away from the Church altogether. I said the bishop's career would be wrecked if Richard testified. Monsignor Carbo's, too, because Carbo was Richard's friend and mentor."

I flexed my fingers. I wanted to hold something with which I could hurt David Ratner very badly. "So," I growled, "you killed Richard to keep him quiet."

The assistant district attorney's face grew even paler, and I could see white all around the pupils of his eyes. *Sanpaku,* some Asians call it—meaning "complete and unmitigated fear." "I didn't. I swear to God I didn't."

"Who did, then?"

"He killed himself—he took his own life." The answer came quickly.

"Where'd he get the gun? Priests don't have guns. Where'd he get it?"

Ratner didn't respond. His head was bowed so low, it nearly disappeared into the concavity of his chest.

"You gave it to him, didn't you?"

He raised his face to look at me, and I was shocked by his dead eyes. Ratner had already put one foot in Hell—and knew it.

"Committing suicide wasn't his idea, was it? He was ready for that subpoena. He knew he'd get in trouble and go to jail himself, but that was okay with him because he'd done something wrong, even though he didn't realize he had. Somebody talked him into it, didn't they?" My fury was boiling over. "The one who gave him the gun!"

I couldn't help myself anymore. I drew back my booted foot and kicked him viciously in the ribs, hearing a few of them snap like pencils. He screamed again and fell over onto his undamaged side.

"Did you meet my brother in the middle of that last night—secretly, down in the basement? Did you tell him where to aim the gun? Or did you do it your fucking self?"

Ratner's voice was almost gone, and I could barely hear him through his gasping and his crying. "I didn't want that, Dominick. I didn't *want* it!"

"But you made sure he was dead before you went home. Didn't you?" Another vicious kick, this time to his stomach. *Didn't you?* My voice echoed someplace, bouncing off the thick trees and coming back to me.

I have no idea how long David Ratner continued to blubber tears and mucus. Time wasn't important to me. Finally, his sobbing wore itself out and he was quiet. Then he said again, this time in a little voice, "I didn't want it."

"What happened then?"

His lips quivered, as if he was trying to speak but nothing would come out. Finally, he said, "I told him—I said we just couldn't let him go to Cleveland and testify. I tried to talk him into shooting himself—swear to God I did. But he wasn't buying any of it. He couldn't. Priests couldn't. So—well, Richard was praying. He was kneeling on the floor down there in the basement, and he had his eyes closed and he was praying in a whisper. I—well, he had his eyes closed. So he never knew—he didn't expect me to . . ."

He lowered his head again, as if I'd been beating him. Then he looked up quickly. His face seemed almost peaceful.

"It was wrong, I know. It was the hardest thing I ever had to do in my life. But I prayed with him, honest to God. I prayed right along with him. I pray differently. But I was there to support him. I prayed with him."

I stepped away from him and put my hand in my jacket pocket. Do-Rag's weapon felt cold against the palm of my right hand.

"Well, I'm not going to pray with *you*, David," I said.

One shot to the back of his head was all it took. I'd like to tell you it didn't even ripple across my conscience, but I had plenty of ripples because David Ratner had caused the death of my brother. That had nothing to do with conscience, not even the way my wet work in Vietnam had made me guilty. This was pure, simple revenge, and it made me feel pretty damned good.

Afterward, I took his wallet, checked it for anything interesting, but all I discovered beside credit cards, club membership cards, a driver's license, and a wallet-size photograph of his family was $128 in cash. I put it in my pocket. The bullet hole in my leg was hurting like crazy. I puttered around until I found some solid rocks to stuff into the pockets of his suit and raincoat before I dragged David Ratner's body to the edge of the backwater and rolled him down the embankment. With a very large dead limb, I shoved him farther into the water, until he sank and disappeared. No gas bubbles marked where he'd last been in the light of the sun. Then I tossed the limb in on top of him to keep him from surfacing too quickly.

Walking out of the hidden grove of willows and backwater, I wasn't sick to my stomach this time—no nausea, no cramping. What I'd done that night and morning had to be done. Italians like me always understand about vengeance.

I got into his car and headed back the way I came—but I couldn't drive it to the lot where he parked every morning. I had a plan in my head, and I hoped like hell it would work.

I pulled the Cadillac off the road behind another stand of

willows, those on the opposite side of the road. Then I took Ratner's shoes and socks and his set of keys, walked across the deserted road to the backwater, and tossed them as far as I could. I was at least two miles from where I'd left him—and there wasn't much of a current.

Then I started walking. After about fifteen minutes, every step I took reminded me that I should have seen a doctor. Fortunately, my thigh wound had crusted over. No matter how badly it hurt, no one could tell I'd been shot just by looking.

By the time I got to the little ramshackle store on SR-87, I was limping.

I bought a package of Hostess Ding Dongs from the laconic proprietor, who didn't wonder where I'd come from, or wasn't curious enough to ask. Fishing in my own wallet, I pulled out a business card, went outside to a phone booth that hadn't been cleaned in years, and dialed the number. The voice that answered was very familiar to me, and that was a fortunate thing, because I'd been thinking about him even before I drove David Ratner out to his final encounter in Frog Alley.

"Mr. Pellegrino?" I said. "Umberto Pellegrino? This is Dominick Candiotti—remember, I had dinner in your restaurant the other night?" I listened. Umberto was thrilled to death to be talking to me—to the son of his friend, my father, and to the brother of his late departed priest. "Sir, I hate like hell to ask you this, but you said at dinner that if I ever needed help, you'd be there for me. Well, I'm hoping you can do me an enormous and time-consuming favor—and not ask me any questions."

CHAPTER TWENTY-SEVEN

The first thing I did when I got back to Chicago was to call an Italian friend of mine from the West Side—he was up in his seventies somewhere and still remembered the days of Al Capone—who knew some discreet doctors, one of whom cleaned out my gunshot wound, sewed up the exit hole, gave me a tetanus shot, and completely forgot about everything after I gave him a thousand dollars in small bills. The second thing I did was to rent a typewriter, an IBM Selectric, from a shop in the northern suburb of Evanston. Then I typed out what I hoped would be an untraceable letter to someone at the Securities Exchange Commission in downtown Cleveland, telling them all I knew about the mysterious Rogan Smythe, his Ohio and Pennsylvania coal mines, and the Ponzi scheme he'd been operating for several years.

After that, I went about my business—my construction business—where I labored designing medium-priced homes for Chicagoans. I was lonely, more than I'd ever been since I got out of the service, and seriously considered buying a dog—a big one, like a Saint Bernard or a Great Pyrenees or a borzoi. I love big dogs. But I love little ones, too—pugs or dachshunds or just plain old raggedy mutts who only want to lick your face. I held off, though, because I thought that any day I'd be visited by someone from the Youngstown Police Department, perhaps Capt. Ed Shemo himself, who would arrest me for murder (or murders), and haul me back to Ohio in chains to stand trial.

I also half-expected someone from the Severino mob to drive by and cut me down with machine-gun fire.

No surprises, though. After three months back home, I'd managed to shove most of the events in Youngstown into an unused portion of my brain, and I stopped worrying about it altogether—until the day after Martin Luther King, Jr.'s birthday.

I'd more or less cleaned off my desk except for a sketch of thirty-four acres in Schaumburg, where we planned on building sixty new homes. I was giving it one last look, studying the terrain, the streams, the existing trees, the hills and slopes. Then I looked up, and Mike LeBlanc was standing in the doorway.

"Hello, Dominick," he said, and smiled.

My first reaction, upon seeing him, was relief that I hadn't purchased a dog. What the hell would I do with the poor guy when I got packed off to prison? "Hello, Sergeant LeBlanc. Welcome to Chicago."

"Thanks, but I've been here before. A couple of times. I've seen the Cubs play at Wrigley. I've gone up to the top of the Sears Tower. I even sat for a while in Grant Park once and watched the Buckingham Fountain. It's a good city to visit. As long as I'm here, can I treat you to dinner?" he said. "There are great restaurants here. I think the best Chicago pizza I ever had was at Lou Malnati's. You been there?"

"All the time. They serve great pizza—not the kind you roll up and eat with your fingers, like in New York. You need a knife and fork. But—I'm not hungry right now."

LeBlanc laughed. "Is the sight of me ruining your appetite?"

"Not at all." I lied.

"Okay, then, let me buy you a drink."

I gave it some thought. If I were to get arrested, I didn't want it to happen at a bar in Chicago, especially one I frequented. I said, "Come back to my place, and I'll buy *you* a drink."

Then it was LeBlanc's turn to think about it. "Why not," he said at last.

I had to drive him to my home because he'd gotten to my office via a taxi. I chose not to think about how he might handcuff me in my living room and call a cab.

We wound up sitting on matching sofas, facing each other, next to a bay window that looked out in the direction of Lake Michigan. We couldn't see the lake from there, but it felt as if we could. Pabst Blue Ribbon and Iron City are the brews of choice in Youngstown, but here in Chicago, where most of the locals also drink PBR or Hamm's, I always enjoy Goose Island, made by a local brewery. We cracked two of them and silently toasted each other. "Nice place, Dominick," LeBlanc said. "Private. You didn't invite me here to shoot me, did you?"

I don't laugh very often, but that one tickled me. "Why the hell would I shoot you?" I said. "You're a cop. I don't shoot cops."

"Well," he said, scratching his chin, "I'm *kind* of a cop." He reached into his inside jacket pocket and took out a leather folder, flipping it open so I could see his identification as a special agent with the Federal Bureau of Investigation.

I'd been right about him from the start—not that it'd help me one way or the other. "I don't shoot feds, either. I used to be one."

"And they made you a major?"

He'd done homework. I wondered if he knew what I'd done for my ongoing assignment as a major. "FBI," I said. "Impressive. All this time you were just pretending to be a sergeant with the Youngstown PD."

"Sort of."

"I thought all the cops were bent, just like everyone else."

LeBlanc gave me an innocent smile. "If somebody in Youngstown is bent, call the police. If the police are bent, call us."

Sure, I thought. "So what brings you to Chicago? The Cubs won't be playing for another three months—and Malnati's has great pizza, but not so good that you'd come all the way from Youngstown for a pie."

"I came to see you."

"Missed me, did you?"

"You left town pretty quickly."

"After funerals for both my brothers in one week, I wanted out of there."

"I understand," LeBlanc said. "I wanted to catch you up on a few things, in case you haven't been reading the *Vindicator*."

"I read the *Chicago Tribune*. This is where I live."

"Well, here's the Youngstown news, just in case you missed it." He drummed his fingers on his thigh. "Let's see—the gang war kicked up again."

"Oh?"

"Somebody killed Polly Severino and two of his soldiers."

"Wow," I said.

"Nobody knows who capped him and his guys—it happened in his kitchen, by the way, and one of the guys got stabbed in the throat instead of shot—but the Severinos got suspicious that the Mangione family was behind it. So one of the Mangione capos got machine-gunned while walking out of Franco's one night. You know how that works. Revenge."

"Too bad."

"Well," LeBlanc said, "it is and it isn't."

" 'Splain, Lucy," I said.

"The FBI doesn't condone murders. We're . . . against them."

"I see."

"But to be honest, I don't give a damn if Polly Severino got killed or not. He's out of the rackets—and out of my hair. Same with the Mangione mob. So I won't bust my ass trying to catch the killers—and I don't think the Youngstown police will, either."

"Life is strange like that, isn't it?" I knew he was poking at me, goading me, and I poked him back, not caring one way or the other.

"Then, of course, the Mangiones had to pay back, too. That's how mob wars get started. So one of the Severino muscle guys headed off for work one morning and was blown all over the street when he turned on his ignition."

I shook my head sadly. "Another Youngstown Tune-Up."

LeBlanc stopped smiling. "I'm sorry. That has bad memories for you."

"It always will," I said.

"It has bad memories for lots of people in Youngstown. Captain Shemo, for one."

"Shemo? Big deal. He can't remember what he had for lunch today."

"Don't sell him short. Sure, he cuts corners, and"—here he rubbed fingers and thumbs together in a "Gimme" gesture—"he takes, too. But before he's a crook, he's a cop, and he won't rest until he finds out who killed *his* cop—who killed Alfonso."

I took a swig of Goose Island because my mouth had gone dry.

"I'm looking into that one, too, Dominick. I carry a badge, and I knew Lieutenant Candiotti fairly well, so I'm looking."

"I appreciate it."

We were quiet for a time, Mike LeBlanc looking out my window. Then he said, "The Cleveland FBI got an interesting letter a few months ago—not signed—pointing a finger at a rich coal owner named Rogan Smythe, for running a Ponzi scheme that has cleaned out most of the big shots in Mahoning and Trumbull counties to the tune of about thirty million bucks. Can you imagine that?"

"I can't imagine that," I said.

"So Smythe got the subpoena that was waiting for your

other brother—Father Richard. He spilled his guts out in Cleveland and will be tried this spring. My guess is he'll do hard time in a federal facility—not a place they send rich guys who pretend it's a country club but without any pussy. A real hard-case prison."

"Rogan Smythe deserves it—except I never heard of him until right this minute."

"You didn't? Well, like I said, it's news. By the way, did you know they started calling it 'news' many long years ago, because the word is made up from the beginning letters from north, east, west, and south?"

"I didn't know that," I said. "I thought it meant that the stories they report in the papers and on TV are new. Therefore they call it news."

LeBlanc laughed. "Trivia, I guess." He thought for another thirty seconds and then snapped his fingers, as if he remembered something. "Hey, didn't you go to college at Youngstown State with a Mahoning assistant DA named David Ratner?"

"I did go to school with him," I said. "I ran into him a few times when I was in town in October."

"He disappeared."

I didn't even try to look surprised. "He did?"

"Also in October. Right off the face of the earth. Nobody knows where he is."

"Maybe he left his wife and kids and ran off with some bimbo."

"Maybe," LeBlanc said, "except they found his car parked off the road up in the northwest corner of the county—an area they call 'Frog Alley.' Heard of it?"

"I've heard of everything," I said.

"Well, that's where they found Ratner's car. No keys, no trace of him but some insurance papers in the glove compartment. Everything wiped clean—steering wheel, door handles, everything. Except for some blood—a little on the driver's seat."

"Pretty gruesome," I said.

"The gruesome part of it all is that he was actually running the Ponzi scheme along with Rogan Smythe."

"He was?" I didn't sound shocked. There was no point to it.

"But he's been gone since October, so nobody worries about him anymore."

"Hmm," I said. "Interesting."

"October was an interesting month. You know what else happened in October? A few days before Halloween?"

"I'm just *dying* to know."

"This has to do with another school friend of yours, I think. Diane Burnham?"

I drained my Goose Island bottle and set it down carefully on the floor. "Yes?"

"She filed for divorce. She's divorcing her husband, Bob."

I cleared the frog from my throat. "Tough shitsky," I said.

"The funny thing is, a few days before she saw a divorce attorney, poor Bob Burnham got his nose smashed all over his face."

"Maybe he ran into a door."

"Or maybe somebody smashed his nose for him."

"Maybe Diane did it. She broke his nose and then divorced him."

LeBlanc considered it. "I don't think she's strong enough to hit him that hard."

"Then I guess we'll never know, will we?"

"I ran into her just the other day. Diane."

"Oh?"

"I mentioned I was going to Chicago, and she said if I happened to run into you, I should say hello for her."

"Tell her hello back, then."

"Why don't you tell her yourself?"

"I live here. I don't live in Youngstown anymore."

"Maybe you should. You're a local guy, you know everybody in town, and everybody knows you. Your name—your family. I asked around, Dominick. It was a damn good family."

"'Was' is right. They're all gone now."

"Except you."

"I'm gone, too," I said. "Gone from Youngstown."

"Diane is still there," he said. "We had a long talk, y' know. She had a rough go of it—from the time you left for Vietnam. I think she loved you back then, and it busted her up that you didn't come back for her. When she married that jerk of a husband, it got worse. She's been struggling a lot of years, just to keep her balance. She's made some mistakes, but she's tried."

"We all make mistakes. You, too, LeBlanc—big-time fuck-ups. But that's par for the course."

He digested what I'd said. Then he finished his beer. "Can I have another one?"

"You like Goose Island?"

"Very much."

"The brewery is less than a mile from right where we're sitting," I said, and went into the kitchen for two more bottles. "I drink it all the time when I'm here. No Iron City stuff for me."

He took a dainty sip and rolled it around on his tongue like a wine taster. "'Iron City stuff.' You put Youngstown down a lot, don't you?"

I shrugged. "I just don't live there, that's all."

"Well, Chicago's a great city, too, but there's good to say about Youngstown. If you opened a branch of your building company there, you'd do very well."

"I do very well here."

"True," he said, and tilted up the new bottle to his lips. Then he licked his lips and sighed contentedly. "But 'there' is home."

"Not for me—not anymore."

"Then you're a schmuck." He took another sip of Goose Island. "Youngstown has problems. Every city does, but in Youngstown it's pretty bad."

"Tell me something I don't know," I said.

"It needs a housecleaning, but it also needs good people to come in there and stand up for what's right. To make it right. People like you."

"Not like me. I don't stand up for what's right—just for what's important to me."

"That's not the way I hear it."

I sighed. Here it comes, I thought. "What do you hear?"

LeBlanc considered answering me truthfully, which would have landed me in prison for the rest of my life. Then he changed his mind. "Nothing I hear, really—just my own instinct."

"Does the FBI operate on instinct? I thought everything's done by the book."

"Maybe," he said, "I read that book already, and now I'm wanting something new—like instinct. My instinct right now is that you take troubles into your own hands. If you move back to Youngstown—even part-time—you can help set the city back on track." LeBlanc smiled. "I wouldn't worry about anyone there being mad at you—any mob guys. Even old man Severino, he likes you. So does old man Mangione. But neither of them know you, uh, well enough for them to get mad."

"Why would anyone be mad at me?" I said. "I haven't done anything wrong."

He nodded, smiled some more. "There are other people who really like you. Your sister, for one."

I laughed. "She wouldn't throw water on me if I were burning."

"She can be a pain in the ass sometimes, I know, but you're the only brother she has left."

"You talked to Teresa about me?"

He shrugged. "We've run into each other a few times."

"Just like you run into Diane Burnham."

"Yep," he said. "My guess is that she loves you, too."

"What are you, LeBlanc? A matchmaker?"

"One does what one can. Captain Shemo—and everybody else on the force—would welcome you back, too. Because of Alfonso."

"Sure, Shemo loves me a lot."

"As I said, lots of people do. Like Umberto Pellegrino, for instance."

That shut me up quickly. I tried not to change the expression on my face, but I felt it melting away like a double-scoop ice-cream cone on a hot August day.

"He runs a hell of a restaurant, doesn't he?" LeBlanc said cheerfully.

"Yes, he does."

"That's a good person to have loving you. He was good friends with your father. He'd do anything for you. Any night of the week, he'll cook you lasagna or pasta primavera or whatever you like."

I took a deep breath before I spoke, fearing I'd suck all the air out of the room. "Did you come all the way here from Youngstown to recite how many people love me, Sergeant LeBlanc—or Special Agent LeBlanc, or whatever the hell you call yourself?"

"I call myself Mike," he said. He guzzled down what was left of his Goose Island and stood up. "Just think about what I said, Dominick. It's a pretty good town. There're problems, sure, but down deep it's very much okay. It'll get better. One of these days, somebody'll breeze in and take over the police department and shake up the politicians and the clergy, and it's going to clean itself up so fast, it'll make your head spin."

"I'm not going to take over any police force."

"No, but you'd make the city just that much better. That's what we need now, people who care about the city and not just about themselves."

"You think so? You think you know everything about me?"

"Nobody knows everything," LeBlanc said. "But maybe I

know enough." He looked out the bay window one more time. "Nice view. Nice place to live." He stuck out a hand. "Thanks for the Goose Island. I'll try to find out if they sell it somewhere around Youngstown."

I shook his hand, wondering why the hell he'd come, and walked with him to the front door. LeBlanc put his hand on the knob, but he turned and looked at me before he did anything about it. "By the way," he said, "how's your leg?"

For a brief moment, my nerves banged around somewhere between my stomach and my throat. LeBlanc obviously knew a hell of a lot more than he'd admitted. I felt impaled on a pin, like a rare butterfly. I squared my shoulders and felt my jaw getting firm. "My leg is just fine, Agent LeBlanc," I said. "How's *your* leg?"

LeBlanc closed his eyes for a moment, then opened them again. They were twinkling. "Take care of yourself, Dominick—and come around sometime, huh?"

I closed the door after him and then leaned against it, my forehead pressing the wood. He knew—the FBI knew—I'd killed Polly Severino and his two bodyguards, and that I'd probably killed David Ratner. Eventually *someone* would find him.

I sat by the window and watched it get dark, drinking quietly. The FBI always does things by the book, going all the way back to J. Edgar Hoover. Yet LeBlanc was throwing that book away to tell me I was off the hook for what I'd done back in October.

He was letting me know I should go back where I was born, where I grew up and learned everything I know. Maybe after my running away from it, this was a way to return and embrace it—my name and family, and my heritage. It *was* a good family, because it produced Richard, a great priest, and even Alfonso, who, for all his kickbacks and his favors to the Severinos, had been a good cop.

I had to think about it some more. You don't change your life around in one Goose Island–fueled evening.

I decided one thing, however, before I hauled myself off to sleep. I was going to get a dog.

ABOUT THE AUTHOR

Les Roberts came to mystery writing after a twenty-four-year stint writing for network and syndicated television in Los Angeles, winning the initial PWA Best First Private Eye Novel competition in 1986, and then writing twenty-five more. He currently lives and writes in Summit County, Ohio, with his longtime love, Holly Albin, both of whom are owned by an elegant Maine Coon cat named Isabel.